Praise for Tim

'This bewitching quee...
Janovsky...is a charmer.'

Publishers Weekly on *Once Upon You and Me*

'Janovsky's latest is an age-gap, forbidden romance that
blends fairy-tale romance with sexier bedtime stories to
deliver pure enchantment to its readers.'

Library Journal on *Once Upon You and Me*

'Tartly humorous and deliciously spicy.'

Booklist on *You Had Me at Happy Hour*

'Janovsky's latest is a work nemesis-to-lovers, 'we're
just friends with benefits until we're so much more'
story, with two adorably awkward protagonists
who it's impossible not to root for.'

Library Journal on *You Had Me at Happy Hour*

'Game show antics, idiots-in-love, and a healthy dose of
steam, this book swept me off my feet. Sexy as hell,
with Janovsky's trademark wit and charm, this book
is everything I want in a romance novel!'

Alison Cochrun, author of *The Charm Offensive* and
Kiss Her Once for Me, on *The (Fake) Dating Game*

'Fans of the fake-dating trope and game shows will find
a lot to like here. Holden is a sympathetic narrator, and
readers will happily root for him as he learns that while
there are no quick fixes for grief, opening up to the
right people can make all the difference.'

Library Journal on *The (Fake) Dating Game*

Timothy Janovsky is a queer, multidisciplinary storyteller based in Washington, DC. He holds a Bachelor's degree from Muhlenberg College and a self-appointed certificate in rom-com studies (accreditation pending). When he's not daydreaming about young Hugh Grant, he's telling jokes, playing characters and writing books.

Also by Timothy Janovsky

Discover more at afterglowbooks.co.uk

ONE WEEK TO WIN THE CHOCOLATE MAKER

Timothy Janovsky

afterglow BOOKS

First Published in Great Britain 2025 by
Afterglow Books by Mills & Boon, an imprint of HarperCollins*Publishers* Ltd
1 London Bridge Street, London, SE1 9GF

www.harpercollins.co.uk

HarperCollins*Publishers*
Macken House, 39/40 Mayor Street Upper,
Dublin 1, D01 C9W8, Ireland

One Week to Win the Chocolate Maker © 2026 Timothy Janovsky

ISBN: 978-0-263-42075-3

0126

This book contains FSC™ certified paper and other controlled sources to ensure responsible forest management.

For more information visit: www.harpercollins.co.uk/green

Printed and Bound in the UK using 100% Renewable Electricity at CPI Group (UK) Ltd, Croydon, CR0 4YY

For those of us with an insatiable sweet tooth

One

DARIO

A chocolate maker, an opera singer and a party boy walk into a reading-of-the-will.

This sounds like the setup for a darkly funny joke, but alas, it is Dario Cotogna's life, and his effervescent grandfather's passing is a mirthless affair.

Inside the well-stocked, regal study at Villa Meraviglia on a scenic hilltop in the village of Montecolognola, in the province of Perugia, Italy, a lawyer sits in wait behind an imposing wooden desk. Above her hangs the Cotogna family portrait, painted back when there were six of them.

And then there were three, Dario thinks as he sits in one of the handcrafted, sixteenth-century wooden chairs in front of the desk beside his mother. His younger brother—taller and wider and hairier, so you'd never guess he was younger—frames her other side. They are half of what they once were. How can Dario dare to feel whole again?

Dario unbuttons his sharkskin overcoat. His closet is full of creations by Gabriele Vitale, the best tailor in walking distance of his front door. No matter the weather or occasion, Dario feels most like himself all dressed up. Today, he broke out his blue power suit with its contrasting yellow polka-dotted pocket square because today is the day he claims his inheritance, steps into his destiny.

The familiar lawyer before him has wide-set, down-turned eyes, black wavy hair that falls well past her padded shoulders, and a hefty sheaf of papers in front of her. A pair of square-framed, plum-colored reading glasses rest upon her tall stack. Her name is Violetta Francisco, and she has known the Cotognas as long as she has been alive. Smiling professionally, she says, "Buon giorno. Allora, cominciamo."

"In inglese, per favore?" asks April Cotogna, the mother. She grew up in America, trained in England, and toured all over Europe. She played the title role in Puccini's *Manon Lescaut* when it came to Perugia many, many years prior. This is how she met Dario's late father, Cosimo Cotogna Jr. She liked to joke that the way to most men's hearts is through their stomachs, but Cosimo Jr.'s heart could only be won through his elephant-sized yet bat-like ears. "Which is good," she'd say, "because I can carry a tune but I can't cook!" The room would guffaw at the gorgeous, lithe diva with golden hair and golden pipes gracing their presence at some party or another.

Despite her vocal training, her years married to a born-and-bred Italian man, and her two multilingual children, she never quite became fluent in the language. The phonetic alphabet was more her friend than any real alphabet ever could be.

"Certo. Yes. Let us begin," Violetta says switching between the two languages effortlessly. She puts on her glasses. They make her look even more severe.

Dario reaches out for his mother's hand, which taps on the

rounded arm of her chair. She squeezes him, which he takes as a gesture of thanks.

Much like the character of Manon Lescaut, April Cotogna was not thought a suitable match for the heir to a global chocolate empire. While Emilia and Cosimo Cotogna Sr. grew to accept April the aspiring opera star who couldn't cook—practically sacrilegious in the Italian culture—there was no guarantee things would stay the same. When Cosimo Jr. died young in a reckless Vespa accident, she feared she and her sons would be cast out from the world they'd come to know. Luckily, Cosimo Jr. made plentiful provisions to ensure that did not happen. Still, that niggling fear must be with her again now that Cosimo Sr. is gone, which is why Dario squeezes her hand back.

Dario is heir apparent. He only needs Violetta to read it aloud from Cosimo Sr.'s last will and testament for it to become a reality. He is keen and ready to take on the massive family business.

Well, mostly ready.

Amorina Chocolates has been his life since he graduated from the University of Perugia. Cosimo Sr. was his de facto father for most of his fundamental years. But Dario earned that relationship, unlike his brother, Emilio, who acted out at every minor inconvenience, spent money without a care, and put the Cotogna family in the press for all the wrong reasons.

Dario understood a man as busy and eccentric as Cosimo Cotogna Sr. could not be understood. That was his power. His hours were erratic, his temperament was calm no matter the blistering amount of work he had to do, and his conversations had a way of veering into riddle if they went on long enough to bore him, which they often did.

However, people liked doing business with Cosimo Cotogna Sr. because you never knew what you were going to get.

When you took a meeting with Signor Cotogna, you might luck into a winning deal and become rich, or you might get tricked into testing a truffle made to taste like puke.

Dario acclimated to his flamboyant grandfather and learned by example, becoming useful around the processing factory, the chocolate school and the company's historical museum. Until one day, sometime in his late teens, while he was taking dictation for a letter to his business associate—Cosimo Sr. did *not* mess with email—the infernal nuisance!—his grandfather looked him in the face and asked, "Ti paghiamo?" *Are we paying you?*

Surprised, Dario shook his head. Tendrils of his shoulder-length chestnut brown hair swished this way and that across his long face.

Cosimo clicked his tongue, shook his head. "Questo non va bene." *That is not good.*

From within his desk, Cosimo Sr. withdrew a small, purple sack. He tossed it to Dario, who caught it. Inside there were golden coins. Shock and awe fizzled like popping candies in Dario's belly, until he reached in and pulled one out. It smushed between his fingers. Chocolate slimed onto his palms from the cracks in the shiny casing.

Cosimo laughed, and laughed, and laughed.

Days later, in the Amorina offices above the museum, Dario discovered his name had been placed on a company mailbox and inside that mailbox was an envelope. It was his very first official paycheck. The rest, as they say, is history.

History is what Cosimo Cotogna Sr. is now.

History is what Dario Cotogna hopes to make.

Holding hands with his mother, in this room of a thousand stories packed onto built-in shelves, Dario waits for the first page to turn on the story he is destined to star in. Patiently, he listens as Violetta talks about how she has been named executor of the will, which makes sense given her family law firm's longstanding relationship with the Cotognas.

Over the next several hours, she details the division of the lucrative, expansive estate including sports cars, art pieces, boats and various heirlooms. It is morbid and mind-boggling, the amount one can accumulate in a lifetime and leave behind for others to sort through and fight over.

"The title of Villa Meraviglia is bequeathed to April Cotogna," says Violetta.

"The title only," April is quick to say, looking to her older son. "As you know, Violetta, I'm never here. I'm always touring. This is your home, Dario. You will continue to oversee it. That's fine, right?"

Violetta nods, which sets Dario at ease.

This is his home. This villa is where he grew up. This is the study where his father worked before he passed away, severing the line of succession and leaving behind a legacy Dario sometimes feels too young to take on with his two modestly experienced hands. His eagerness to make impactful change on the family business does not outweigh his ballooning, clinically diagnosed anxiety.

This villa, due to that generalized anxiety and his acute agoraphobia, is also Dario's fortress. Which works in a morbid way given the village's medieval beginnings. Dario's world has not extended past the borders of Perugia since *the incident* he tries not to dwell on. His therapist keeps reminding him that increased exposure to his triggers is key to treating his agoraphobia, and he's made small strides.

Outside of the villa, Dario can go to the Amorina factory for work and to Lake Trasimeno for a sail and a stop at Isola Polvese, but ever since his nonno got sick and then passed away, he's put his mental health on the back burner. Because if as a child, you touched the stove while it was still hot and came away with a burn, you would know not to touch it again. Perhaps, like the skin on our fingertips, Dario Cotogna is too sensitive for the scorching stovetop of the unknown, and *the incident* was the universe's way of imparting a tough lesson.

Violetta proceeds. "On to the matter of the Amorina company."

Dario's heart takes off with the speed of a thousand horses. He grips his mother's hand again, needing to be grounded in what is both a bittersweet and significant moment.

Violetta's red lips turn down, and she sets her glasses aside. The air in the room grows warmer, and it has nothing to do with the bright sun shifting positions through the nearby windowpanes, creating lines of mustard yellow across the tan, lacquered floor. Dario hitches forward in his chair, which creaks with age beneath him.

"There is a small matter we need to discuss," she says, going off-script. Dario has known Violetta since he was an infant. She used to babysit him. Judging by the creases between her eyebrows, whatever the matter is, it will not be small, but it almost certainly will be unpleasant.

"What is it?" Dario asks, not sounding the least bit brave.

"According to the will—" Violetta begins, voice professional but eyes brimming with sympathy "—Dario Cotogna is to be the temporary successor of Amorina Chocolates."

"Temporary?" he asks, confusion bursting out of every syllable in the blasted word.

She ducks her head back to her paper, evidently needing the safety of legalese to deliver this next part. "The will states that you get to be permanent owner of Amorina under one stipulation—you get married by your thirty-second birthday." She offers no explanation, just a weak, sad smile.

At present, Dario is as far from married as one could be. He is out of the dating pool, shut off from the world on this hilltop. But he is quite close to turning thirty-two. Less than a year away from it.

"I'm confused," he says, letting go of his mother's hand and standing. Emilio snort-laughs. Dario shoots him a fiery glare that he hopes shuts him up. Though he knows not even a knife to the throat would shut Emilio up.

When they were younger, people often mistook them for twins. They had the same modest height, the same hush puppy hazel eyes, and the same rosy, round cheeks. If you found one running mud-stained through the garden, the other was always close behind, roaring like a monster in a game of make-believe only the two of them understood.

But as Emilio put on weight, grew a full beard and spoke with a lower register, Dario stayed the same. His voice remained high and bright like his mother's. His cheeks got patchy at best. His body never became a trunk to boast a family tree on, instead remaining twiglike and shaky to any sudden breezes.

People treated Emilio like a man, including their venturesome father, and Dario like the second-born late bloomer. Time and difference and eventually distance put an end to their playful, brotherly bond. These days, they regard one another more as side effects of their parentage rather than true siblings.

"You have one year to marry, or you forfeit your inheritance," Violetta says.

"That old bat!" Dario shouts, pacing across the floor.

He stops long enough for Violetta to produce a crisp envelope from the outer pocket of her fine leather attaché case. "He told me to give you this."

His grandfather's inscription in practiced cursive on the front of the envelope says: *In case he calls me an old bat.*

The card inside the envelope simply reads in Italian: *Chocolate tastes sweeter with a little love.*

Dario, seconds away from ripping out his hair, says, "This must be a joke."

Violetta whips out another envelope. The outside reads: *In case he says this must be a joke.*

Dario's eyes jump to the words on the card. *Love is no joke.*

"He can't do this!" Dario shouts.

A third envelope. A third card. Cosimo Sr.'s written: *I can, and I did.*

Dario holds the three cards—a losing hand in whatever game his grandfather is playing—and flaps them about. "What am I supposed to do with these?" he asks. Exasperation echoes through the study.

He did not need to look at the outside of the next envelope to deduce what his grandfather wrote there. The envelope, unlike the others, is thick and weighty. Inside is not a card but a letter. A letter that unfolds dozens of times like a king's scroll, sweeping across Dario's newly shined shoes.

Tesorino,
As you know, my dearest nonna began Amorina Chocolates from her two biggest loves: sweets and her sweet, your great-great-grandfather. Since then, love has been the main ingredient of both our recipe and our business model. It is my belief that love is the reason Amorina Chocolates has had such success and staying power in the candy industry.
Since this is so...

There's a plan, already in action. A harebrained plan. A plan that is so outrageous that Dario steps away from his mother and brother who have been reading over his shoulders. As he moves to the window, he nearly tears the scripture like a roll of toilet paper when he steps on its outlandish length. Bathed in fresh sunlight, he tries and fails to make sense of this testimony.

But wasn't that always the way? He understood that his grandfather could not be understood. Even in death, there are no exceptions, no differences. Cosimo Sr.'s powerful specter hangs there, suspended in the room. Dario half hears his booming laugh right in his ear.

Dario does not have the energy to read on. His eyes keep glazing over, and his mind keeps running seven words ahead. He cannot absorb any of this, too stuck in the aftershock, mired in the barbed wires of grief. "What happens if I say no to this? All of this?"

"It says it in—"

"Please tell me," Dario says, hands clasping the pages so tightly he crumples them a little. "I'll go back and read it. Read it all. I promise." He means this, he does. Because this is the last correspondence his grandfather has written him. He would cherish it for all eternity if it weren't so set on catapulting him straight out of his comfort zone and into a thicket of never-ending panic attacks. "But right now, please just tell me."

Violetta nods before putting her glasses on again. "Should Dario Cotogna not accept the terms of this will, the line of succession will skip to Emilio Cotogna immediately."

Dario's hand flies to his mouth, dropping the scroll. He is going to be sick.

"Fuck yeah," Emilio says, fist-pumping the air.

"Em, not now," says April, crossing to Dario. She wraps him in a hug that should be comforting but is not. Not even her familiar floral fragrance, underpinned by the dark chocolate they were all snacking on moments ago, calms his nerves.

"I'll contest it," Dario says, stepping out of his mother's embrace. The heir apparent of Amorina Chocolates needs to be strong. He can do this alone, just as he's done everything. Alone is how he is best. Minimizing the probability of betrayal and hurt and mistakes is the name of the game.

"Do you really want to take this to court?" Violetta asks.

The time, the money, the headache! Dario refuses to drag his family through that, but *why*. Why, from beyond the grave, must his grandfather punish him like this?

"No," Dario confesses.

"Good boy," says April.

"Yeah, *good boy*," Emilio mocks, rosy cheeks jiggling with laughter. April smacks him on the arm. "Ow."

"Oh, please." She rolls her eyes fabulously. She does everything fabulously. Why could Dario not have inherited that from her? He would be fabulously married by now and this would be a total nonissue.

Dario swallows the fight hardening in his throat. "What do I have to do to make this happen?"

Agoraphobia drew strict boundaries around his world. Cosimo Sr. was aware of them before he passed. He might have been quirky, but he was never cruel.

"Nothing. You say the word and the whole plan, overseen by me, gets set into motion today."

Dario stares out the study window. The in-ground pool sparkles in the sunshine. Beyond it, Lake Trasimeno swans with life. Boats speckle the wavy surface along with its famed islands, most of which are crawling with over-tanned tourists in funny hats saying grazie mille in unpracticed accents because they're on vacation, seeing the world. Because why not.

Why not? That's the new question that sails through the break of Dario's thoughts.

He's never been able to outwit his grandfather. This time, he should not even try. Instead, he must choose to accept.

"Va bene," he says, without any true idea of what he's agreeing to, "I'll get married."

Two

CHARLIE

Death tickles Charlie Moore's doorstep.

The single-story, two-bedroom, one-bathroom house he shares with his parents and grandparents in Slatington, Pennsylvania, sags into its foundation like a shingled, forgotten mausoleum on the literally named Cemetery Street.

Many years ago, on a walk home from school past the white-painted church with its foreboding bell tower, Charlie's erstwhile friend Max asked, "How can anyone live on a street where people go when they die?"

Charlie stopped whistling, shrugged and said, "We get on just fine."

Nothing feels fine now as Charlie straddles the property line between the weather-battered headstones and the rusted mailbox with peeling numbers on its side. He doesn't need X-ray vision to know what's inside the hefty envelope from the local bank stamped URGENT: OPEN IMMEDIATELY in violent red lettering. His heart twists.

Foreclosure looms over the house on Cemetery Street, like a wrecking ball set to swing with his family and their belongings still tucked inside.

Unable to stay still when it's nearly dinnertime and he has mouths to feed, Charlie marches up the overgrown grass, a phantom funeral procession close behind him playing an awful dirge.

The outside of the house on Cemetery Street has seen much better days, but the inside fizzles with warmth and personal touches. Every wall is covered with framed, sepia-touched photos. The bulbs in the old light fixtures blaze in the gray overcast of a soon-to-be-stormy summer day. The shoe rack overflows with sneakers, work boots and snow boots that should've been brought up to the attic for storage many months ago, but who has the time? The pantry is mostly stocked, and the well-loved kitchen table where they sit down for meals and trade stories and play games of gin rummy stands as the one family heirloom that hasn't been lost or sold.

How can anyone live on a street where people go to die? he thinks again.

Easily, when love practically flows through the electrical circuits.

However, the Moore household might be no more, once the bank comes to collect. Charlie sets the teakettle on the weak burner and one of two frozen meals in the microwave before opening the letter, even though it's addressed to his parents and he already knows what it says.

Under the *brrrr* of the microwave, Charlie clicks his tongue at what he reads. One more month of missed payments and the bank will be forced to file foreclosure proceedings with the court.

Upset rises thick in his throat. Not only is he upset with the bank and a cruel repayment system set against people like his family, but he's upset *with* his family, too. His parents promised him they would seek out a mortgage modification before it got to this.

They can't pay the back mortgage, and they certainly can't pay a lawyer to represent them in court. What then? Will they be thrown out on the street?

The beep of the microwave finishing nearly scares him out of his heavily tattooed skin. He sets the letter down and singes his fingertips on the scorching plastic of the container. Thankfully, he doesn't drop it, or one of his grandparents would have to go without dinner.

Will that become the norm? Will they continue to be food insecure?

Charlie's head whirls with the unthinkable. They already make do with so little. His grandparents claim the primary bedroom. His parents live out of the spare. And he camps out in the living room.

Max annoyingly comes to mind again as Charlie's eyes sweep over the plastic, scratched TV stand, the vacuum-lined popcorn carpet, and the well-loved brown couch at the foot of which a folded fitted sheet and a feather pillow sit. "How can anyone sleep in a room meant for living?" he recalls his old friend asking.

Charlie sighs. How will they get by now?

At the door to the main bedroom, Charlie uses his exposed elbow to knock twice. On the inside of his forearm is one of his many tattoos. It is a house cat with a pair of scissors in one hand, a tongue clutched in the other, and a lit cigar dangling from the corner of his open mouth. A speech bubble overhead says, "I got it."

He has always had a penchant for sardonic comics and an

artistic eye for the alternative. At sixteen, as an act of rebellion after being denied permission, Charlie did a stick-and-poke star holding a water gun on the inside of his ankle. The first time he wore no-show socks that summer, his grandmother damn near keeled over from shock. Especially after he said, "It's a shooting star!"

"How could you, Charlie?" his mom said.

"You said I couldn't *get* a tattoo," Charlie replied without an ounce of arrogance or moodiness. "You didn't say I couldn't tattoo myself."

To this, nobody could argue. A loophole had been detected, and he earned a dash of begrudging respect from his elders.

But as he did more online research into what it took to become a tattoo artist, he learned about "scratchers"— self-taught, at-home tattooers who disregarded apprenticeships and licenses and, sometimes, even the sanitation necessary to prevent basic blood-borne pathogens. While he'd gamble on himself, he wasn't about to put anybody else's health at risk.

From then on, Charlie vowed to play by the rules so he could take a true shot at his dream career. He honed his drawing skills through YouTube tutorials and told himself he would eventually bring his design portfolio to the local tattoo parlor in search of an apprenticeship.

But, at eighteen, he learned that apprenticeships were not feasible for someone like him with so little money and so little free time, so instead of giving tattoos, he got them. Lots of them. When he was able. They didn't fill the hole where his dream used to be, but his time under the needle came close, and he liked the way they looked on his body once completed.

"Come in," calls Grandma Moore through the bedroom door in a weakish voice.

Charlie schools his expression and uses his hip to twist the loose knob. The door sails open and slams against the wall behind it. Grandma and Grandpa Moore sit up in bed, backed by two tall towers of slouchy pillows.

"Your hair!" Grandma exclaims.

Charlie nearly reaches up to scrape a hand over his newly dyed buzz cut before remembering the tray of food. "Oh, yeah. I did it this morning."

"It's so blue!" she adds.

"Yeah." He chose the color because it matches his favorite Gatorade flavor from childhood. Bright, vibrant, sugary. After bleaching his locks several months earlier, he needed a change. His body was nothing if not a canvas for self-expression.

Good thing his hair doesn't have magical mood ring properties, otherwise it would have turned jet-black to signal stressed and anxious. He can't worry his grandparents about the mortgage until he can question his parents and launch a plan of action.

On the small TV screen across from the bed, a new show on the Food Network starts. It's one of those travel shows where an über glamorous person jet-sets all over the world trying different foods.

"I'm Larsa Vanderbell, and *this* is *Europe Your Way*. Today I'm in Florence. Would you believe me if I told you that the best sandwich in the entire city came from a walk-up window? Sounds fake, but let's find out what that means. Come along!" A tall, conventionally beautiful woman wearing slender heels on cobblestone streets struts ahead of the camera, then eats a focaccia, tomato and fresh mozzarella sandwich that looks handmade by angels.

Charlie lifts the lids on two steaming microwave dinners. The soggy meatloaf and flaccid carrots underline how mouthwatering the food on the screen is. Everything they eat either comes cold in a bag from the store or hot in a bag from the drive-through. Such is the way in their neck of the woods. And in their tax bracket.

"Goodie, meatloaf. My favorite," says Grandpa, tucking the paper napkin into the top of his worn white T-shirt so he doesn't dribble. Charlie mirrors this for Grandma. The gout in her fingers flares often, so it's easier for him to feed her than risk the inevitable spills. At first, she refused. After several soiled blankets, she grew amenable to Charlie's hands-on assistance.

Charlie cuts up the frozen meal for her as the show plays out across the room. Larsa's *mms* and *uhhs* are broken up by pre-recorded voiceover of her detailing the history of the family-owned eatery. Grandma and Grandpa's eyes never leave the TV. They have the slightly detached glaze Charlie has only ever seen on kids scrolling through their phones. If only his family could afford professional elder care. Someone to safely get them up and out into the fresh air.

All they'll have is fresh air once the roof is ripped off right over their heads.

Charlie imagines a bank giant clomping across Slatington, picking their house up in his greasy palm, and crushing it inside his meaty fist.

"Have you ever been to Europe?" Charlie asks, deploying small talk to stave off the unpleasantness roiling in his stomach.

The absolute best part about living with and caring for his grandparents is that he has the chance to ask them all the important questions many grandchildren don't get to before they go.

Grandpa shakes his head. "Oh no. My parents immigrated from Wales and never crossed the ocean again. Money was tight. By the time I came along, the slate industry was dwindling away. My brothers always joked I was an accident of the bad economy. A jaunt on the continent was out of the question," he says.

Charlie's great-grandparents came over and got swept into the slate belt in Pennsylvania. The men worked the quarries, mining for blue-gray slate with flint striations. It was hard, manual labor that tormented their bodies, but it paid, and even though they lived in tenement buildings, they were together. They made do. Their eternal mantra.

Grandpa went into the same shrinking line of work once he came of age, but by then opportunities were scarce and conditions seemed worse. The train lines hauling slate disappeared and alternate materials being mined undercut the main export of the area.

Still they worked on. Sweating beneath the beating Pennsylvania sun. Returning home to meals of cabbage stew cooked by frugal wives who taught or typed or sewed to add a bit to the household income and keep the children healthy. It was not glamorous or comfortable, but it was the only way they knew.

Charlie yearns to give his family a better, more leisurely life, like the one Larsa on the TV lives.

"If you could go now, where would you go?" Charlie asks.

"With what money?" Grandpa says with a laugh, which sours Charlie's attitude more.

"It's a hypothetical, Grandpa," Charlie says, stuffing down his impatience.

Grandma chews on a carrot, presumably in thought. "Italy," she says after a swallow. "I love this program. This Larsa is fabulous. She seems to love Italy the most. All that art and history. Not to mention those fountains!"

"I'm not sure I could get around in a city like that," says Grandpa, slapping at the crutch beside the bed. Beside that is his wheelchair. Those uneven streets and old buildings without ramps or elevators would prove difficult for him.

The slate industry not only took most of the Moore men's youths, but it took Grandpa's right foot. Fifteen years ago, a loading machine malfunctioned. A large piece of slate was dangling over the bed of a truck when a chain came loose, crushing Grandpa's foot beneath it. The whole thing had to be amputated, putting him out of commission in the only line of work he'd ever known.

"You heard the boy, it's a hypothetical," Grandma says with a wistful sigh. Wistful mostly because there was a time, right after Grandpa lost his foot, where the burden of finances went from slate slab to featherlight thanks to the lawsuit payout.

How then were they close to losing their home on Cemetery Street?

Charlie does not want to think about Uncle Buck, his dad's only brother, and the great disappearing act he pulled.

Instead, Charlie sets his mind on how to fix this, for all of them.

Three

CHARLIE

The large linden tree out front of the house on Cemetery Street is the one thriving thing on this plot of land. It is a welcome burst of green in the last flecks of what little daylight they have between sporadic summer showers that turn the lawn to mud.

Charlie shortcuts through the still-damp, too-tall grass, making a note to break out the mower over the coming weekend.

The family car pulls up to the curb. Dad rolls down the window. A day's worth of graying stubble dots his gaunt, pale cheeks. He does warehouse work for a beer company. "Sorry we're running late, kiddo," he says.

Charlie is twenty-eight. He will probably be retired by the time Dad stops calling him kiddo. He gets it. He has got a boyish face. Thin with round cheeks and a smattering of charming freckles. And he has never left home. Too needed around here. Except when conversations turn to finances, clearly, judging by the hole the foreclosure notice is burning in his back pocket.

"No worries," Charlie says, running through a list of ways to transition into this impossible conversation.

"Loving the new hair. Blue looks good on you," Mom says from the passenger seat, sounding tired. Her own hair is pulled up in a ponytail, which draws attention to the dark bags under her eyes. Their hours are long in that flat, windowless building several towns over, but at least they ride to work together. Country music—their favorite—spills out of the pickup truck's radio.

"They're cutting hours again, so we're trying to stay a little after our shifts to show some initiative," Dad says. Even in a senior position, he still gets paid by the hour. They live at the mercy of a time card and a changing schedule. Life can be unfair and unpredictable.

"Want a ride?" Dad asks, already reaching for the door handle.

Charlie waves him off. They can't have this conversation about losing the house over a quick ride in the car. And, what? Was he supposed to leave the foreclosure notice for them to find in the center of the kitchen table as if it were a surprise bouquet of flowers from a secret admirer?

No, he will hold on to it.

At least for the night.

What can his parents do about it now when the bank is already closed?

Tomorrow, in the light of another sweltering summer day, things will be clearer, and he will know what to say. How to fix this. They can carry the burden together.

"Okay. Be safe," Mom says, blowing him a kiss.

★ ★ ★

On the other side of trickling Trout Creek, Slatington stands stilled in a different decade. When the slate industry and opportunity up and left, so did advancement, modernity. Hope, too. At least that's how it currently feels.

Past a gas station in a more open parking lot is an industrial space reminiscent of an auto body shop. It's called Drink Dash. The road sign is partially burnt out but everybody who wants to find it already knows where it is. Charlie has not seen a new customer in nearly eight months.

Drink Dash is a drive-through liquor store. Because nothing goes together better than drinking and driving.

The same folks roll through like clockwork buying their Jim Beam and their Sam Adams. Charlie wonders if these men's names are used to make the consumption of alcohol feel more personal. Especially if you're doing it alone and in a high volume.

He veers up the center drive, kicking at a stray rock with his orange high-top sneakers. He pretends the rock is a miserly banker running scared from him and his inevitable, fantastic solution to this foreclosure fiasco.

After clocking in with his old-timey punch card—*cha-ching*—he takes his seat inside his glass booth with the sliding window. Beside him are the frozen cocktail machines, the munchy snacks and the cash register.

From his backpack, he pulls out his tiny sketchbook. Ever since his school days, Charlie has drawn illustrations he thinks would make sick tattoos. Everything from his sardonic cartoons to lifelike interpretations of animals or people. Today, he uses the sketchbook for something entirely different—a list of ideas for saving his family home.

1. Get a second job

No, that won't work. Caring for his grandparents takes up all his daylight hours. Even if he got a work-from-home gig, their internet service is spotty at best. He could never get any work done with all the outages and breaks he would have to take.

2. Start an OnlyFans

While Charlie likes sex, and showing off his inked-up body when the occasion arises, he shares a house with his parents and grandparents. Completely unsexy. Besides, privacy is in short supply. Nobody is going to pay premium prices for shoddily lit bathroom nudes.

3. Win the lottery

He makes tips here. They sell scratch-offs. If he did one a shift, the odds might be...*pretty good?*

4. Sell an inessential organ

He has at least one or two parts pumping away in there that he could give up for the right price. Speaking of parts...

5. Sell my sperm

Charlie bangs his head on the table, feeling lower than low and hoping the impact might pound a good idea into his brain. Somebody clears their throat. Charlie looks up to find a customer waiting to pay.

Not just any customer, either.

It's Dennis, forty-two, from two miles away.

At least that's how Charlie remembers him given what was listed on his profile for the hookup app he uses.

Dennis is a regular. He wears jeans, splattered boots and a stained T-shirt. A toothpick dangles out of his lightly chapped mouth, remains there even as he smiles within the frame of his scratchy beard. After they met up last, Charlie had a hard time explaining away the redness all over his mouth the next morning. "Must be an allergic reaction to something I ate," Charlie said, only to be met with his mother saying, "But you ate here, and we didn't cook with anything new." His shrug seemed to stop the forward inquisition, but he was certain she knew what he'd been up to after his shift the night before.

"Rough evening?" Dennis asks.

"You could say that," Charlie replies, not wanting to get into it. He closes his notebook so Dennis can't see his sad list. "How are you?"

"Good. Family's good. Work's work." His bulky body built by manual labor bursts from the confines of his T-shirt. Charlie recalls how warm and eager it was against his own, yet also how impersonal the whole ordeal felt. He could've been anyone in the back of that Honda parked alongside the trailhead, and Dennis would've been just as happy. Charlie could've worn a cat suit, a ski mask and black gloves through the whole encounter so long as Dennis finished.

"When does your shift end?" Dennis asks. His true question is as explicit as Drink Dash's neon signs advertising every alcohol brand known to man.

"I'm closing," Charlie says.

He nods once. "What's that? One a.m.? Two? You know I'm a night owl."

"I'm pretty beat," Charlie says. His mind is on everything but sex right now.

"Have one of these," Dennis says, slapping a canned energy drink down on the counter. "My treat. It'll perk you up before I do."

Charlie resists the impulse to roll his eyes. "I'm good, thanks."

"Aw, come on." He sounds half-defeated. And already a little buzzed.

"Seriously, I'm good."

"Another night, then?" Dennis asks.

"Another night," Charlie says as noncommittally as possible.

Dennis sighs, pulls his purchases back through the cubby. "Just these, then."

Charlie calls out his total.

"Did you get it all?" Dennis asks.

"Friends and family discount," Charlie says, giving the guy a break alongside a warning. "As long as you promise not to open any of these on the ride home."

"I'll take that deal." Dennis slips him some cash. "And you can keep the change for being so handsome."

Once Dennis has driven off, Charlie debates what to do with the five-dollar tip. He could put it toward the foreclosure fund he has already begun cobbling together in his mind. But five dollars is a drop in the massive bucket of what those papers said his family owed.

Tonight, he could stand to treat himself.

From the snack display, he selects a fancy Italian chocolate bar called Amorina. He's loved it for as long as he can remember. The rich bitterness of dark chocolate tinged with vanilla is to die for. He will spread the squares out across the hours of his shift to savor it while he hatches a full-fledged plan.

He rings himself up with the employee discount and skins off the candy wrapping that is bulkier than usual. There is a big red word stamped on the inside that demands his attention. *CONTEST!*

Intrigued, he reads on:

For over 100 years, inside every Amorina chocolate bar wrapper, we've written you, dear customer, a love note. This tradition began as a nod to our founder and my dearest nonna, Eleanora Amato, who wrote letters to my beloved nonno, Vincenzo Cotogna, using the wrappers of candies just like ours. Now, it's your turn to share the love.

Charlie undoes origami-style folds that accordion out until the wrapper is as big as an amusement park map.

My grandson, Dario Cotogna, is looking for his love match. He seeks a spouse to share his life and fortune with. If you're single and twenty-one years of age or older with a valid passport, we invite you to write him your very own note. Tell him what you love about Amorina chocolates and what love means to you in 1,000 words or less. The five most compelling responses, judged by a panel of chocolate lovers and relationship experts, will receive one of five all-expenses paid trips to Perugia, Italy, to tour the newly reopened museum and stay in a luxury villa with a private chef for one week, all while vying for the heart and hand of one of the most eligible bachelors in all of Italy!

More information can be found on the Amorina website.

Rules and restrictions may apply.

Buona fortuna!

"Whoa," Charlie murmurs to the empty store, "this is completely ridiculous."

How strange, too, that he was just talking to his grandparents about going to Italy. Together they fantasized about those cobblestone streets, beautiful fountains, marble statues and fresh focaccia. Here, his favorite chocolate company is offering a chance to go for free. *Purely coincidence or a sign from the universe?*

Curious, he goes into the corner outside the sightlines of the security camera and opens his phone to scan the QR code. Up pops the Amorina website with the contest rules. Entries are due tomorrow at midnight. There is a whole page below that looks like an online dating profile.

Name: Dario Cosimo Cotogna
Age: 31
Height: 5'5"
Eye color: Hazel
Sexual orientation: Pansexual

Next to the baseball-card-esque stats are several photos of Dario. He is debonair with chestnut brown, chin-length hair and a wide array of colorful suits that make him stand out in even the most crowded frame.

He isn't unattractive, but he is hardly Charlie's usually tall, burly, blue-collar, boot-wearing type.

He continues reading.

Dario Cotogna was born and raised in Perugia, Italy, where he presently resides. He has worked for Amorina Chocolates since he was fifteen years old. He took a small break from the business to study Food & Sustainability at the University of Perugia, where his passion for a more modern Amorina flourished, much to the chagrin of his stalwart nonno. He is passionate, good-humored, hardworking, and loves to dress up no matter the occasion.

Likes: Menswear, sailing, hiking, bike rides, listening to music, watching TV, homemade pasta, time with family, his beloved dog, environmental advocacy

Dislikes: cold weather (you must love to cuddle), dancing (he has two left feet), crowded and small places (best he tells you about this one himself)

Charlie assumes Dario didn't write this profile, or even approve it, for that matter. Why would he publicize so much personal information?

He also can't help but notice one key detail is missing from the listing, so he launches a Google search and nearly chokes when he reads Dario's net worth.

With money like that, Charlie could save the house on Cemetery Street with funds left over for a beach cottage and a cabin in the mountains and a penthouse apartment in whatever major city he chooses.

His whole family could retire on that money. They could travel the world on that money. They could frolic in a swimming pool of gold coins.

Do they even still make gold coins?

He reopens his notebook and writes: 6. Marry a billionaire chocolate maker

He likes hiking, bike rides, dogs, and who doesn't like homemade pasta? He lives in shorts and T-shirts, so he's no expert on men's fashion and he's never been much for music outside of what his parents enjoy, but that doesn't mean he couldn't learn to love these things.

Then, feeling foolish, he immediately scratches the idea out.

There is a .01 percent chance they would even choose him if he entered. He should not waste his time on frivolities.

Who marries a total stranger anyway?

He leans forward in his padded rolling chair and looks out

through the window, into the empty liquor store where the ancient fridges whirr and the sickly lights flicker. A metaphorical tumbleweed blows through the desolate, dusty space.

Honestly, if pressed, he could.

He *could* marry a total stranger.

Maybe it's better when you don't really know the person you marry, anyway. They can't let you down when they inevitably unmask their annoying quirks and faults. Randomness could lead to happiness, couldn't it?

At present, Charlie's best romantic prospect is Dennis, forty-two, from two miles away, and his family situation is as dire as it gets.

He has so little to lose by entering this contest, and a whole world to gain if he wins.

Why not take a chance?

Four

DARIO

Two weeks later

On a blazing afternoon in the middle of July, the scent of freshly baked focaccia lures Dario from the guesthouse. A new, white tent presides over the villa's green, grassy rear lawn that separates his room in the barn house from the main house. The grandiose nature of the frilly tent gives the impression that the circus arrived at the village overnight, blown in on a strong Adriatic breeze.

Are his guests arriving to meet the ringmaster or the century's saddest clown?

Regardless of whether he is ready or excited, today is the day that five total strangers descend upon his home for a week-long stay with the hope of…a love match?

That seems too impossible, even for his nonno's fancies. What are the odds that he would find the elusive, magical recipe for love buried somewhere in hundreds of thousands of short, written testimonials?

The word *recipe* peppering his mind gives him a whole-body shiver even while embraced in the sun's radiant warmth. A recipe is what ended his last serious relationship. He learned the hard way that it wasn't only his heart that needed guarding like a precious family heirloom when it came to trust and vulnerability.

Angelo, the Cotogna family's geriatric Maltese with the size and plucky spirit of a newborn puppy, darts through the parted flaps of the tent. He sniffs at the square white table before hiking up his back leg. "Angelo, no!" Dario appeals. Either Angelo's hearing is shot, or he ignores his owner and nightly cuddle buddy before dashing off.

Dario closes his eyes and keys into the blades of mowed grass poking up between his toes. In a moment, he will have to slip into his Italian leather loafers and greet his prospective spouses like a world-renowned host, but he takes a moment to relish being barefoot while wearing his new five-piece, seafoam green suit.

Seafoam green is Dario's favorite color. Once he became the sole inhabitant of Villa Meraviglia, he had all the door and window frames painted with it. He needs the armor of his favorite color to buoy him. The last few years have left him depleted and sorely lacking in social practice. How does one make small talk when the problems he faces seem so large?

When he opens his eyes, the sight of Violetta spooks him. She wears all black even in this heat.

"Just the reaction I love to get," she says, deadpan. Dario apologizes for his overreaction. He supposes he should get used to people coming and going around here. "I have come to oversee the arrival of your guests and to get them to sign proper documentation."

Ah, so she is here as a lawyer and not as a family friend. "Grazie."

"I am also to deliver these to you." She passes him a stack of envelopes tied up with an Amorina bow. "They are from your grandfather."

"Don't tell me this is some additional scheme of his."

"Non lo so." *I don't know.* "They were sealed and given to me with instructions."

Dario sets the bundle on the table. As soon as he undoes the ribbon, the whole tower falls apart. Each envelope is inscribed with a day. There is one for every day his guests will be here. "Veramente?" *For real?*

Violetta nods. "Signor Cotogna was nothing if not a planner."

He lets out a gusty sigh. "Too bad I can't just marry you."

She does not even pretend to laugh, which he appreciates. "You have been saying this since you were five." Before she was a lawyer, she was a babysitter. Ever the cliché, Dario developed a massive crush on her. So did Emilio. They would fight and fight and fight about it, despite her adamancy that she preferred older gentlemen. "Business and pleasure should stay separate."

"Is this not business?" Dario gestures around at the tent and the focaccia. He points at her leather attaché case, overstuffed with legal documents. "It all seems pretty transactional to me."

"View it as you wish." Violetta blows a stray hair out of her eye. "I'll be inside preparing the paperwork if you need me."

Alone again, Dario takes a seat under the tent. There are trapezoidal centerpieces set out before him with tiny utensils and a wide array of finger foods on the shelves for a proper aperitivo. It is a long-standing Italian tradition dating all the way back to the 1800s with Roman roots. Small bites are

paired with alcoholic drinks to jump-start your appetite before a big, savory dinner.

The spread is robust. Fresh focaccia, olives, prosciutto, figs
and jam. Bruschetta is on a display all its own next to veggies,
a cold salad and a rich-looking quiche made by Paola. Paola
has been the Cotogna's personal chef for longer than Dario
has been alive and he is almost certain she will outlive him.

When he was a kid, Dario hated the cultural tradition of the
aperitivo. While the adults gabbed and sipped wine without
a care in the world, he munched on potato chips and moaned
that he was hungry for something more substantial. Having an
aperitivo felt like a giant tease. As an adult, though, he thinks
of the aperitivo like extended foreplay before really good sex.
Not that he has had really good sex since Preston, and Preston is as good as dead to him.

A clank ratchets him from his thoughts. Across from where
he sits, on the triangle of grass on the other side of the stone
path that wraps around the house, a bar has been erected. Behind it, a handsome man with salt-and-pepper hair and a fabulous mustache organizes the liquors, mixers and garnishes.
There are plentiful wines and beers, and also the ingredients
for an Aperol Spritz or a Negroni. A small glass bowl of salted
nuts sits near the front edge of his workstation.

Dario's stomach begs for even the tiniest morsel, but it
would be rude to start eating before his guests arrive, so he
picks up the day one envelope and unfolds the stationery he
has handled a million times before.

Caro Tesorino,
Today begins your new adventure. Bravissimo for agreeing!
Love, in the stories I've been told and the one I lived with
your nonna, is a matter of time, place and spirit.

I have given you a time: one week rolling into one year rolling into forever.

I have given you a place: Villa Meraviglia, the site of many fond memories and a million more to be made.

Unfortunately, unless I am now un fantasma favoloso, I cannot provide the spirit.

That must come from within you, Dario.

Strangers can only become friends and friends can only become amanti if you possess an openness of spirit, a joy for the possibilities.

Now go. Greet your guests with a smile, a hug and a delicious meal. See what cooks up between you.

Con affetto,

Nonno

Despite having sworn his tear ducts were depleted over the last couple of months, he softly cries. His nonno was always looking out for him and his well-being, even if he chose the strangest ways to do so. Dario has to trust that this is going to work out for the best.

Moments later, a musical horn blares out front. So engrossed in the letter, Dario didn't even hear the big car coming up the drive.

From the outer pocket of his jacket, he produces a tan handkerchief to wipe away his tears. The handkerchief is monogrammed CCS. He runs his thumb over his nonno's initials. It's a small way to keep his nonno close to his heart through this wacky plot.

A sleek black Mercedes van idles a few feet away from the side gate. The bartender from earlier appears behind Dario with a tray of champagne flutes. The driver—Fabrizio, a favorite of his nonno's—comes around and slides open the back door. Dario's heart climbs up into his throat and backflips off his Adam's apple.

He has seen these people in photographs and read their ruminations on love, but meeting them in person still makes his hands clammy and his back sweat. Good thing he remembered to put an undershirt and deodorant on.

The first guest to step out of the van wears board shorts, a blue T-shirt advertising his own band called California Storm Clouds, and Velcro sandals. His skin is dark, and his hair is free-form dreadlocks. His easy, charming smile is tinted with melty chocolate. An Amorina wrapper is balled in his right hand and a sticker-covered guitar case is gripped in the other.

"Hey, man. I'm Beau Garner. Oh, shit. Sorry." Laughing, he shoves the candy wrapper in his pocket, then pulls Dario in for one of those very bro-ey greetings: part handshake, part hug, all awkward.

Dario stumbles backward. "Ciao. It's a pleasure to meet you." Beau wrote lyrics to a song as his contest entry. He fronts a relatively new, modestly popular indie group back in the States that Dario enjoyed listening to online even if he's unfamiliar with most popular music. He favors opera and classical over other genres. Perhaps his nonno should've been more specific when he said Dario liked music.

The bartender waves the tray of champagne before Beau in offering.

"Don't mind if I do," Beau says and then, clearly perked up by the bubbly, breaks into a song about landslides and supernovas that Dario has never heard before.

"Bravissimo! Did you write that?" Dario asks.

"I wish! That was 'Champagne Supernova' by Oasis. Do you guys not have Oasis over here?" Beau asks. Dario doesn't have a moment to respond before Beau barrels on by singing a song about a woman named Sally that he also doesn't recognize. "Oh, man. Let me play for you later. There's so much music I can introduce you to."

He ventures into the yard singing yet another song Dario can't identify.

The next guest is short, white and pale. She wears red lipstick that matches her red hair, which hangs down in long waves that clear her rib cage. She's dressed in an unassuming floral shirt and a light tan jacket. She introduces herself as Michelle Trottier. "Lovely to meet you. You're a fashion student in Paris, yes?"

"Aix-en-Provence," she corrects, demurely shaking his hand. "Have you seen the latest episode of *The Luxurious Ladies of Provence*?"

Dario curls his brow. "What is that?"

The demureness evaporates into the air. Her wide eyes go wider, making her look like a Walter Keane painting. "Are you joking? Only the best French reality show on TV!" She whips out her phone to show him her wallpaper. A gaggle of women in lavish gowns pose before a glittery background. They are all attractive, if somewhat plastic-looking.

Dario Cotogna is as pansexual as a person can be. His first kiss was with a guy, his first time was with a woman, and his first real relationship was with a nonbinary person. Like with all the best chocolates, the wrapper does not matter so much as its contents.

"Your information section said you liked watching TV. I can't believe you haven't seen it," Michelle says. "On the most recent episode, Juliette—the one in the middle with the big hoop earrings—was filmed outside my new apartment! I nearly dropped dead when I watched the episode. When had they filmed it? Had I been home and missed it? I rushed outside and took this." She shoves a side-by-side comparison photo in his face. On the left is Juliette taking a phone call, looking stern yet glamorous. On the right is Michelle in a similar yet less expensive version of Juliette's outfit, holding the same pose. "My friend took it. Do we not look alike?"

Dario doesn't see the resemblance. "Of course. Uncanny!"

Michelle beams. "You must watch at least one season while I'm here. You'll be hooked. It'll be our thing!"

He is confused why someone would want to travel all this way just to stay inside and watch a TV show, but she's beautiful and he'll need to be amenable if he plans to find a spouse among these strangers.

"Your wish is my command. I look forward to it. It is a pleasure to have you with us," he says as she accepts a champagne flute and flits into the yard.

A lumbering, square-faced, white man emerges next. He dons a blue polo shirt and slacks. On his wrist is the largest, gaudiest watch Dario has ever seen, and he is very rich, so that's saying something. The man's golden hair is parted to the left and shellacked into place with a ton of product.

"Guten tag!" he greets.

His handshake is firm and a tad abrasive. Dario's fingers cramp. "Ansel Voight, thank you for making the *time* to be here with me."

The cheesy joke sails right over the head of the German watch salesman.

"The pleasure is all mine," Ansel says. "What is that you've got on there? Is that a Panerai?" He points his nose down at the watch Dario wears.

"Good eye," Dario says, twisting his wrist in the light. Every day, he straps on one of his late father's watches. He possessed an impressive collection of Florentine watches with Italian leather bands and titanium bezels with vintage-inspired dials. The brand has ties to the Italian Navy, and as an avid sailor, Cosimo Cotogna Jr. loved the waterproofing and practical design as a status symbol without all the flash. It keeps Dario connected to him in the same way the hankie keeps him connected to his nonno, and it serves as a reminder that time is never guaranteed, so he needs to make the most of it.

"'99?" Ansel asks, grabbing Dario's wrist and bending down quite a way to get a closer look. As a short king, Dario has always been taken by tall people. He likes his bed partners climbable.

"I believe so. Si," says Dario. Ansel's large hand is warm and inviting. He glances up with an impish smile and arrestingly clear pale blue eyes. Dario's heart patters. Maybe this won't be all bad.

"Finely crafted and well-minted, but nein. It doesn't suit you. Let's talk more about this. A lovely wrist like yours deserves a statement piece," Ansel says before planting a charming kiss on the back of Dario's hand. A heat rushes to his cheeks. Does he say this to all his customers?

Selina Velasco bounds onto the scene next. She is a skyscraper of a woman made to look even taller by her high-waisted slacks and sand-colored platform heels. A tailored crop top with a low neckline hugs her slender frame. Her deep-set, dark eyes have smoky makeup around them. She wears huge, dangly earrings in the shape of the quince fruit.

"Cotognas," Dario says with a smile, pointing to her jewelry.

"You noticed," she says, eyelashes fluttering. She turns her head and extends her neck to give him a better look. He contemplates what it might be like to trail kisses up and down that soft-looking skin.

"What a sweet touch. Did you make those?" he asks.

"Sí. Te gustan ellos?" she asks.

Since he knows a little bit of a lot of languages given his

line of business, he replies in Spanish to try to impress her. "Ellos son muy hermosos." *They are very beautiful.*

"*Eres* muy hermoso," she says with the radiant smile Dario mooned over in her modeling portfolio. She's even more beautiful in person. Her nails are long and painted white and he'd like to feel them tracing down his cheeks. "Before the sun goes down, I have to take a picture of my outfit to post. I promised the designer. Where is the best spot to take it?"

"Just around the house. You can get the hills and the lake in the background," he says.

She leans in and air-kisses both of his cheeks.

Not wanting to miss Selina posing for those pictures in his own backyard, Dario starts to follow her before someone clears their throat behind him.

When he turns back, he is shocked at the sight of his fifth guest, Charlie Moore, whom he'd forgotten all about for a moment.

Charlie is the first man Dario has ever seen with blue hair. It was blond in his photos, no? Currently, it is buzzed short and dyed bright. He stands at a sensible five-foot-ten in a pair of orange, lace-up sneakers, green shorts, and a white tank top with a wrinkly, button-up linen shirt thrown over it. A small nose ring on his right nostril blinks in the sunlight.

While Charlie's head is pitched back, mouth agape, taking in the grandiosity of Villa Meraviglia, Dario plays connect the dots with the plethora of tattoos going up his arms, across his collarbone and down his legs. He loses count of them by the time Charlie speaks.

"You really live here?" Charlie asks without so much as a hello. There is a gentle scrape to Charlie's voice. It's a bit nasal and reminds Dario of a bouncy ball, rising and falling in random arcs.

"For my whole life, I have," Dario says.

"How old is this place?" Charlie asks, not moving an inch from his spot on the gravel driveway.

"Oh, centuries," Dario says. "It got a renovation when my parents married and moved in to start a family, but all the original materials and stylings were kept, maintaining the architectural integrity. My great-great-grandmother was born here."

"That's some history, huh? Is it haunted?" Charlie asks.

Only with memories, Dario thinks but says, "Not to my knowledge."

Charlie frowns. Dario hopes he hasn't dissatisfied his guest already. These people came from all over the world to stay here, to meet him. Disappointment is the airplane of fear crop-dusting this endeavor and he would like to cut the engine on it as quickly as possible.

"All good," Charlie says. Their gazes finally meet. Dario likens Charlie's eyes to molten chocolate, so brown and rich. "I'm Charlie, by the way."

"I'm Dario Cotogna," he says. "Won't you come in?" The iron gate squeaks behind him.

Neither is sure which of them should go first, so Dario and Charlie end up squeezing through the gate together. Their shoulders brush. They let out little uncomfortable laughs, though Dario secretly thrills at the touch. This reminds him of courting back in scuola secondaria di secondo grado, when he was beginning to blossom into his own.

"I'm clearly underdressed," Charlie notes, obviously inspecting Dario's suit.

"Not at all. You're perfect as you are," Dario says, surprised at how suave he sounds despite his flirting skills sitting dormant for some time.

The pink flush that instantly appears on Charlie's cheeks coupled with his blue hair makes him look like a delicious tower of cotton candy.

"How do you say 'thank you' in Italian?" Charlie asks.

"Grazie," he says.

"Grazieye. Grayzey-aye," Charlie tries then laughs at himself.

"Grat-zee-ay. Grat." Dario motions with his hand toward Charlie to repeat after him.

"Grat."

"Zee."

"Zee."

"Ay."

"Eye," Charlie says with his gaze laser-focused on Dario's mouth.

"Ay," Dario repeats slower.

"Ahye," Charlie tries again, mouth really making a meal of the wrong-sounding syllable.

Dario stifles a laugh. "Once more. Ay."

"Ay."

"There! Now, put it all together. Grazie."

"Gratezie."

Dario offers an encouraging smile. "Closer."

"I sound like a hick, don't I?" Charlie asks, slipping his hands into his pockets. It's not a self-conscious gesture so much as a self-aware one.

"A hick?" Dario asks.

"You know, like, unintelligent, unsophisticated, a total bumpkin." His head bobbles.

"Bumpkin? Like a pumpkin?" His confusion increases as their strides lock.

Charlie's blush deepens. "I think my Pennsylvania is showing. A 'bumpkin' is somebody from the countryside."

"Is Pennsylvania the countryside? I've only been to America a handful of times, and never to Pennsylvania," Dario says, surprised by this easy conversational rhythm they fall into.

"You're not missing much," Charlie says. "Especially in Slatington. It's a bit of a one-stoplight town."

"We have no stoplights here in Montecologna," says Dario. Flashes of his father's untimely end emerge from his subconscious even after twenty years. He elbows them back down.

Charlie, having clearly caught Dario's far-off expression, looks away out of courtesy. "It's more of a phrase that means it's a small town with not a lot going on in it. This—me winning the contest—is the first exciting thing to happen to someone from Slatington in years."

"Is this your first time in Italy?" Dario asks as they cross the pool deck on their way to the tent where the others are already snacking away.

"This is my first time out of the country. It was my first time on an airplane ever," Charlie says. "I knew they gave you in-flight pretzels or whatever, but they served me a whole meal! It wasn't very good, but it was still cool. Eating in the middle of the sky like that."

Dario is taken by the innocent wonder radiating off Charlie. "Why don't we get some good food in you here? There's plenty to choose from." He gestures at the impressive spread Paola and her team have whipped up.

Charlie's eyes brighten. "Grazie, Dario."

"That was it! Exactly right," Dario says, clapping Charlie on the back in an overly familiar way. He steps back, afraid he's gone too far, but Charlie flashes him a big, bright smile as they enter the tent together.

Five

CHARLIE

Charlie downs the last drops of his Negroni as an old woman who barely clears five feet shuffles out into the night. She wears a spotless apron over a short-sleeved shirt with lemons on it. Her hair is as white as her apron and mostly tucked back into a bandanna, and from her droopy ears, two pearl earrings dangle. She does not speak a lick of English, and nobody expects her to.

"Buona sera, a tutti. Mi chiamo Paola. Per il nostro primo piatto abbiamo un'insalata di rucola condita con finocchi e pomodorini all'olio d'oliva e limone," she says. Charlie understands none of it, but he politely accepts the plate of greens coated in a citrusy dressing anyway.

At first bite, dormant taste buds on his tongue galvanize. Pleasure centers he has never accessed in his brain flicker on. He thought the focaccia was mind-blowing, but this? A whole cherry tomato bursts with freshness between his in-need-of-a-checkup teeth. The dance of flavors is divine, and he eats faster, almost as if he's afraid his plate is going to get taken away before he's finished. He audibly *mmm*s through his chews.

A soft chuckle comes from across the table. Dario, their gracious and well-dressed host, has his fork set aside. Is he overheating in that dapper, seafoam green suit in this over-eighty-degree weather? His shoulder-length, chestnut brown hair curls a bit at the edges, yet there's not a single bead of sweat on his face. Only a charming smile. Directed right at Charlie.

"Am I being too loud?" Charlie asks, wiping his mouth with the back of his hand. "My manners are a little rusty." He remembers the cloth napkin on his lap and wipes his mouth again to save face.

First impressions are important. They seemed to click when he got out of the van, but any number of uncouth quirks could turn Dario off.

There's too much riding on this for him to not put his best foot forward.

Marriage, as a concept, has never really appealed to Charlie. While he understands the legal and economic benefits, it's a bit archaic, and he's never seen it as the ultimate declaration of undying love the way some of his peers do. In equal quantities, he knows miserable married couples and blissful unmarried couples. Signing his name to a piece of paper alongside a wealthy stranger doesn't seem like such a bad trade if it gets his family out of the early grave they've dug for themselves.

"Not at all. I'm glad you're enjoying yourself," Dario says. His eyes crinkle slightly with his growing smile.

"I've never met a salad I actually liked," Charlie says. The wilty, premade bagged stuff from the grocery store makes his stomach sad and leaves him hungry all afternoon.

"Typical American," says Michelle with an over-the-top eye roll.

Beau chuffs at this from the other end of the table. "You think all we eat is McDonalds, don't you?"

"No," Michelle says. "I'm sure you eat Chipotle, too."

Selina lets out a spicy *ooh*.

Ansel chimes in. "Care to comment, Charlie?"

"I'm more of a Burger King fan myself," he says earnestly.

Everyone laughs, even though Charlie didn't think he said anything funny.

"Who can talk about fast food when we're eating *this?* In Charlie's defense, this is a really good salad. How long has Paola been cooking for you?" Selina asks, even though she's barely touched her food. She is far too busy taking photos of it from every angle, poring over them to decide which one to post on her social media story so she can rack up impressive numbers of views.

"Since well before I was born. Paola's like a nonna to me," says Dario, straightening in his chair.

"Che cosa?" Paola comes up beside him. Several suited servers line up at her back.

"Sei come una nonna per me," he repeats in Italian.

She smiles, revealing a few missing teeth.

"Mio tesorino" she coos before swapping out his empty salad plate for a fresh plate of mouthwatering pasta. Food is clearly her love language.

Thick noodles cradle a hefty white sauce dappled with finely grated cheese and specks of black pepper. The aroma is enough to send Charlie into a state of sheer bliss. He picks up his new, clean fork and feasts.

Ansel is the first person to break the strong spell of the spaghetti. "Dario, this is truly your home?"

"Si. This is my home. I live right in there." He gestures toward the stone barn adjacent to the main villa.

Charlie questions aloud why Dario lives in the smaller of the two structures on the expansive property.

"I am only one person. I do not need all that space." Dario stares down at his plate, swirling his noodles.

Charlie wishes he hadn't asked. Clearly, he struck a nerve.

"You're really going to let us stay here?" Michelle asks. Charlie hates to admit that he was thinking the same thing and glad someone else spoke it first. Seems like a wild invasion of privacy. Not to mention a massive inconvenience. But then again, when you have this much, it would be wrong not to share it.

Dario nods.

"Why?" Ansel asks. "I assumed we'd all be in a luxury rental in Perugia proper. This is so much like *Der Bachelor*!"

"It's for the promotion, obviously," Selina says. "Nobody here knows branding better than me. Amorina is a chocolate brand that started in the home. What better way to underline that than inviting potential suitors into the home of the new head of the brand? You are the new head of the brand, right?"

"Since we have such a short time together, this is also easiest for me to get to know you," Dario says, but sounds as if he's holding back.

"This is just like when Juliette Boucher from *The Luxurious Ladies of Provence* launched her own shoe line and gifted the other luxurious ladies a lifetime supply of Boucher Booties," says Michelle.

"But we're not getting a lifetime supply of chocolate," Ansel says. "It's not at all like these Lavish Ladies."

"*Luxurious* Ladies," Michelle corrects under her breath. Then louder: "If one of us marries Dario, then we can have all the chocolate we want, right?"

"Right," Dario says, clearly having a hard time following the rapid volley of conversation across the table. Charlie is right there with him. The varied accents don't help either.

"You said *if* one of us marries Dario. Isn't one of us *going to* marry you?" asks Beau.

"There are no expectations on this experience. It was simply my grandfather's final wish for me to meet people from all walks of life from different parts of the world that I may not have crossed paths with otherwise. There are no obligations. You are all here to relax and enjoy. If at any point you decide you are not interested in me, that is completely fine and you are still welcome to stay the whole term of your winning," he says.

This isn't a surefire thing? Charlie sags a bit. He got on the plane under the assumption he had a one-in-five chance of being engaged by the end of the week. He was floored that he was selected in the first place—reading and rereading the email to make sure it was not some sort of awful joke.

In this case, his game plan for winning Dario over might need to be more aggressive. Beau's got the voice, Selina's got the looks, Michelle's got the style, and Ansel's got the charm. What does Charlie have?

"I did not notice any release forms in the paperwork we signed earlier," Michelle says, changing the subject.

"Why would there be release forms?" Dario asks.

"I assumed a camera crew would be documenting this…" She peers around as if she may spot hidden cameras among the landscaping disguised to look like birds or flowers.

"This is all private," says Dario with a new firmness. "While the contest did drum up a lot of excitement for Amorina, I do genuinely wish to connect with all of you and see, um, what cooks up."

Paola and her staff arrive with the final course, Amorina

tartufos. Inside a hard shell of Amorina chocolate are tiers of gelato in the colors of the Italian flag. Cherry for red, vanilla for white and pistachio for green.

The conversation veers away from Amorina and the marriage scheme. Everyone goes around and talks about their jobs and their families. Charlie stifles several yawns in a row. The time difference and the jet lag are catching up to him, but he will be damned if he lets a bite of this heaven-on-a-plate go to waste even if he is stuffed to the gills.

The stars are out by the time they emerge from the tent, full and happy. They carry small glasses of ice-cold, electric-yellow alcohol.

"What's this called again?" Michelle asks, sniffing the rim. Her upper lip curls.

"Digestivo. This is limoncello, a lemon liqueur straight from the Amalfi Coast," says Dario.

"Salud!" says Selina.

"It's meant to be sipped," says Dario, but it's too late. She downs the drink like a shot.

Charlie tips the glass to his lips. "Tastes like adult Gatorade," he says. "They don't sell anything this fancy at Drink Dash, where I work."

Beau and Ansel smoke nearby. The nubs of their cigarettes look like extra stars in the twinkly, cloudless sky. They all sway to piped-in music. Charlie feels buoyant on his feet for the first time in a long time. The lake glistens beneath the moon high above the village. He's just arrived, and he already never wants to leave. If only his family were with him.

"What's that Italian song about the moon hitting your eye?" Beau asks, scanning the group. Then, as he seems to love to do, he breaks into song. Without a lick of self-consciousness, he sings "That's Amore" in a buttery, melodic voice.

"That's an American song," says Charlie when Beau forgets the lyrics and trails off.

"And what horrendous stereotyping," says Dario with a good-natured laugh that rolls through the entire group.

A little while later, Charlie stands in the center of the downstairs sitting room. The walls are a tan stone, and the ceiling is curved brick. A fan spins overhead, spreading the scent of fresh-cut flowers through the air.

Beneath his shoes, a rust-colored carpet bunches up. Three Negronis, pasta, a tartufo, and a lifetime's worth of focaccia churn in his stomach. He hasn't eaten that well in God knows how long. The flavors linger on the length of his tongue. Trying to pick a favorite one is like trying to decide which family member to save in a house fire.

A house fire would not be a half-bad idea if nobody were inside and he were able to make it look like an accident for insurance purposes...

No, that's the Negronis talking.

"Two of you will have to share a room," says Violetta, the lawyer overseeing the contest, once all five of the winners venture inside the villa. Earlier, she served them dozens of legal documents to sign before they could touch the aperitivo spread. Charlie was so hungry that he was almost tempted to eat the paper. His initials started to look like wingdings. For all he knows, he signed away his first-born child, eyes glazing over around page seven.

"Not it!" shouts Selina, already dashing toward the exit and up the outdoor stairs. Charlie is impressed she can move that fast in those towering, expensive-looking shoes. And with jet lag and alcohol in her, no less. How did she even know which direction to go?

Beau puts his hands up, looking over at the others. "I already settled my stuff in the bedroom down here."

Michelle says, "I'll take the single upstairs, then."

"How is that fair?" asks Ansel, the oldest of the group and somehow the most immature.

"I am a woman," Michelle says, concern building a wall behind her thin voice. "You do not expect me to sleep in a room with a strange man I do not know."

"Macché! Signor Voight, you see the situation," Violetta says.

"You are here to date a man you do not know," Ansel argues. "We all won the contest. We should all get the same amenities." Perhaps the bartender overserved him. Spittle leaps out of his mouth, visible in the lamplight.

"Mi dispiace. There are two twin beds in the last bedroom. That is how the villa is laid out," says Violetta. Beau, clearly uninterested in further confrontation, backs into the downstairs bedroom and shuts the door behind him. Seconds later, the pluck of guitar strings floats out through the wood.

"I don't mind a roommate," says Charlie, hoping this squashes the issue. "I didn't bring a lot of stuff, so I won't take up too much space."

When Charlie was the last to arrive at the meet-up location at the Florence airport, he felt out of place. Everyone seemed glamorous, with their hard-shelled, metallic, rolling suitcases. All he had was a beat-up, blue duffel bag from back when he played basketball. A couple shirts, a couple shorts, enough underwear to get him through the week without needing to do laundry, his sketchbooks and his pencil case.

"You may not, young man, but I am past forty. It is nothing personal, of course. It is a matter of principle," he says as if any of this is going to get them on his side. As if his words can magically make Violetta carve out a new room in this centuries-old villa and drag one of the beds into it for him.

"Come va?" Dario asks, appearing beside Violetta.

Charlie rights the rug beneath his feet. Dario remains unruffled in his shiny loafers and full suit despite how humid the day was.

"I was telling these men they will need to share a room, and Signor V—"

"I was just telling Violetta here what a beautiful home you have. We have such luck to stay here," Ansel says, changing his tune and flashing a smarmy smile.

Charlie turns to Michelle. She looks back with disbelief. But this is only day one, and given the bedroom situation, he thinks it best not to upset Ansel or risk an uncomfortable sleeping arrangement by voicing the truth, so he shrugs in acceptance. His focus is on wooing Dario, not making enemies.

"Grazie mille, Ansel. Are you needing anything else?" Dario asks, appearing more tired than he was when they arrived. All that socializing. Charlie considers himself an extrovert, but international travel can really kill your personal battery.

Ansel shoots Dario with a loaded smile. "Not right now."

"Let me know if you do," Dario adds.

"I will," Ansel says, eyes flecked with mischief. He exits toward the outside stairwell.

Michelle slaps her palms on her thighs. "I'm tired. I'm going to head upstairs to whichever room Selina didn't claim. Bonne nuit," she says, proffering a small wave.

A charge lingers in the room once it's only him and Dario. Charlie blames the slight buzzing of his skin on the limoncello working its way through his system and not the appealing lean Dario does in the room's arched doorframe.

"I wanted to say thank you for your hospitality. This place

is beyond my wildest imaginings. I can't even conceive what the museum looks like," Charlie says.

"You'll get the chance to see for yourself tomorrow. You should rest up before then after all those travels," Dario says.

"I promised I'd call my family when I arrived. I got so caught up in dinner that I forgot. Do you have the Wi-Fi password?" Charlie couldn't afford the pricey international plan his cell service required for him to make calls out here, but he knows he won't be able to sleep if he doesn't update his family.

"Of course. Video call or voice call?" Dario asks.

"What time is it?" Charlie does the mental math. They are six hours behind in Pennsylvania. "Video."

"The connection is stronger out in the barn house. Happy to let you in, if you're okay with that," Dario says.

"Cool, yeah. Thanks."

They head back out into the yard. The staff at the villa works quickly and silently to pack up the food and take down the tent. Charlie follows Dario as he weaves through the workers, noting that his gait seems to lack the confidence of someone who has just inherited a global chocolate empire. From the profile and the pictures accompanying the contest notice, Charlie visualized a broad-smiled, aggressive salesman mixed with European elegance. Someone more like Ansel. Dario has softer edges than he expected, which is intriguing.

The rounded, windowed doors of the barn house open into a large room with a king-size bed at its center. At the foot of the bed, a tiny white dog perks up from sleep. It yaps immediately upon seeing them.

"Tutto bene, Angelo. Charlie è un nostro amico," Dario says, leading Charlie inside. "Meet Angelo. The only Cotogna who can't have chocolate. He's friendly, just excited."

Charlie laughs and scratches the dog on the top of his head where his fur is tufted and soft.

In the left corner of the room there is a wooden chair beside a tabletop where a TV rests. "Will this work?" Dario asks.

Charlie nods and sits. There is a piece of paper on the desk with the Wi-Fi password written on it. He keys it into his phone and calls his mom, but she doesn't pick up. "That's weird. She should be home from work by now. I'll try my grandpa."

"Your grandpa lives with your parents?" Dario asks.

"Both of my grandparents do. They're mostly homebound for health reasons," Charlie says. A framed photo of Cosimo Cotogna Sr. catches Charlie's attention on the bedside table across the room. "I was really sorry to hear about your grandpa's passing."

"Que? Oh, grazie." Dario stands at the propped open doors. The jangle of Angelo's collar echoes outside as he circles for a spot to pee. Dario stares into the night, but it doesn't appear that his eyes land on anything.

"You must miss him," Charlie says. Thoughts of his own grandfather passing invade his brain, but he shuts them down. Grandpa has such strong will that he might outlive Charlie at this point.

"Si. Yes. We all do." He presses his back into the wood of the door, so it swings and squeaks.

"How is it being the new head of Amorina?" Charlie asks.

Dario's facial expression fluctuates rapidly.

A loud chime erupts from Charlie's phone. His mom's contact photo appears on the screen.

Dario looks relieved to not have to answer. "Take your time," he says before shutting the door.

An uncomfortableness fills Charlie's belly. Did he say something wrong?

He answers the call before the final ring.

"Charlie! You made it! Tell us how it's going!" Mom says,

the first and closest face in a crowded rectangle of them. Grandma and Grandpa are in the back peering over. Dad is poking in from the side.

"Yeah!" Grandpa says, hungry for information. "Tell us everything!"

He goes to speak before realizing he can't tell them *everything* because in his duffel bag, nestled beside his passport, is the foreclosure warning from the bank he never gave his parents.

His acceptance into the contest happened quickly—a total whirlwind of good news—and he felt it was a sign from the universe that everything would work out. If he can secure a marriage to Dario over the next week, there is no way Dario won't pay off their debt *before* the bank can legally file a foreclosure claim with the courts. "Where to even begin?" Charlie says.

Six

CHARLIE

The next morning, Charlie gapes at the whimsical AMO-RINA CHOCOLATE FACTORY AND MUSEUM sign towering over his head as he steps out of the van with his fellow contest winners in tow.

The building fans out in all visible directions. Its exterior is a Technicolor dream of brick and tubing and pluming smoke-stacks. The scent of rich chocolate spills out from every crevice in the brickwork. His whole body lurches forward.

The stately front doors fling open, revealing Dario in a new fuchsia five-piece suit, the same color as the Amorina logo. The vibrant suit is paired with tan-heeled white shoes, a white shirt and a red-striped tie that matches his jaunty pocket square. On his head is a tan fedora with a red ribbon wrapped around it, and his hair winds out from underneath. He stretches out his arms in greeting, revealing steampunk-style half gloves on his hands. Charlie must admit that the ensemble is sort of doing something for him. Much showier than the stained T-shirts and ripped jeans his usual hookups live in.

"Benvenuti nella fabbrica di cioccolato Amorina," says Dario with the pizazz of a carnival barker. "Welcome to the Amorina Chocolate Factory. Today I have the pleasure of guiding you through the newly refurbished and reopened museum. Come in."

Charlie leads the charge inside, childish glee bubbling up to the surface of his skin. Beau and Ansel are close behind. Selina turns Michelle into her personal photog, demanding she capture a video of her entering the storied factory.

Inside, the floor is a tan tile and in the center is the Amorina logo, which is a fuchsia heart draped in melty chocolate. Dario stands in the center of it, backed by a wall of sepia-tinted photographs charting the company's entire history. Workers crisscross behind him with smiles on their faces, showcasing what a fun place this must be to work.

Charlie wishes his entire family could be here to experience this with him. This is his first time away from home for any extended period, and in the background, homesickness is an adhesive bandage slowly being torn from his skin.

This is all for them, he reminds himself. And if he's having fun while here, so be it!

The tour starts in earnest in a large, colorful gallery room. Boxes and cases display photos, preserved artifacts and golden placards. Charlie tunes up his listening ears, eager to learn about the company behind his favorite candy.

Dario details with a clear voice and bright eyes how in the early 1910s, his great-great-grandmother Eleanora Amato decided to use her family's meager Umbrian bakery as a launch pad for her artisan chocolate business. Later, it grew into an empire with the help of Vincenzo Cotogna, the neighbor boy with a nose for business.

"The Amato and Cotogna families would tell you their children were destined for one another from birth, but Eleanora and Vincenzo were adamantly against the idea for the longest time," says Dario, gesturing them toward a display in the front corner that prominently features a portrait of the two of them. "You see, my great-great-grandfather's family was in the pasta business, huge factories that employed hundreds." He gestures to a scale model of a factory, not dissimilar to the one they are inside but less fanciful. "He was enamored with Eleanora's dark chocolate recipe, as were many in Umbria and beyond, so when he returned from World War I he had the idea that they could turn her small business into an industrial enterprise, an entire chocolate empire."

The group moves over to an interactive exhibit with a sign above it that reads: Dove tutto ha avuto inizio… *Where It All Began…*

A backdrop photo of La Pasticceria Amato hangs unwrinkled behind a 1920s-model car propped up on tall wheels, calling to mind a monster truck rally Charlie once went to with his dad at the Allentown fairgrounds. Two massive headlights poke out of the cone-shaped hood, and they gleam in the studio lights that are set up in the corners of the squared-off area.

A woman dressed in an Amorina polo with her black hair pinned up shows them a rack of period-appropriate costumes, hats and props to the right of the car. "Who will go first?" the woman asks in heavily accented English.

Most of them decline the photo op, except Selina who struts in front of the camera.

"I never say no to a hot set," she informs the group. In the car, on the way, she had shown them all her entire modeling portfolio—from Paris runways to perfume ads. During an internet search last night, Charlie learned that she is one of the world's preeminent trans models, really moving the needle for representation in the fashion industry. She also plans to launch a line of her own handcrafted earrings, of which she presently wears a pair. Two giant chocolate bars hang from her ears. "My followers are going to love this."

She rifles through the rack, flinging her chosen pieces at the worker, deeming her the wardrobe assistant, even if the employee appears unwilling.

Charlie grows restless as Selina toils over an outfit for ten minutes or more. Noticing a nearby bench, he takes a seat and pulls out his sketchbook and pencils to distract himself. The shapes of the old-timey car inspire him, and while pictures on his phone are great, he has challenged himself to do as many flash tattoo designs as possible while he is here as a more active memory book.

The swipe of a pencil across paper always puts Charlie into a state of flow, mind and hand moving in perfect harmony.

By the time Charlie is on to shading the hood of the car, Selina is adjusting the lights to suit her needs despite the protests of the worker not to touch them because they're hot. Dario, clearly displeased by the delay, checks his watch and announces that they should keep moving.

"Go on without me," Selina says, pulling a compact mirror from her purse as she sits on the hood of the car, oblivious to a sign telling her not to. "I have to get this right. Perfection is part of the job."

After a short nod, Dario waves the rest of them on. Charlie glances back over his shoulder, wondering *Is Selina Dario's type?* If so, there is no way he can compete for Dario's attentions. He knows he has his attractive features, but he's far from stylish. He only packed one pair of shoes. Selina brought a whole second suitcase full of them. And she somehow looks just as beautiful in a feathered hat and beaded flapper dress as she does in platform sandals and a modern, low-cut jumpsuit.

In contrast, Charlie thinks he looks like a dog playing dress-up when he has to put on anything nicer than jeans.

At the next bay of history, Dario talks about how it wasn't until his great-great-grandparents started Amorina with an eye trained on growth that their longstanding friendship and new business relationship turned into something more romantic.

"While unheard of in those days, Eleanora was the one to make the first move," Dario says, a winsome smile spreading across his face. *Is Dario Cotogna a romantic?* Charlie needs to take note of these things so he can tailor his approach. Make up for his lack in other areas. "During one of their lengthy meetings with the suits in power, she wrote him a note on an empty chocolate wrapper. This became their primary mode of communication. It turned from friendly notes to love notes, creating the basis for the love notes that we have printed inside our wrappers ever since the beginning of Amorina."

Charlie has always adored those little messages. *You are starshine. The world is kinder because of you. You lead with love, and I follow.* They are always written in Italian first and then a dozen or so other languages beneath. He enjoys picking up different words or phrases from foreign tongues, sounding them out for an audience of the empty liquor store. It gives him a sense of connection to the greater humanity.

The next interactive exhibit is a Write Your Own Wrap station. Several computers are set up in a row beside a large printer. On a pedestal nearby is a pyramid of glistening, gold-foiled chocolate bars. "Go on. Try it out for yourself," says a petite blonde woman.

Everyone nabs a stool and brainstorms messages.

Michelle settles on "Love is the finest luxury," while Beau writes a near-perfect lyric, "Even the sweetest bite is better with you by my side." Off he goes on a tangent of creative genius, pouring poetry into his phone, forgetting to send his wrapper to print. Michelle fiddles with the font, accompanying images and layout of the wrapper, clearly utilizing her designer's eye to create visual balance.

Ansel, however, seems more interested in the woman in the tight Amorina polo than the activity. "Do I spy a Junghans Max Bill Damen on your wrist?" he asks, sidling up beside her. Charlie would have never noticed the slender, unimposing tan band she has on.

"Si." The worker seems to perk up at the attention, and a blush spreads across her already-rosy cheeks when he asks to see it. He plants a kiss on the back of her hand.

"Did you use the quick hook system to match the strap to your work outfit?" he asks, one eyebrow raised in total flirt mode. Charlie tries not to make it obvious that he is watching every second of this juicy show.

"It's like you were there when I got dressed this morning," the worker says, her voice upbeat and airy.

Ansel's upturned mouth grows wolfish. "I wish I had been there when you got dressed this morning. You wear it well. All of it," he says, eyes scanning over her while she giggles.

Is Dario seeing this? Does he care?

Charlie focuses back on his screen, trying to shed the proximal ick slicked to his skin from that overheard exchange.

A slideshow of messages scroll across the screen before taking him to an open dialogue box. He can either type in his own message or use the pre-scripted prompts that have blanks to fill in and a list of words beneath each empty line. He chooses his own simple message: *I hear love in every step when I walk beside you.*

"That's beautiful," comes a voice from behind Charlie.

Dario stands over him. Even sitting, Charlie still comes up to Dario's collarbone, marking their height difference. "I can't take credit for it. My grandma wrote it in a card to my grandpa for their anniversary right after he lost his foot."

"Oddio! I'm sorry to hear that," he says, hand floating onto Charlie's shoulder. This might seem overly familiar from anyone else in the group, but Charlie understands that Italians are expressive, feely people, and he unconsciously leans into the touch. "How did it happen?"

"I'm from an old mining town. A piece of slate fell on his foot and, sparing you the gory details, yeah. Factory production is dangerous work," he says, then recalls where they are and what Dario does. "I'm sure I don't need to tell you that."

Dario nods contemplatively. "Still, that's a hefty price to pay for going to work."

"Thankless, low-paying work at that," Charlie says, unsure why he is disclosing all this other than he feels like he has known Dario a lot longer than a day. Maybe it's that cherubic face that makes him want to spill his whole life story, or the fedora that makes him feel like he's speaking to a newspaperman from the 1950s. A hat like that would usually make Charlie cringe, but in Italy, on Dario, it seems suave.

"Safety and fair pay are important parts of factory operations in food production. I make it my mission to ensure those two facets never go unattended at Amorina," Dario says, eyes brimming with kindness and true care for those that work under him. "I can hardly imagine what your family has gone through."

Charlie shudders at this. Spilling his whole story—*everything* his family has gone through—would require a lot more time than he has and a lot more liquid courage than is appropriate for a midday museum tour. He can't quite come out and say, *I want to marry you so we don't lose our house*, now, can he?

Charlie smiles and says, "Yeah, but we make do. There is always hope. My grandpa may have never walked again, but then he came into some settlement money and got a prosthetic."

"That explains the walking sentiment." Dario juts his chin back toward the computer screen.

Charlie expands his smile. "The card is tacked up on a corkboard in my grandparents' room. I see it every time I bring them their meals. Like I mentioned, they're mostly bedridden these days."

"The prosthetic doesn't work?" Dario asks with a surprising amount of genuine interest. People with the kind of wealth Dario was born into don't usually need to cultivate qualities like curiosity. It heartens him that Dario has done the work of self-betterment so many seem not to bother with.

"Prosthetics get worn down over time. They're supposed to be replaced every three to five years, I think. At this point, it's almost definitely been over five years. From what I understand, prosthetics with their government-issued insurance are near impossible to get these days. There is finding a prosthetist that takes Medicare, paying the twenty percent—that's if you met your deductible—co-pay, waiting for the custom prosthetic," Charlie says, remembering what financial burdens they were already under before the foreclosure warning. Debt is a hungry, stinking sinkhole.

"The American health care system has always baffled me. What ails your grandma?" he asks.

"She has gout, and when it flares, which it often does, she finds it fiery and painful to get up and move about. My grandpa is so devoted to her that he wouldn't ever think to leave her alone in bed when she's in a state like that." Every day, Charlie sees what true love looks like, for which he counts himself immensely lucky. Especially because when he figured out his sexuality, he assumed that kind of simple, happy love wasn't meant for him. That he was doomed to a lifetime of bachelordom. This week probably won't change that, but there's hope that it could, and he clings to that.

Dario nods in understanding. "That love note rings bittersweet now."

Charlie considers the black text on the white background again. "Yeah, I guess so." His smile fades away.

"Are you familiar with the poem 'Footprints in the Sand'?" Dario asks.

"I don't think so," Charlie says.

"It's a religious poem. My family is very Catholic. Or *was* before… I don't practice, but the poem has always stuck with me," Dario says. "It's about a man who walks along a beach and sees scenes from his life. Through most of it, there are two sets of footprints in the sand on his journey, but during the lowest and hardest moments of his life there is only one. He asks, 'I don't understand why, when I needed you the most, you would leave me.' God says, 'When you saw only one set of footsteps, it was then that I carried you.' Sounds like that's the kind of relationship your grandparents have."

"It's the kind of relationship my parents have, too," he says before turning back to his computer screen. Charlie finalizes the layout of his wrapper by choosing a font and sends it to the printer. Since the worker is still busy flirting with Ansel who is leaning in, towering over her with all the smarm of a businessman, Dario grabs the chocolate from the pile and the paper hot off the press, then delicately wraps and seals it shut.

"For you," he says, hand outstretched. "A keepsake."

And he's not sure why just yet, but Charlie knows he's going to treasure this single chocolate bar forever.

Seven

DARIO

Giving a tour of the Amorina Chocolate Factory feels natural, even after the time away. Dario's heart beats in time with the careful words he shares with his potential suitors. Every time he reengages with the history of this place, his passion for the family business ratchets up, as does his pride for the work he wants to do for the rest of his life.

Easier said than done when a wedding stands between him and his destiny.

They are a little over an hour in, and he has already lost two participants, which feels like a bad sign. Selina is surely off in the café already, editing the perfect picture to post. Ansel, who Dario thinks is handsome in a way he does not want to admit to himself, stayed behind with Chiara since he never made his custom chocolate bar. Dario tries not to take Ansel's overt flirtation with Chiara to heart. Again, this all comes with no expectation, and he is a modern queer man who understands that interest in another doesn't mean lack of interest in him.

"Our next stop is all about Amorina's appearance through the ages," he explains to the remaining trio. They enter a room plastered in old advertisements and blown-up, colorful images of Amorina boxes from years past. "Our famous packaging has undergone subtle changes over the years but the central image of the fuchsia heart with the chocolate drizzle has remained a constant."

Some families have a coat of arms; the Cotognas have this—a chocolate-covered heart that represents over a century's worth of love and legacy.

Earlier in the day, before he took his private car to the factory, Dario opened Cosimo Sr.'s day two letter, which was entirely on theme.

Caro Tesorino,
In any new venture, the first step is always the hardest.
    The story of my grandparents' love affair cemented itself long ago. The love notes in the wrappers have found purchase in the minds of candy lovers all over the world. Did you know that the story is not true?
    Take a moment to catch your breath.
    They had passed notes back and forth on empty wrappers out of a want to not waste paper, which I know you'll appreciate given your fervid passion for sustainability, but they weren't love notes. They did not do it because they were so passionate about each other that they simply had to get the words down before they died on their tongues. It was covert, the messages were urgent, and the wrappers were there.
    The truth lies mostly in that my nonna made the first move. After years of dancing around the topic and many business partners not wanting to associate with an unmarried woman in the

workforce, my nonna made a batch of her chocolate the old-school way and incorporated quince fruit into the bar.

Inside the wrapper she wrote: I'd like to marry my recipe with your last name.

They were not pawing at one another. They were not madly in love. They were companions and business partners who liked each other's company and sought to expand their opportunities through matrimony.

This, however, does not make for particularly good marketing copy.

They took bits and pieces and crafted an angle around it.

Through that angle and that marriage, love grew, deeply and truly.

Love is not always the aperitivo. Sometimes it's the digestivo.

You've opened your home to new people. Are you ready to open your heart as well?
Con affetto,
Nonno

The letter pops back into mind as he shows his guests to the next interactive exhibit: *Make Your Mark-eting*. After watching several television commercials for Amorina chocolate dating back through the 1960s, a staff member invites everyone to grab a prop, step in front of the green screen and try their hand at playing the Amorina spokesperson.

Beau goes first. He improvises a melody using the words that scroll by on the teleprompter. Beau's handsome face and voice are enchanting, but Dario can't tell yet if it's a spell he could live happily under forever or a siren song luring him toward the cliffs. Out of all his suitors, Beau seems more interested competing for attention than Dario's heart. But it's still early days, and Dario definitely wouldn't mind a lifetime of private concerts from Beau Garner.

Charlie trips over every line of the script, shrinking into himself as he reads with a robotic cadence. While Charlie may not be a great public speaker, Dario is enraptured by Charlie's tattoos. They become more alive under the blazing lights. Every time he moves, each cartoon figure dotted along his arms does a special dance.

Michelle has the employee switch the teleprompter to French. Excitement bubbles off her as she steps on the red-taped *X* in front of the massive camera attached to a tripod. On the monitor, B-roll footage of the factory processing chocolates rolls behind her.

The rather timid woman melts away as she speaks, her hands moving in time with the turns of the text. Going off script, she flips her red hair with aplomb as she concludes, "Je m'appelle Michelle Trottier et je suis aussi douce qu'Amorina." She blows the camera a kiss, gives a wink.

Charlie leans in and whispers to Dario, "Do you know what she said?"

Overwhelmed by the encompassing scents of coconut and mango wafting off Charlie, Dario struggles to answer. "Uh, she said, 'My name is Michelle Trottier, and I'm as sweet as Amorina.'"

Charlie snorts, shaking his head. A note of vanilla mingles in with the coconut and mango. "So you speak French?"

"Un peu. A little," he says. There is a smudge of white on the bridge of Charlie's pear-shaped, pierced nose. He must be wearing an aromatic sunscreen. Dario wants to slather himself in that scent when he gets home. It knocks his nervous system into overdrive in a new way. He never pictured himself being attracted to someone so edgy and alternative, but Charlie's nearness makes him feel like a brand-new engine roaring to life.

"Perfect Italian, perfect English, and a little bit of French.

How are you so good at languages?" Charlie asks, keeping his voice low so it doesn't get picked up on the recording.

Michelle is dissatisfied with her first take, so she requests another go before the group moves on. She starts facing the backdrop before flipping around with a flashy smile when the camera operator's countdown ends. Dario suppresses a laugh at the theatricality.

"I went to a Montessori school. It was split instruction, so half in Italian and half in English," he explains, eyes tracking Beau as he wanders off, clearly bored by Michelle's holdup.

"Wow. I went to public school where we took maybe a couple semesters of Spanish and called it a day. I tried downloading one of those language game apps a year ago out of boredom and realized I didn't even remember all the days of the week," he says and sighs audibly.

"I've heard some choice things about the American school system. My mom is American, so we mostly spoke English at home," he says.

Michelle takes it from the top again, trying yet another tagline at the end. She must be practicing for her inevitable *Luxurious Ladies of Provence* audition. Though he can't imagine they'd cast a twenty-two-year-old fashion student. But with him as her husband...

Is that why she entered this contest? Is he the clout she needs to lead the televised life she so admires?

"What about the French? How did you learn that?" Charlie asks, whisking him out of that uncomfortable line of thought.

"French and other languages I picked up while working for my grandfather. You can't run an international chocolate company without knowing the languages of your business associates," says Dario. A pang of grief strikes him in his still-fragile heart. There was much more he wished to learn from his nonno.

"Don't they have interpreters for things like that?" Charlie asks.

Dario bobbles his head, recalling conferences past. "My grandfather was big on making business as personal as possible. He felt meetings were more genuine when you spoke to a potential partner in their native language," he says, fumbling slightly over the phrase "potential partner."

That's what this whole setup is about. Charlie is easy to talk to and undeniably attractive, but does that make for a proper life partner? His pop of blue hair and his doodled-upon body parts don't paint him as the portrait of a traditional Cotogna man.

While Dario would never judge a person solely based on their appearance, he is aware that the world does so easily and vocally, especially on the internet. The way Dario presents is a direct reflection of the Amorina brand and the same would go for his spouse.

Charlie doesn't fit the premade mold of an Amorina man, and he shouldn't be set on a public pedestal to be scrutinized for expressing himself in such unique ways. That kind of confidence deserves admiration. It's already earned Dario's. But there is a potential for proximal hurt that sends Dario back and away from contemplating the possibilities with Charlie too hard.

Five strangers. All still in the running. It's far too soon to pick frontrunners when his heart remains frazzled.

"Shall we move on?" Dario asks, clapping his hands together. The sound is dulled by the leather gloves.

Michelle twirls one strand of auburn hair. "Is it okay if I stay here for a little longer? I haven't gotten it quite right yet." The camera worker seems annoyed by the repetitiveness, and a line of other guests unaffiliated with the contest has formed, but Dario wants his suitors to be happy.

"Of course. Take as much time as you need," Dario says.

The final part of the reopened museum is new. He has never given a tour of this room. Amo-Random-na says the sign over the entryway. "Bad name," he mutters to himself, pulling a tiny notebook and fountain pen from the inside pocket of his suit jacket. He leaves himself a memo to get that name updated and the sign replaced.

In the center of the room, in a temperature-controlled box beneath a giant spotlight, is the world's largest Amorina chocolate bar. Other displays showcase funny facts from throughout the company's history. The most notable is in the back corner.

"A little-known fact is that the world record for most chocolate bars eaten in a minute was set with Amorina chocolate bars," Dario says, pointing up at the face of a happy white man shooting the photographer a thumbs-up with a brown, smudgy ring around his mouth.

"How many was it?" Beau asks, interest piqued.

"Three bars," says Dario.

"I can beat that," Beau says, eyes squinted and head cocked back.

"Care to put that to the test?" says a man in a formal outfit appearing from behind a sign that says, Try Your Luck! "I represent Record Holders International. I'm happy to oversee any challenge to the official record."

How much are they paying this official representative of an international organization to hang around the factory museum? It is not even that busy. This must have been one of the many ideas that got floated in meetings right after Cosimo Sr. passed. Dario, too bogged down by his fear of what came next, signed a lot of documents he didn't read as closely as he should have.

Beau cracks his knuckles, then his neck, and steps toward the table. "Hell, yeah. Let's do this."

"Are you sure that's a good idea?" Dario asks, aware of what the quick consumption of chocolate can do to the human body.

"Oh, man. You just made it an even better idea. I'm a bit of a hothead when it comes to people telling me I can't do something," Beau says, rubbing his hands together. "I don't back down from a challenge. You probably didn't know that I started my band on a dare."

"Really?" Charlie asks.

"A friend of mine started a band a few years ago, and I went to his gig at this hole-in-the-wall venue where the drinks tasted like toilet water. The band was okay. They needed more practice, and some of their songs sounded like direct rip-offs of other, bigger artists. After the show, he asked what I thought, and I try to be an honest guy. I said, 'Look, man, congrats. It takes a lot of guts to get up there and do what you just did. Here's where you might improve…'" Beau says.

Dario and Charlie share a look, both clearly knowing where this story is headed.

Beau adds, "He got real mad, pointed a finger in my face in front of our whole friend group, and said, 'What do you know? You're not even a musician. Like you could do better. You can't even commit to a job.'"

"Harsh," Charlie says.

"Meh, I'm a career nomad. I've been a parasailing instructor, a diamond inspector, a short-order cook, a volunteer fireman, a for-hire sculptor and a limo driver. When I encounter a new challenge, I run toward it and leave everything else behind," he says.

"Music was the new challenge?" Dario asks.

Beau nods with pride. "The next morning, I went to a secondhand shop, bought a beat-up Martin D-28 and taught myself everything I needed to know about music. Luckily, one of my previous challenges was writing poetry and selling a piece to a literary magazine. I had notebooks full of poems, which I turned into lyrics, which I turned into songs. The California Storm Clouds is a challenge that stuck longer than others."

Dario bristles, afraid he might be another one of Beau's challenges. Perhaps he's only here to prove he could woo Dario. He could add "husband of a billionaire" to his over-stuffed résumé of accomplishments.

"Now this? I've been eating chocolate since I came out of the womb. This will be a piece of cake," he says, then pauses to correct himself, "This will be a piece of *chocolate*. Ha! Four bars of chocolate. I'm going for the gold."

"There's no gold. Just a certificate," the man says.

Beau waves the man on, dons the branded bib and unwraps his loot. Behind the employee is a big stop clock with bold, red numbers that ticks with each blink of the colon.

"I don't think this is going to end well," Charlie whispers, leaning in again.

That scent. That voice. It banishes thoughts of Beau's intentions and gives Dario goose bumps along his arms. A lump forms in his throat. He swallows it back, nauseous for himself and for Beau. "Only time will tell," he says.

"Your time starts…now!"

Beau's limbs are a blur. He cracks the bar into quarters and shovels them into his mouth. Bits of chocolate fly into the air, landing on the table, skittering off the edges.

Two bars down, with one and a half to go, Charlie grips Dario's forearm, ripping his attention away from the unfolding scene. That large hand crawling with tattoos bunching the fabric of his expensive suit jacket makes his heart speed and his cheeks heat.

The representative shouts that time is up. Dario snaps back to Beau, whose mouth and hands are smeared in chocolate.

His eyes appear watery, and his brow crinkles like one of the discarded wrappers.

A silver platter swirls in front of Beau. On it are wet wipes and a T-shirt that reads I Tried to Beat a Chocolate-Eating World Record and All I Got Was This T-Shirt… On the back, near the neck, is the Amorina logo.

"Swore I had that," Beau says, fists balled in apparent frustration. He gets up from the bench too fast and sways. From under the table, the representative produces a black metal bucket right in time. Beau hunches over and vomits into the bin.

Dario and Charlie quickly turn away, shoulders hunched and heads down.

In their tiny huddle of two, their eyes shift toward one another and lock in. Charlie's clear brown irises capture him, and the faintest trace of a smile confuses him. Until Charlie laughs, low and throaty, broken up by weak apologies. "I don't—" he hiccups "—mean to laugh, but…"

Dario peers over his shoulder. Beau is escorted out of the museum toward the nurse's station, holding his own bucket of puke like an extra tragic consolation prize.

The dam of Dario's laughter bursts. He doubles over alongside Charlie. Their jubilant sounds echo in the now-empty showroom.

"Does he get to keep the bucket?" Charlie asks between guffaws.

"I'll see to it personally that he does," Dario says, leading them away from the unpleasant lingering smell and toward the final stop on the tour, The Tasting Room.

The employee stationed at the entrance asks how many to be seated. Charlie's eyes tunnel past the employee and into the lounge that features long tables and zanily patterned booths. Childlike wonder bolts off Charlie.

Dario realizes none of the others ever caught up with the tour. It's clear where their priorities lie. Dario should be disappointed, but he's not because the present company is too good to begrudge.

"Want me to round up the others?" Charlie asks, clearly trying to be helpful.

"They'll find us when they're ready. Table for two, please," Dario says to the employee, and to his surprise, he really likes the sound of that.

Eight

CHARLIE

The Tasting Room is like the automats of old his grandparents used to tell him about, except only for chocolate.

Each table is pressed up against a wall of rainbow-colored, rectangular compartments. A tablet pops out from the table and asks what you'd like to try. Dario prompts Charlie to go first.

"What do I say?" he asks, amazed at the technology.

"Anything your heart desires. We have old treats, new treats, and treats not yet put to market. If we don't have what you're craving, our taste lab will concoct something close to what you desire," he says, leaning forward on his elbows, letting his chin rest on the backs of his clasped hands. The posture and the direct eye contact make Charlie's heart squeeze a little.

Charlie rolls through his memory bank of favorite flavors. Saliva floods his mouth. While he's partial to the classic Amorina bar, he is not averse to trying something specially made for him. "How about dark chocolate with marshmallow and peanut butter?"

The words appear one at a time on the tablet. A rainbow circle whirls before the name "Snowtop Truffle" glitters across the screen. Whizzing sounds emanate from behind the wall and then a drawer pops open. A springy tray slides out with a single truffle on it. It is about the size of a quarter and pointy at the top like a mountain peak. The marshmallow is drizzled across the smooth exterior.

"It's almost too pretty to eat," says Charlie.

"It's meant to be eaten," says Dario. "I would be offended if you let it go to waste."

Charlie was not expecting this much alone time with the chocolate maker right off the bat, but he won't look a gift horse in the mouth. Unless that mouth is trying to steal his Snowtop Truffle, which he devours whole. The outer shell melts on his tongue, and the sweetness of the chocolate and marshmallow topping give way to the saltiness of the smooth peanut butter that must be made right here on the premises because it's so fresh.

"These are artisan batch chocolates, made closer to the way my great-great-grandmother made her first chocolates in the family bakery. From the stories I've heard, she was very experimental with her concepts, so I asked my grandfather to hire a group of young, excitable chocolatiers to breathe fresh life into Amorina," Dario explains. "Who better to give them ideas than the chocolate lovers who come from all over the world to try out our Tasting Room?"

"That's a brilliant idea," Charlie says.

Dario's cheeks grow pink beneath his smattering of light facial hair. "That's how I pitched it to my nonno. Selfishly, it's a bid for a better sustainability score for the company and a healthier global impact. There is a ton of waste in chocolate production. It is a greenhouse gas intensive food. I don't want my family business to be the reason my children suffer an inevitable heat death."

"You want children, then?" Charlie asks, filing this tidbit away.

"I meant if I have children." Dario's ears pinken the same shade as his cheeks. "I like the idea of keeping Amorina in the Cotogna family, should there still be an Earth to keep Amorina going on by then."

"You're making me feel guilty about wanting to order another chocolate," Charlie says, eyeing the wall of wonder hiding such scrumptious delights.

Dario makes a clicking sound, and his eyes spark with some idea. "No guilt needed for this next one. Let me order for you," Dario says before whispering some Italian words into the microphone on the tablet.

A single square of chocolate appears on the next platter.

Charlie inspects it, sensing he's missing something. "Isn't this just the regular Amorina bar? I mean, I'm not complaining. I love them…"

"Try it and you tell me," Dario says, something unnamable glinting in his eyes.

Charlie lets the square linger on his tongue. The flavor remains rich and decadent, but he can tell that the recipe isn't right. "I like it. It's good. But it's not a typical Amorina bar. I've had enough of them to tell. Is it…sugar-free?"

"Close!" Dario says, seeming delighted. "I have hired a team of scientists to research uses for more of the cocoa fruit. Seventy-five percent of it gets thrown away in the production process like the husks and the pulp. That kind of waste is unconscionable for an operation as big as ours. I have tasked this specific team with developing creative ways to reduce our eco footprint by adding those parts back into the chocolate-making process. Here, they've created a syrup as a sugar replacement meant to replicate our standard flavor."

"Hmm," Charlie says before licking his fingers clean. "Pretty tasty knowing all that."

Clearly pleased, Dario orders Charlie another. When Charlie bites it, the initial flavor is jarring. "Oh, uh, I'm not sure about this one."

If he were not trying to win Dario's affections, he might spit the rest out in one of the compostable napkins stacked nearby. Instead, he muscles through and swallows with a weak smile.

Dario nods, orders a second, and tastes it himself. He barely conceals his own cringe. "What about it isn't working for you?" he asks.

"It smells like chocolate, but it tastes too tart? I'm not sure that's the word I'm looking for," Charlie says.

Dario pulls a small notebook from his pocket and writes down the word TART. He underlines it several times, which makes Charlie feel like his opinion is important.

"That's good data to have. You see, cocoa only grows in specific climates. Due to global warming and deforestation, it's becoming harder to import. What people don't realize is that the familiar flavors of chocolate come out through the roasting and fermenting processes, not so much the cocoa bean itself. Here, our scientists and artisan chocolate makers are working to find a substitute for the cocoa bean. What else can we roast and ferment to make chocolate?" he says with mounting enthusiasm. "It might take years to perfect, and many of our competitors are ahead of us, but I think it's worth the investment and time if we can lessen our carbon footprint with a subset of cocoa-less products."

Charlie was never any good at science, but this all makes

overwhelming sense to him. "For a chocolate maker, you seem very excited about not-chocolate."

A glittery feeling spangles inside Charlie's chest. The whole plane ride over, he assumed he would meet with some stand-offish, Lothario billionaire only concerned about the dollars and cents of selling candy. Dario clearly cares about the world at large and is kind of a nerd about it, which is…*hot?*

Dario licks his pink lips.

Oh, yeah. Definitely *hot.*

"Not-chocolate is, dare I say, the future of chocolate." A shadow of contemplation falls over Dario's face.

"Sounds fake, but I like your passion," Charlie says. "Mind if I order a normal chocolate now to get this taste off my tongue? It's starting to sour on me."

"By all means," Dario says. "Change does not happen in a day."

A pleasingly pink confection with swirls of white and grooves of flower petals pops out of the wall. Sweet hibiscus leads the flavors marching along Charlie's tongue. "Delicious. I'm even tasting some vanilla in here."

"We haven't come up with a name for that one yet," says Dario.

"A rose by any other name would taste as sweet. That play takes place in Italy," Charlie says, recalling his freshman year English class where he played Romeo in his graded scene presentation. He got an A, but everybody who actually memorized their lines got an A, so that wasn't saying too much about his acting skills. He thought he might need to deploy every ounce of those acting skills to show interest in the chocolate maker, but Dario has made such a strong impression that every interaction has been effortless and comfortable, no performing necessary.

"The scene is laid in fair Verona. Not Perugia," says Dario.

"But you could call it The Juliet, or something. I don't know. Just an idea," Charlie says, self-consciousness creeping into his voice. Dario is a professional, international business-man; he doesn't want to hear Charlie's silly thoughts about candy names.

"I really like that," Dario says, and it sounds sincere. But Charlie still clams up, afraid he's overstepped. Dario opens his notebook again.

"What's in there?" Charlie asks, unable to stanch the flow of his curiosity too long.

"Pages of ideas. Everything from the good and the bad, to the outlandish and the simple. My grandfather used to do it, so now I do it as well. He used to say, 'Tutto fa brodo,' which means 'Everything makes broth.'"

"Broth?" Charlie asks, slightly stumped by the connection.

"Every little thing counts toward the big picture. The small-est idea can be the biggest innovation if you believe in it," says Dario, smiling in a way that makes his handsome face even handsomer.

Charlie has always found passionate people deeply sexy. Plus, there is a manliness to Dario's slightly crinkled eyes and facial hair but a boyishness to his rounded, bouncy cheeks and colorful outfits. At once, Dario seems both wise beyond his years and as playful as a newborn kitten. That duality is in-triguing; it makes him want to lean in and look closer. What other contrasting traits might make up this successful man?

"I keep a notebook on me at all times, too," Charlie says, producing his sketchbook with a small charcoal pencil wedged through the spiral, top-side binding.

"Great minds," Dario says, eyebrows rising and smile ex-panding.

"You must really love this business," Charlie says.

Dario looks away contemplatively. "I do. I really do. I love it so much that I've agreed to marry for it."

"You don't want to be married?" Charlie asks, reading into his dark tone.

"I'm not sure. I did once…" Dario says. "But now I'm being strong-armed into it. In order to inherit all of this, I have to wed. It was in my grandfather's will."

"How does he expect you to fall in love so quickly?" Charlie asks.

"I'm not sure he does, and I'm not sure I can. I'm not even sure that's the point of this…exercise," Dario admits.

Charlie orders another chocolate as he considers how this changes his perception of the competition. If Dario's not after passionate love, and all he wants is stable companionship, Charlie knows he could be a solid companion.

"You must really love chocolate then at least to go through all of this," Charlie says.

Dario snaps his head back to the table. His strangely sexy fedora nearly falls off his head. "I don't know about that. I admire chocolate. I revere chocolate. I understand it. I sell it well. But I don't think I love it. Not anymore at least."

"Since your grandfather passed away?" Charlie asks, then worries he is bringing it up too much. Living on Cemetery Street has made him immune to those pressing, worrisome thoughts about death that others often have. Maybe that makes him morbid, but he prefers to think of it as acceptance. No sense spiraling over the inevitable.

Grooves river across Dario's forehead. "No, it was before my grandfather passed away. You see, I was in a—"

"None of these work. I should've brought my lighting from home," Selina says, interrupting their heart-to-heart by plopping down in the seat beside Dario. Her head tilts down toward her phone, fingers scrolling through the photos she took.

Charlie notices the Amorina logo painted on the chocolate bar earrings she wears. It's a cute touch.

"You missed the whole tour," Charlie says, toying with his napkin. He wishes they hadn't been disturbed, because Dario snaps out of confidant mode and back into tour guide mode.

"The what?" she asks, thumbing through various filters on a fancy app Charlie has never seen before.

Dario clears his throat before tapping at the tablet. "Selina, would you like to try my—"

"I never want to see another piece of chocolate again," says Beau, shuffling into the tasting room. He sports the T-shirt he "won." His face has a sickly coloring to it, and his eyes are bloodshot from puking.

"Might be hard to do here," Charlie jokes, but Beau does not laugh. Instead, he slams down into the chair next to him and flops his head into his hands.

Michelle runs in with excitement. "Look! Look! Look!"

She swivels her phone toward the table. Everyone turns their attention except Beau, who curls further into himself. On the screen, the edited video of her fake advertisement plays. She hams it up for the camera. She reminds Charlie of a girl in his high school English class who pretended to trip during every line in her Romeo and Juliet scene presentation just to get laughs.

"It looks great," says Dario, smiling sweetly. This man is earnestness incarnate.

Selina leans in. "You look oily. Can they edit that?"

Michelle snaps back. "Do I? I am not sure they can now."

"In that case you look beautiful," Selina says. The table goes silent at the slight.

Other visitors chatter nearby while enjoying their choco- lates. Their table remains church house–quiet with Selina and

Michelle engrossed in their phones and Beau too grossed-out to raise his head.

Dario's hazel eyes bulge at the unfortunate scene, giving Charlie a better look at their unique color makeup. They are blooming sunflowers with their soil-brown rings, verdant green centers, and flecks of yellow spindling out from his pupils. Charlie used to go to the local farm in autumn with his family to frolic among the fresh fields of sunflowers and then pick a basket of apples to take home. Those were some of his happiest childhood memories. Strange that Dario reminds him of home when he is so far away from it.

"Perhaps it is time for a riposo?" Dario asks the group.

"What's that?" Michelle asks.

"It's like a siesta," says Selina. Her phone pings and dings, and she dips out of the conversation again.

"Si. It's an Italian custom. A little midday nap to fortify you for the evening," explains Dario.

"Count me in," says Charlie. He needs it after last night. Ansel snores, and it took a while for him to adjust to his lawn-mower of a roommate, despite the lavish plushness of his bed and the silky feel of the zillion-thread-count sheets. Comfort could only take him so far into dreamland.

Beau groans in assent.

In the distance, Ansel approaches with the employee from the message station hanging on his arm and his every word.

"What did we miss?" Ansel asks when he arrives tableside.

Charlie scans the group. "We'll fill you in on the ride back."

"Splendid. Chiara here just finished her shift. I was telling her all about your beautiful villa and she said she's never seen it," Ansel says to Dario as if all bosses invite their employees to their places for private tours. "I told her she simply had to. Can she join us for dinner?"

Dario appears flummoxed by the request but tries to be

acquiescent. "If you would like, Chiara. You're more than welcome."

"Grazie! Fammi prendere la borsa," she says before flouncing away.

"I'll help," Ansel says, though Charlie's certain Ansel has no idea what she just said.

Dario hits Charlie with that hapless yet winsome look again. Charlie laughs to himself. Their eye contact lasts a little longer and burns a little deeper this time around.

Nine

CHARLIE

"Where's Chiara?" Charlie asks when he makes it to his shared room in the villa. After so much chocolate, he is in desperate need of that riposo.

Ansel whirls around like a tornado, tidying up. Stray socks and underwear fly into his bag.

He straightens and shushes Charlie. "She's in there," he tilts his head toward the shut bathroom door. "Can you hang on to this for me?"

Charlie accepts whatever small object is on offer. When he uncurls his hand, he holds what looks like a gold wedding band. "Are you married?"

Ansel shushes him again. "What's it to you?"

"Nothing," Charlie says, rolling the ring around in his palm. It looks expensive, and has a bit of heft to it. "Just... didn't the contest rules say you had to be single?"

"Did it? I barely read it," he says. "I saw 'free Italian vacation' and had my assistant write something up to enter me."

"Your assistant wrote your entry?" Charlie asks, a bit peeved by this. He worked hard on the illustration he ultimately submitted. It took him all night to get it right and then transfer the images to clean paper, which he scanned at the local library to submit electronically the next day.

"I am a busy man. A busy man who needed a vacation from both his business and his family," he says in a sharp, low whisper. "This stays between us." He shoves Charlie to the door so fast that Charlie nearly drops the ring. Before slamming the door in Charlie's face, Ansel hangs one of his argyle socks on the doorknob and says, "See you at dinner."

So much for a midday rest.

Like everyone in his family, Charlie never went to college, but somehow he's having the formative experience of being sexiled, except in a foreign country in a lavish villa. Life is weird sometimes.

He bumbles down the stairs in search of a salty snack after all that sweet chocolate. Would they be doing aperitivos again? The enticing smells of homemade cooking waft out of the brickwork kitchen. Charlie expects only to find Paola, but Dario is in there too, wearing an undershirt and an apron, turning the pasta crank with surprisingly muscular biceps alongside the short woman.

The distinct sound of squeaking bedsprings and muffled moans come from above. They exchange a curious look, and then speak in hushed Italian.

"Non penso che funzionerà," Dario says.

Charlie lives in tight quarters with his entire family, so conversations are expected to be overheard. He stops and listens in since he doesn't understand what they're saying anyway. The melodic cadence is novel and exciting to his ears.

"Basta!" Paola smacks the back of Dario's hand with a wooden spoon. "Abbi fede."

Their banter warms Charlie's heart. The domestic scene only adds to Dario's charm. Charlie could see himself with flour-coated hands kneading dough on Sunday afternoons in this kitchen alongside these two.

"Qualcuno ha attirato la tua attenzione?" Paola asks.

"Mi piace l'americano di nome Charlie," Dario says.

Charlie perks up at the sound of his own name. Without even thinking, he launches one of the translator apps on his phone and presses the speech-to-text button.

"Perché allora sei pessimista?" Paola asks. *Why then are you pessimistic?*

"Non è il tipo di ragazzo che sposi." *He's not the kind of guy you marry.*

Charlie's heart plummets into his stomach. He thought they had connected today. Is it his looks? His manners? His upbringing?

He reads the translation again, wondering if he misread it, but accidentally hits the text-to-speech button. A robotic male voice starts to speak, threatening to give away his eavesdropping. Paola bangs a pot on the way to the stove, inadvertently saving the day.

Charlie rushes out into the yard and sits on one of the loungers beside the pool. The soft moans of pleasure emanating from the cracked upstairs window only worsen the situation.

From his pocket, Charlie fishes out Ansel's wedding ring. It must have cost a pretty penny. Even his mom's wedding ring, which was an heirloom passed down through many generations, isn't anywhere near this shiny, nor holds a stone as big.

Just because he doesn't see marriage as the be-all and end-all of romance doesn't mean he wants to be preemptively excluded from it. Blue hair and tattoos and a lower-class up-bringing shouldn't be markers that he isn't husband material.

Out of sheer curiosity, he slips Ansel's wedding ring on his left hand's fourth finger. It is a squeeze, but it slides all the way to the base with a bit of a pinch. He could be biased, but it looks and feels like it belongs there. Commitment, for better or worse, in sickness and in health…he might want that.

He *needs* that, if he has any hope of saving the house on Cemetery Street and caring for his parents and grandparents.

Certainly he can turn Dario's impression around. He has a whole week to prove that he's the kind of man who can make a house a home and can shoot the shit with the best of them.

He lies back and closes his eyes beneath the late afternoon sun. If he rests for a minute or two, perhaps the hurt and angry feelings throbbing in his chest will subside. The caressing breeze sweeps him into sleep.

Seconds or hours later, the clatter of plates stirs Charlie awake.

The catering staff is setting up an outdoor table on the veranda beside the sitting room connected to the main house. Their loud work has replaced the sex sounds spewing from upstairs. For a second, Charlie forgets all about Dario's slighting words.

Blinking against the last of the daylight, Charlie lets rip a loud yawn and rubs his eyes. The cold smoothness of Ansel's wedding band swipes across his left eyelid.

He goes to remove it—he was supposed to be keeping it safe, not playing make-believe with it to prove something to himself—but it won't give. That pinch earlier must have been more of a struggle than he realized, so lost in his head and his emotions. The gold band won't budge an inch. The Italian heat must have caused his finger to swell, and now he is super screwed.

His mind rushes through a list of possible solutions, but not fast enough, because Paola appears on the veranda in her apron ringing an antique cowbell. "È ora di cenare!"

DARIO

Betrayal burns hot down Dario's throat like a limoncello shot.

Charlie is *married*. He lied on his contest entry.

When Dario spotted him lounged out all alone beside the pool through the small, circular window in the kitchen, he decided he could step away from dinner preparations with Paola to keep his guest some company, only to find Charlie fast asleep. *Wearing a wedding band.*

The gold ring glinted off his ring finger, plain as day.

Dario kicks himself for getting caught up in this ridiculous scheme. The only one of the five persons gathered here he truly connected with today concealed the truth from him, then flaunted it out in his yard for everyone to see. He refuses to be made a romantic fool again.

Still exuding that post-sex glow, Ansel and Chiara scarf down their dinners. Paola was none too happy about having to fix an extra plate, and Dario was equally irked about one of his potential spouses sleeping with one of his employees under his own roof. He's never considered himself the jealous type and he told his guests to have fun while they were here, but still, it seems like bad manners given the circumstances. They *at least* could've been quieter about it.

Violetta joins them again. Seated at Dario's right hand, just off the head of the table. He called her earlier in a frenzy.

He felt it prudent to have a professional on hand should legal threats start to fly when he confronts Charlie about his deceit.

Michelle, clearly still upset with Selina over her comment about her skin earlier, shoots pointed glances her way as she picks at her food. Completely uncaring, Selina raves about Paola's cooking.

Charlie, who has chosen a seat far away from Dario and sits suspiciously on his left hand, attempts small talk with Beau who is still looking green and faded from his cocoa-smeared defeat this afternoon.

Dario hates to sour Paola's potato tortellini, one of his favorite dishes from childhood, with pointed confrontation, but he barely picks up his fork, too nauseated with this new information. Eventually, he stands, fury flickering millimeters from the surface of his skin. He taps his knife to his glass. "I have an announcement to make."

A hush falls over them like a torrential downpour. Even the music cuts out.

"I know you all wondered why Amorina was hosting this contest to meet me in the first place. I take the business and my duty to it very seriously. In the spirit of transparency, I need to tell you all that my inheritance is staked on me marrying before my next birthday as per my grandfather's will," he says, slapped anew by the clause that has caused this emotional chaos and unburied a romantic wound he thought he had entombed well enough. "My grandfather felt that the world of modern dating was overstuffed with choice—given apps and what have you—and concocted this to bring together a small selection of sensible matches for me under one roof. I am taking this experience with you all seriously, but it has come to my attention that not all of you feel the same. One of you is a liar. One of you is already married."

Questioning heads snap around in all directions before a fist slams the table.

Ansel's face transforms from a glowy flush to a ruddy red. "You told?" His harsh eyes are trained on Charlie, whose shoulders are sloped over his plate.

"I didn't!" Charlie holds up his hands. "I swear, I didn't!"

"Che cosa?" Chiara says, a hand rising to her sauce-slicked mouth, green eyes wide with shock.

"Wait, Ansel and Charlie are married?" asks Michelle.

Selina rolls her eyes. "On what planet?"

Beau shakes his heavy head at the table. "Can everyone bring their voices down a notch or two, please?"

"This is an outrage!" Ansel shouts even louder than before.

"Great, thanks. That's perfect, guys," Beau mutters before dropping his head to the table again and covering his ears with his palms.

"Why are you wearing my ring?" Ansel growls across the table.

"*Your* ring?" Dario asks, but the question gets swallowed up in the murmurs and growing commotion.

Charlie cowers. "I was just trying it on. It got stuck, and I got scared!"

"You're married?" Chiara asks Ansel, affronted.

Ansel huffs out a breath. "If I had known this dinner was going to turn into a trial, I would've brought my lawyer."

"Let me assure you, nobody is on trial here," Violetta says, the calm, collected voice of reason at this table where emotions have already shot sky-high. "We are simply getting to the root of a raised issue. The Terms and Conditions clearly stated that all entrants must be unmarried, otherwise they could be rightfully disqualified and have their winnings revoked."

A sheen of sweat forms over Ansel's nose. "Who reads the Terms and Conditions?"

Everyone at the table raises their hands, except him and Selina. Clearly noticing she is the odd one out and not wanting to be lumped in with Ansel, she says, "My talent agent read it for me. I trust her."

Dario reels with uncertainty. "What were your intentions here?"

"I'm married. I have kids. I wanted a vacation! Sue me!" Ansel says, then grows pale. "Don't actually sue me."

"Bastardo!" Chiara yells as she throws her full wineglass in his face and stomps out of the backyard. Michelle perks up, clearly trying to tamp down a smile over things getting juicy, just like on her favorite TV show.

Ansel stands, failing to dry himself with the small linen napkin. His shirt stains a bloody red. "This is getting out of hand."

Violetta glances to her stack of papers, obviously also perplexed by this turn of events, before slipping them into her attaché case. What a waste. In his hasty misunderstanding, Dario had asked her to secure Charlie's departure when Ansel was the deceitful party this whole time. He should not have cast premature blame. Nobody in the villa is going to trust him or his judgment now.

"Signor Voight, I will book your passage home at once," Violetta says, producing a work laptop and setting it on the table beside her plate.

Michelle seems nearly giddy with the way Ansel's anger morphs into rage.

He says, "Geh zum Teufel! I am leaving?"

Violetta nods. "Si. You qualified under false pretenses. Therefore, you are no longer eligible to receive the prize of this stay."

Ansel shakes his head in open-mouthed shock. "The whole world is going to hear about this!" His snarl is sad. The watery embitterment of an overworked white man who thinks the world owes him way more than it does.

"I'd like to remind you of the ironclad NDA you signed, Signor Voight," says Violetta. Her gaze, cast up from her laptop screen, is ice-cold.

Disgraced, damp, and out of fighting words, Ansel retreats into the house to pack.

The table stays quiet for a long moment as everyone processes what just happened. Dinner is definitely over. Tortellini grows soggy in its fragrant sauce.

"Here," Selina says, walking over to Charlie. She takes a bit of the oil from the dish used to garnish the fresh bread and wipes some of it on either side of the ring. Holding his wrist down with one hand, she uses the other to slowly work the ring back and forth until it gets slippery enough to glide off.

Michelle claps for Selina despite their squabble earlier, clearly not reading the vibe of the group. Selina sets the ring in the center of the table so they can all stare at the offending token that shot their dinner to hell.

"You thought I was married?" Charlie asks Dario.

"I saw the ring. I assumed," Dario says, hearing how weak both his voice and his reasoning sound.

"You could've asked me before all of this," Charlie says, waving at the table. The only person here who seems to have enjoyed the massive spectacle is Michelle, and even she's eased off a bit since Ansel's angry exit.

Dario hangs his head in shame. He inherited a flair for the dramatics from his grandfather and his mother. Still, it's no excuse. "You are right. That was my mistake."

A chair scrapes across the stone. Dario can't bring himself to look up and see whose it is.

"You think you would've known the ring wasn't mine since I'm not the kind of guy you marry, right?" Charlie says.

Dario rears back. Had Charlie overheard him in the kitchen with Paola?

The blatant offense etched on Charlie's face tells all before he turns and storms back into the villa.

The ensuing silence could strangle them all.

"Scusi," Dario finally forces out to the remaining few before crossing the lawn toward the barn house. He needs to be alone. He flops down on the bed in anguish.

The *why not* chasing after him at the will-reading switches to a *why bother*.

Why bother trying to satisfy his dead grandfather's wishes. There is no way he is going to meet the marriage deadline to inherit Amorina. Maybe he shouldn't inherit it if he is prone to letting his emotions cloud his judgment as quickly as he did today.

Public confrontation was a bad move all around. Not only did he read the situation wrong, but he hurt Charlie's feelings.

Charlie, who'd never been on a plane or a vacation in his life. Charlie, who seemed to care about Amorina unlike the others. Charlie, who has the warmest chocolate eyes and kindest smile of the bunch.

Not the kind of guy you marry. That is not exactly what he meant. He likes Charlie as he is, and he fears if he were to bring Charlie center stage, the audience viewing his life through a proscenium might hurl their waiting tomatoes at them. Though, maybe Dario is more worried about optics and the metaphorical dry cleaning bill for his five-piece suits rather than about Charlie's well-being.

God, he is an asshole.

And assholes don't deserve inheritances, promotions, weddings, or partners like Charlie Moore.

Dario might as well give up now. Emilio can run the business. Run the business right into the ground for all he cares.

He is too, too tired to care.

Ten

CHARLIE

The next afternoon, Charlie stands behind his designated workstation in the Amorina School of Chocolate.

Selina pins her chef's hat in place. Beau uses some of the cooking utensils to bang out a beat on the worktop. Michelle bobbles about in chunky, open-toed shoes and large pieces of costume jewelry, overdressed for what is evidently going to be a messy day.

One down, at least, Charlie thinks, noticing Ansel's empty station. Not that he has any better of a shot with Dario after all that occurred last night. He should have kept his temper in check at the table to demonstrate his maturity. But his hackles rose to an all-time high.

Dario enters the room wearing a white chef's coat. His name is stitched in gold script on the left breast beneath the Amorina logo. The lapel of his coat is striped to look like the Italian flag. His hair is tied back in a tiny bun, which draws attention to his expressive, puppy dog eyes. They brighten when they land on Charlie in the back row. Charlie refrains from reading into it.

"Buon pomeriggio a tutti," Dario says, sporting a show-man's smile. "Today we begin our journey into the art of mak-ing Amorina chocolate. But first, I'd like to apologize again for the theatrics last night. I do not normally operate that way. I think the newness of this experience has churned up some feelings I wasn't aware were sitting under the surface. I deeply apologize for my behavior."

A chorus of "It's okay" rings out from the others, but Char-lie holds back. There is a personal conversation to be had that the whole room need not be privy to. He shoves his hands in the apron pockets, still feeling like the least likely person in the room to end up marrying this man when he obviously needs it the most.

Once he wrestled himself to sleep, he suffered an awful nightmare where he stood in front of a packed church waiting for a nameless, faceless someone to march down the aisle. Bit by bit, his tux got stripped away by an unseen force until he was naked and shivering before the congregation. The ruinous winds stripped all the decorations, tore the church to pieces and sent the gatherers soaring. At the end of it, he stood in a roofless, windowless church covering his unmentionables and wondering what curse he must be under to be so unmarriable.

"Ansel left the villa this morning. If any of you, at any point, become overwhelmed or uncomfortable with the pa-rameters of this week, you need only to tell me and I shall see to it other accommodations are arranged for you, or that you are ferried safely home as promptly as you wish," Dario says. Charlie avoids a direct line of eye contact, shifting be-hind Beau. "Now let us begin."

★ ★ ★

An incredible amount of math and science go into the production of chocolate. The numbers and calculations and history make Charlie's head spin.

Using a large knife, Charlie chops twenty-four ounces of chocolate up into tiny bits so it will melt quicker. Once done, he puts most of the chocolate into a big, clear bowl and sticks it into the microwave hooked up below his workstation. The bowl swirls under the buttery yellow light at half power. Every minute on the dot, he takes the bowl out and stirs the gooey deliciousness with an Amorina-branded spatula. The fragrance is heavenly.

"This process is called tempering and the method we're using is called seeding," Dario says as he walks around the room at a steady clip. A heat spreads over Charlie's neck as other types of *seeding* banner through his mind, causing the front of his shorts to strain. Earlier, Dario demonstrated cracking open the shell of a cocoa bean. The clean break. The pleasing crunch. Charlie wonders what else Dario could turn out with those strong fingers.

Dario continues, "For chocolate to be considered true, real chocolate, it can't have any other fats besides cocoa butter, so we're heating this chocolate to melt all the fatty acid crystals." He pushes up his sleeves and drops a thermometer into Selina's chocolate bowl. "We want to get this chocolate to roughly forty-seven degrees Celsius. Roughly one-sixteen Fahrenheit for you Americans." Selina videos the whole thing and captions it: "Isn't Dario Cotogna as hot as this chocolate?"

Dario blushes for everyone to see. So does Charlie when Michelle catches him glancing too long at the exposed, chorded muscle of Dario's forearms. He may still be irked about last night, but his hormones have not gotten the memo.

The beep of the microwave catches him completely off

guard. *Crap.* When he opens the door to the microwave, he gets hit with a swirl of smoke and an overwhelming campfire smell that reminds him of youthful bonfires at backyard hangouts. He coughs as he stands.

"Oops," Charlie says. Dario appears beside him. "I think I burned it."

"Quite all right," Dario says, taking the bowl from Charlie. "Happens to the best of us. We have plenty of chocolate to spare. You can start over." Dario goes to the front of the room and returns with some pre-chopped chocolate in a new bowl. Charlie sets it in the microwave.

"Do you think we could start over, too?" Dario asks in a low voice. "I would like to apologize and explain where I was coming from."

"I think so," Charlie says, taken aback at first by the forwardness but still ever the believer in second chances. And thirds and fourths, honestly. He is in no position financially to back away from this potential arrangement when his family's security is on the line.

"I'm sorry for making assumptions and hurting your feelings. I wish I had behaved better." Dario stares straight into Charlie's eyes. It's disarming. "I'm quite a bit out of practice when it comes to meeting new people. I let my emotions get the better of me. It is just, you see, I enjoy you, Charlie."

The hairs on Charlie's arms stand up. "You enjoy me?"

Dario clears his throat as he squats down to extract the chocolate bowl. At least one of them is paying attention to something other than their accelerating heartbeat. "Si. Your presence, your conversation, your look. I saw the ring and this overriding jealousy ran through me." He sweeps his eyes around the room, boosts his voice back to teaching level. "Please go ahead and add the wafers to your bowl. These are the seeds. Mix until the wafers dissolve, and the overall temperature reaches thirty-one degrees Celsius. What this does is attract the loose crystals of fatty acid in the non-tempered chocolate to crystallize the way the tempered wafers are."

"Can we go back to the part about you being jealous?" Charlie asks, lesson thrown to the back of his mind. "What could you possibly be jealous of me for? You have all this."

"Not of you, exactly. I was jealous of whoever put that ring there. Whoever got to welcome you home at the end of a long day," he explains as he stirs with his own spatula that has his name inked into the handle.

Someone should put a warning on Dario's chef's jacket. Caution: Contents are hot *and sweet*!

"There hasn't been anyone like that in a long, long time. Really, ever. The only people I come home to are my parents and my grandparents. I promise you that," Charlie says, glancing away. Shy suddenly, and afraid he sounds pitiable. He is a launched ping-pong ball of emotions. "I think that's why I got so upset that you told Paola that I wasn't the kind of guy you marry. I know I shouldn't have been eavesdropping, and I'm sorry for that, but still. Yeah."

"That was my own insecurity talking," Dario says, a fetching, refreshing portrait of sensibility. "I reflected last night and realized that. My family is highly visible, and in this industry, people talk. When we spoke yesterday, I worried being with someone like me might invite gossip into your life."

"I have learned the hard way not to care what people say. I mean, look at me. I can't walk around like this if I can't handle some choice words," Charlie says, trying to sound as confident as possible. He may project coolness with his hair and tattoos, but he can suffer extreme bouts of self-consciousness when he gets stressed or upset. His self-expression doesn't double as self-preservation. He knows it makes him a brighter moving target.

Dario adds the tempered chocolate wafers to the ready bowl. Charlie stares into the surface of the dark chocolate as if it were a reflecting pond. His past ripples about in the bowl.

"Thick skin is abundantly important in my family. I take it you're speaking about a specific experience?" Dario asks.

"Yeah. Back in high school. But I don't want to take up your time," Charlie says. Except when he checks on the others, Michelle is the only one still working. Beau has disappeared, and Selina has gone live on social media with what little service there is in the building. She boisterously responds in Spanish to comments from her adoring fans.

Dario points his nose down at the bowl. "We've got at least ten minutes. Tell me about it. If you'd care to."

Should he? Revealing too much too soon might be the wrong move. Yet the expression on Dario's face is so expectant that Charlie can't help but feel that Dario prizes vulnerability.

"I only ever had one serious relationship," Charlie says, both excited and nervous to be sharing this. "His name was Max. He was my best friend. We started fooling around my senior year of high school, and things got serious. So serious that I wanted to tell people about us. We agreed the week before graduation, we'd start by telling our friends. Only, I came to school that Monday and all of our friends were being cagey with me. Max didn't even come to class. I texted him a million times to no response. I figured he had a doctor's appointment he didn't tell me about. He could be forgetful like that. At lunch, I got up the nerve to tell our friends that Max and I were dating. That was the plan. The whole table went silent. My heart sank. Finally, our closest friend, Freida, brought me out into the hall and told me that I couldn't sit with them anymore because I was lying, that I 'wasn't the type of person Max goes for.'"

"Oh, Charlie," Dario says, face falling. "Mi dispiace."

He shrugs. "I was so confused. We had an accepting friend group, for the Slate Belt crowd. I mean, I wasn't expecting any of them to come to Lehigh Valley Pride with me and Max or anything, but still. My parents and grandparents came around to it easily when they caught me and Max uh…*tempering by seeding* in the barn earlier that year."

Dario snorts out a laugh that catches Selina's attention. "Sorry. This is serious. I don't mean to—"

"No, laughing is good. Laughing is much better than the pity face you were giving me. I promise. I prefer it. You look handsomer like this," Charlie says, reaching out to place an assuring hand on Dario's shoulder.

Dario reddens at the compliment before saying, "Okay. Go on."

"I went to Max's house after school, but his mom told me he was sick and didn't want to see me anymore," says Charlie, thrust back to that day, and how small he felt on their rain-soaked porch. Like a worm displaced by the storm that still thundered in the distance. "I could see in her eyes that he'd told her the same lie he'd told our friends. That I was trying to 'turn him.' He was the one who lied and yet somehow, I was the one being branded Char*lies*, as if that's even a creative insult."

Dario shakes his head as he finishes tempering the chocolate. "That's a hard thing for a young person to have to go through."

"It was. I gave up on guys in any serious way after that. Working, taking care of my grandparents, and my illustrations keep me plenty busy," he says.

"You do more illustrations like the one you submitted for the contest?" Dario asks.

"Tons more. I post them online as tattoo inspiration, for myself and others. My dream is to one day become a tattoo apprentice at a real parlor so I can learn the trade and tattoo my art on others," Charlie says, eager to share more now that he's gotten the Max incident off his chest.

"I'd love to see these tattoo designs while you're here," Dario says. "But first, I should find Beau and we should begin molding our bonbons. Talk more later?"

"I'd like that," Charlie says, spirit renewed.

Eleven

DARIO

In his mess of a morning, Dario forgot to read his grandfather's letter.

Post chocolate-making lesson and another scrumptious dinner under the stars with his suitors, he sits at the desk in the barn house while Angelo gulps down his own dinner from a noisy, nearby bowl. Dario opens the next envelope in the series.

Caro Tesorino,
Sharing knowledge is an underrated love language.

Every Cotogna has learned the precious art of crafting chocolate, no matter what part of the business they go into. It is a way of linking to our history through our hands.

Take careful note of those who treat the task with interest. Not seriousness. Seriousness can be feigned. Interest cannot.

Interest lives in the eyes, the open ears, the posture that says 'I'm ready to learn.'

If they are willing to learn about Amorina and the storied art of chocolate making, they are willing to learn about you, tesorino. Have faith that, as in the chocolate tempering process, like crystals link together to create the creamy, rich treat of love, the right ones will flock to you and follow your example.

Has anyone caught your eye? If an interdimensional postal service has been founded since my passing, do write. Sono sulle spine!

His grandfather's words leap off the page and into the air. He closes his eyes and manifests his nonno's voice in the room. Missing him hasn't gotten any easier, but these letters have been such a salve.

To avoid a hearty cry, he pulls a sensible, one-piece men's swimsuit from his wardrobe and dons a swim cap to keep his hair healthy and free of chemicals. A late-night swim will clear his mind as it always does. And if he sheds a tear or two, his face will be too wet to notice.

As he steps outside, a splash from the pool deck surprises him. Someone else must have had the same idea as him. Minus the crying part. As he gets closer, Charlie's slim, tattooed frame shows beneath the surface of the water, gliding from one end of the pool to the other in the honeyed light.

Relief caught him by the toe when Charlie accepted his apology during the chocolate lesson. From his nonno, he learned early that when mistakes are made, apologies must not be withheld. Damage done to a relationship must be tended to with swiftness, otherwise, the mold of misunderstanding festers until the whole thing must be thrown out with the trash.

He treasures how honest Charlie was with him earlier about high school and that Max fellow. It makes him want to snap off a part of himself like a square of chocolate to share with Charlie.

Charlie holds his breath for a long time, becoming fishlike beneath the soft ripple of the water. Dario submerges slowly. As soon as Charlie comes up for air, he lets out a yelp.

"Scusi. I did not mean to scare you," Dario says.

Charlie glances from his face to his chest. "Are you wearing a wetsuit?"

"It is a one-piece," Dario says. Made of black material, the swimsuit has short sleeves and legs that stop above the knee. Around his middle is a white band, and above is a quarter-zipper that he keeps drawn all the way up.

"Once again, I feel severely underdressed," Charlie says with a nervous-sounding laugh, glancing away. Dario tracks his eyes to the pool deck, where a wet pair of swim trunks lie crumpled in a ball. *Is he…*

"Naked," Dario says aloud without thinking. *Smooth. Real smoooooooth.*

Charlie moves to grab them. "Sorry. I didn't think anyone would be out here this late. I will put them back on—"

"No!"

"No?" Charlie stops, quirking a questioning eyebrow.

Dario huffs out an awkward breath. "I only meant that you should be as dressed or as…undressed as you would like to be." He attempts to keep his eyes above the water line so as to not seem like some overeager creep.

"I don't want to make you uncomfortable." Charlie angles away.

Dead puppies. Car crashes. The heat death of the universe.

Dario narrowly avoids popping a boner right there.

"I'm comfortable if you're comfortable," Dario says, regaining control of his words and his hormones. The last thing Charlie needs is an eyeful of Dario's uncut cock straining against the clinging, black spandex. "You have a lot of tattoos," Dario observes, hoping to lead the conversation into safer territory. Normal territory. Not 'shouting "Naked!" at his house guest' territory.

"I do," Charlie says, smiling with pride and extending his arms.

"How many do you have?" Dario asks after clearing his throat.

"Over the years, I've lost count," Charlie says in a way that almost invites Dario to do the dirty work of searching him head to toe and taking a formal tally.

"What are they of exactly?" Dario asks instead of fantasizing about playing connect the dots along Charlie's skin with his newly quivering fingers.

"They're mostly bastardizations of idioms or phrases I find funny," he says. "I like the interplay of words and illustration."

There are flames and animals and ghosts parading up and down his body parts. None of which should go together. But on Charlie, somehow, they all tell a twisted, interesting story of an uninhibited mind allowed to run amuck with creativity.

"Which tattoo is your favorite?" Dario asks.

Charlie turns his head a bit to reveal the area right behind his left ear. There at the edge of his buzz cut is a tearful eyeball cartoon. It holds up a hand and in its palm is a lowercase letter *i*. There's a bow on top of the dot, as if the letter were a gift.

"Maybe this one?" he says.

"An *i* for an eye," says Dario with a low chuckle. It is clever and grotesquely cute at the same time.

"People don't usually get them," Charlie says, brushing his hand over the art. Dario imagines what it might be like to run his tongue over the very same spot and how Charlie might react.

"Does that bother you?" Dario asks.

"Not really. They're not for other people. They amuse me. I think there is this misconception about tattoos that they are meant for the viewer. I could not disagree more. My tattoos are for me, a mode of growing my artistry."

"These are all your art?" Dario asks.

"Most. Some are collaborations with my local tattoo artist," Charlie explains. "Every artist has their medium. Some choose canvas or clay, I chose my own skin. Don't ask me why. I'm no psychiatrist."

"When do you have time to make your drawings?" Dario asks, desiring a peek behind the curtain of creativity. While his job requires ingenuity and quick thinking, it is not the same as making art. He's always wished he had a more visual mind.

"I'm bored at work a lot since I do the overnight shift. I've had to become a bit of a night owl because of it. We're not supposed to use our phones—the owner has cameras set up after some former coworkers got greasy-fingered—so I play around in my sketchbook," Charlie says. "The one you saw back at the factory. All my best ideas come late at night, which is probably why I'm still awake right now. My mind thinks it's playtime."

Dario skirts around thoughts of a different sort of *playtime* with Charlie Moore. "That makes sense."

"What are you doing up?" Charlie asks.

Dario says, "My routine has been thrown off. I don't think my body knows what time it is unless we're eating a meal."

Charlie nods and waves his hands along the water's surface, creating small ripples. "D'ya know I've never swum in a private pool before?"

"Non esiste! No way. How is that possible?" Dario asks, though he feels like a jerk after doing so. Charlie has already expressed that he doesn't come from means.

"None of my friends had pools growing up. The only time

I got to swim was at the YMCA or at a public pool every now
and then, but they get so crowded that there's no room to really swim. You just stand there, cool from the waist down,
sweating from the waist up," Charlie says. He cups his hand
and splashes some water across his chest. The beads cling and
glisten, sluicing down his torso in tantalizing trails, creating
micro magnifying glasses over his ink.

"That sounds…" Dario begins, "different." He cringes over
the word choice, afraid it underlines something he should care
less about. Just because Charlie comes from humble beginnings, and Dario was born into generational wealth, doesn't
mean they are not both human beings who need companionship and care.

"Do you know what else I've never done?" Charlie asks.
Dario's mind fills suddenly with filthy fantasies, of first times
and fresh experiences. He widens his eyes in lieu of a response,
trying to breathe and reroute his traitorous blood flow. "Had
a swimming race!"

Dario exhales out a big breath, and hopefully his horni-
ness, too. "Is that so?"

"Back in high school, I always wanted to try out for the
swim team, but it involved a lot of traveling and suits and caps
that my parents couldn't afford," Charlie says in an unguarded
way. "There's a dormant competitive spirit inside of me begging to bust out."

Something was begging to bust out of Dario as well, and it
certainly was not a competitive spirit. But a race would distract him well enough, so he agrees to it. They meet in the
deep end of the pool where they lay out the rules. Three laps.
First person to slap the tile at the end of the third wins.

"We do not have a judge," Dario points out.

"We're adults. I think we can play fair," Charlie says. "Only
I have an advantage."

"What's that?" Dario asks.

Charlie gestures to his naked form. "No lag."

"Right." Dario wishes Charlie weren't drawing *more* attention to the places his eyes have been avoiding.

"You could also shed your suit."

"I'm good," Dario says. "Thank you. This is how I'm comfortable."

Charlie smiles, nods, and doesn't pry, which Dario appreciates.

After a countdown, they crest through the water like two Olympians. Dario settles into the familiar, rhythmic stroke. He keys into his breathing and does a near-perfect somersault turn in the shallow end to swim back.

The contest churns up memories of childhood and his brother, Emilio, and how much fun they used to have in this pool, back before their father's death poisoned their relationship. Back before inheritances pitted them against each other in fiercer ways than any childhood dare ever could. Winning a chocolate empire was much higher stakes than winning the privilege of naming their pet frog.

On the third lap, they both reach for the edge of the pool at the same time, slamming their hands down under a wave of water that splashes out of the pool and covers their eyes.

"Who won?" Charlie asks.

"I think we tied?" Dario says, jumping on one foot to get water out of his ear.

"Figures," Charlie says with a laugh.

"Figures, what?" he asks when he can hear right again.

"I was going to suggest that the loser owed the winner a kiss," Charlie says, scraping his upper teeth along his bottom lip. "If you still enjoy me…"

Dario fights to catch his breath. "Wouldn't that mean we'd both won?"

Charlie moves closer; their toes touch. "Would it?"

Boldness is an arm to Dario's back, pushing him toward the tattooed American with the alluring pink lips. "Let's find out," he says.

They kiss, and it's like their hearts are now in a race to see which can beat faster. Charlie's lips are so soft that the slight taste of chlorine doesn't bother Dario one bit. It's the kind of kiss he could never come up for air from. He'd happily drown inside this moment.

Their tongues twist together as Dario gasps against Charlie's mouth. There is no hiding his erection now as it strains up against Charlie's inner thigh in search of another's touch.

Someone else clears their throat from closer to the house. "Do you two mind? Some of us are *trying* to sleep!" It is unmistakably Selina's feminine register, and it sends them sailing away from one another.

"Scusa," Dario calls back.

"Don't wear your lips out, Dario," Selina chides, rolling the r in *Dario*. He flushes hot to know she saw that steamy, legato make-out. "Save some for me tomorrow."

The door to the house clicks closed behind a satisfied Selina. He sighs with relief. But then…

Out of the corner of his eye, he spots an orange speck against an otherwise dark yard. "Is someone over there?" Dario calls.

Beau steps into the light, a lit cigarette dangling from his lips. He wears pajama bottoms and no shirt. Charlie must become freshly aware of his own nakedness, because he cups his hands in front of his cock.

"My bad, guys. I came out to smoke before bed and wanted to give y'all some privacy, so I went over there. I promise I didn't see anything!" he says.

"Va bene," Dario reassures him. "We got…a little carried

away." He is embarrassed now. Nowhere in his grandfather's letters did he set parameters for what sort of physical connections he should be exploring with his houseguests. Has he crossed an unjust line?

"You do you. I'm off to hit the hay." Beau stubs out his cigarette on the arm of a nearby chair before slouching inside.

Dario turns back to Charlie to discover the moment they were sharing has fractured.

"I should get to bed, too." Charlie is already halfway out of the pool. The pale, fuzz-dusted orbs of Charlie's cheeks are round and bitable in the moonlight as he ascends the ladder. Dario's teeth aren't the only thing he could sink into that gorgeous ass.

"Don't want to go for best two out of three?" Dario asks, half joking. Half wishing they could go back to before when they were making out and a chorus of angels was harmonizing in his head.

Charlie chuckles. "Another night, Candy Man."

Candy Man. Dario has never had a pet name before. It sends shivers down his spine and he's not even the one that's naked against the night air.

"Va bene," Dario says. "Buona notte."

"Buo-no…uh, what you said." Charlie leaves him with a smile and a still-stirring erection.

Twelve

CHARLIE

Last night, Charlie had not been prepared for how hot Dario looked in that low-cut, old-timey, one-piece swimsuit. Today, he's even less prepared for how hot Dario looks in a sailor's cap.

Shiver me timbers, Captain! Charlie would get down on his hands and knees and swab the deck if Dario Cotogna asked him to.

Dario's hair naturally curls at the ends from the Lake Trasimeno mist spraying up against his sailboat. His outfit consists of a smart, navy blue, double-breasted suit with brass buttons over a striped collared shirt and huge aviator sunglasses. They are mirrored, so Charlie has no idea if Dario sees how often he's checking him out and swooning, which is probably for the best.

Charlie already thought Dario competent and accomplished yesterday during the chocolate-making workshop. Before the room, Dario discussed the growth patterns of Theobroma

cacao—a type of evergreen tree—with conviction and au-
thority. He did not even shy away from dour topics such as
the effects of climate change on places like Ghana and Ivory
Coast, where much of the world's cocoa is harvested.

Presently, Dario steers the sailboat, which was once his father's, toward a pop of land on the south side of the lake called
Isola Polvese. Charlie lounges, snug in his orange life vest, on
the seat of the boat between Michelle and Beau. Beau wears a
wide-brimmed hat that smacks Charlie in the head each time
he looks around to check out the view—or more accurately, to
check out Selina, who drapes herself in a sarong on the deck
of the boat, relaxed and growing tanner by the millisecond.

Michelle clutches the nearby handrail, clearly scared of falling overboard.

A charcuterie plate gets passed from Dario to Charlie. He
throws a fresh grape into his mouth and savors the juicy burst
of flavor.

The main sail catches the wind as if Dario set an expert trap
for it and ensnared it to his will. For the most part, their ride
is smooth, but that doesn't stop Michelle from dashing below
deck to puke up breakfast.

"At least it wasn't me this time," Beau jokes.

Everyone is too sun-drunk to let out more than a brief
chuckle.

Charlie checks the time on his phone. They've been sailing for forty minutes already.

The lock screen on his phone is a photo of his family on
Thanksgiving. Charlie stacked up a pile of books on the table
and propped his phone against it with the timer on. He rushed
to kneel in front of his grandparents; his parents stood behind
their wheelchairs. "Say 'giblets'!" he cried before the smiley
moment got captured.

Last night—that heated moment in the heated pool that

spurred a hot solo session up in his Ansel-less room after—makes this whole marriage plot seem possible. Pheromones were practically floating on the surface of the water, drawing them into each other with the kind of chemistry that can't be faked or ignored. The other thing that couldn't be ignored was Dario's hard, enormous dick pressed to the inside of his leg as they'd kissed.

Short kings always pack the biggest surprises, and Charlie can't wait to get Dario alone again.

The clouds overhead are thin white wisps slashing across a cornflower blue sky. A bit of mist hangs on the horizon, giving the rich brown hills a sense of movement, like they are a litter of overgrown, sleeping cats curled up together in a basket; their backs rise and fall with each slow, passing breath.

Eventually, they come to a stop on a sandy beach dotted with permanent umbrellas made of straw. People lounge in their shade, smiling and watching boats come in for anchor.

Beau passes out bottles of water from the cooler to everyone before they disembark.

They start up a dirt path that snakes around a squat visitor center. A bird with inky black feathers and a bright white beak skims the tops of the foliage before landing in the nearby water with a splat. Michelle, who's trying and failing to get her land legs back, identifies it as a coot.

"Where are the picturesque gardens and villas? The decadence? The opulence! I need it. I *crave* it," Selina says, casting a disapproving eye around the reedy expanse interspersed with purple sprigs of wildflowers.

"In the sixties, a count owned the island and built a villa using existing structures, but in the seventies, the island became public again. This is a protected wildlife oasis overseen by the province of Perugia," says Dario. Charlie can sense Selina rolling her eyes even behind her humongous sunglasses.

The day swelters around them, but Charlie holds excitement close to his chest. This is his first time on an island. Land-locked Pennsylvania has nothing on this sort of natural wonder. He relishes getting to watch Dario play tour guide again.

Their first destination is a pentagonal fortress with watch-towers at every corner. Sandstone and limestone stack up into the sky. Dario leads them inside, where they climb centuries-old stairs to the top walkways that give them an aerial view of the lake and the surrounding land. The factory was stunning, but this structure takes Charlie's breath away. He snaps a photo on his phone.

"Would you mind taking one of me?" asks Selina, coming up beside him and glancing at the picture he took. "I had to fire Michelle. I think she's purposefully trying to make me look bad now after my oily comment. I thought I was being helpful. I didn't realize she'd be touchy about it."

"Sure," Charlie says, stowing his phone away and accepting Selina's.

"Where do you want me?" she asks.

He glances around for the perfect spot, nervous he's going to do a lousy job. "How about by the watchtower?"

Once she's situated, she smooths down her top and pokes a long leg out from the part in her sarong. "Tell me when."

Selina, a total professional, tilts her head up to find her natural light. The sunrays kiss her already-bronze cheeks like they are thanking her for existing. Charlie counts down from three, then takes a bunch so Selina has options.

"You have a good artistic eye," Selina says afterward.

"You think so?" Charlie asks, uncertain of the compliment.

She nods and flips her long black silky hair over her shoulder. "You wouldn't believe the number of photographers I've shot with who don't understand lighting or composition. When I'm working solo, I'm the subject of the image, but everything in the frame needs to tell a story, especially in fashion editorial, which I'm doing more of. I can't stand artists without confidence or vision."

"I can understand that," Charlie says as they walk on, feeling bad about how he assumed she was singularly self-involved. It sounds like her quest for beauty isn't out of narcissism but about creative satisfaction. Charlie relates to that life goal.

Up ahead, Dario looks out on the lake with reverence, a small smile playing on his lips.

"I feel the same way about men," Selina says almost conspiratorially. She whips around so she's in front of Charlie. He trips over his own feet at the sudden roadblock. "Tell me. Is Dario a confident kisser?"

"Oh, um—" Charlie fumbles for words. He's never been one to kiss and tell.

"¿Fue tan malo?" Selina asks.

Even though Charlie doesn't remember much Spanish from his school days, he understands her meaning from her torqued expression.

"No, it was good. It was nice," he says, uncertain what she's looking for. He's not about to explain how his heart thundered, his pulse raced and his head spun with newfound feelings. That would be too embarrassing.

She purses her lips like she doesn't believe him. "Who made the first move?"

"I did," he says.

She sighs. "I assumed so. I do prefer to be chased, but my mother would say 'Selina, ponte las pilas.' I need to get going if I'm going to get my man. Hasta luego, Charlie!"

Down the walkway, Selina hooks Dario's arm in hers, tugging him into a stroll. Once they disappear from Charlie's line of vision, a stab of jealousy punctures him in the gut.

Last night, as he kissed Dario, it was easy to forget all about the other contestants. Easy to forget that they were not the only two people on the entire planet. But now, without a clear view of what's happening between Selina and Dario, Charlie's mind runs wild and his stomach sours.

Selina has high-up connections in the fashion world and legions of followers to sweeten the marriage deal for the chocolate maker. Charlie has no dowry to speak of. No platform or influence or flair for public image. Plus, Selina hasn't seemed all that serious about Dario until now, acting more like someone who just enjoys flirting as opposed to someone who could settle down if a proposal were made.

Next to the fortress is the Church of San Giuliano. Charlie kneels and prays for patience and objectivity to get him through this week. He signed up for this, and it is going to be an uphill battle.

Literally.

The next part of the hike takes them up through a picturesque olive grove. Stout, bushy trees bracket them as they weather the incline. Beau splits off from the water-glugging pack and stomps through the tall grass. He plucks an olive from a low-hanging branch.

"I wouldn't do that if I were—" Dario starts.

Too late.

The mushy lump of a barely chewed green olive slides off Beau's outstretched tongue.

"Fuck, that was putrid!" he shouts.

He rushes back to the group, obviously in search of the cooler, only to curse that they left it on the boat.

"Here." Dario offers up his untouched water bottle. Beau's gratitude is telegraphed in his eyes. "Olives need to be cured after picking to remove the compound in them that makes them bitter."

Beau flicks his tongue like a lizard. "That was nasty! How do I untaste that?"

Dario chuckles like this is adorable.

Charlie ignores the devil on his shoulder telling him to forget this competition and the foreclosure of his childhood home and make a new home on this island where he can live alone, off the grid forever, outside the reach of jealousy and capitalism.

"I may have something that will help you," Dario says to Beau. From his pocket, he unfurls a handkerchief. Inside are a few grapes, olives and roasted nuts from the charcuterie on the boat. "I thought I might need a snack on our hike."

He feeds Beau one of the grapes as a palate cleanser. Beau acts like an Egyptian king on a gilded throne. They share an intimate laugh. Charlie looks away and walks past, even though he isn't sure he is leading them in the right direction.

Some ways on, past a stone farmhouse, at the top of the island, they enter the ruins of the Church of San Secundo. They pass through the mighty, arched entrance. The side walls and roof are long gone. All that stand are columns. A ghost of a house of worship.

It reminds Charlie of the nightmare he had a few nights ago about the storm on his wedding day that tore away the church and his clothes right along with it. He battles fears that this place might be an omen about what's to come for the house on Cemetery Street.

If his family gets evicted, will the city tear it down and expand the graveyard? Build a new fast-food joint? Leave it to rot beneath vandalization and overgrowth?

Charlie shudders to think of it. Not that he loves the house itself with its peeling wallpaper and loose molding; it's everything it stands for—the foundation of his family—that he cares for. He'd hate to see that left in shambles.

And yet, Charlie runs his hand along the fractured lumps of stone that have withstood time, almost like he can absorb the history and majesty of this place through his fingertips.

"It's beautiful," he muses aloud. He does not expect Dario to be standing close enough to overhear him.

"Beautiful? You think it's beautiful?" Dario asks. It's the most they've spoken since their kiss last night.

"Don't you?" Charlie asks. "I mean, this is practically in your backyard. Maybe seeing it all the time makes it less special."

"It is not that." Dario shakes his head. His seaman's cap has been replaced by a different hat, another fedora from what must be an impressive collection. How he pulls those off, Charlie may never understand. If Dario were American, he'd probably be mocked for wearing them, but somehow, here, in those hats, he embodies an unmatched old-world elegance that makes Charlie swoon. A feeling he didn't even know he was capable of.

"What is it, then?" Charlie asks.

"Whenever I come here, I feel sad. I imagine what the rose window looked like and how the pews were arranged and how grand the altar must've been before all the battering and erosion it suffered."

"You talk as if a building has feelings," says Charlie. If the house on Cemetery Street had feelings, Charlie is sure it would have a severe case of depression, what with its stripped siding and faulty hot water heater. But the love and warmth that exist inside it? That is what Charlie is here in Italy to save.

"Maybe I'm projecting." Dario shrugs, stepping over a low-lying stone.

Charlie follows around the half wall, unwilling to let this fleeting moment of privacy go while the others are occupied. "You don't strike me as a pessimist."

"Not in business, but in life—emotionally—I can be," he confesses. "You see, I had my own Max not that long ago, and he left me like this." Dario gestures at the debris of the formerly glorious church.

Instead of asking Dario what happened, which he wants to do but fears won't go over well, Charlie extends his hand. "Come," he says. They step back inside the no-longer-there nave.

"What are we doing?" Dario asks, hand warm inside Charlie's.

"Look up," Charlie says, recreating a moment from his childhood.

Dario uses his free hand to shield his sensitive eyes from the glare of the sun. "What are we looking at? All I see is sky."

A heron soars through their line of sight.

"There is the problem. My grandpa would say that it's not just sky. It's wide-open sky. It's possibility. He once told me, 'The sky's the limit? We went to the moon! There is no limit.' This church, you're seeing rubble. I'm seeing possibility. Without a roof, this could be rebuilt into the tallest building in the world. It could become a sanctuary, a resort, a haven, a monument," Charlie says. "Just because something once was great, doesn't mean it can't be again."

Charlie doesn't realize how hard he's squeezing Dario's hand until Dario squeezes it back. And any jealousy he felt over Selina and Beau slides away.

DARIO

Sometime later, they've circled back to the beach, which means it is lunchtime.

They return to the boat to grab their spread. Dario leads

them to the special spot he's picked out for them. Charlie nabs the picnic basket with the cheese and bread. Michelle carries the bag with the blankets and towels. Beau grabs the cooler. Selina claims she did her nails last night and can't risk her manicure, which, in fairness, looks spectacular, so nobody complains.

Dario takes them to the garden of aquatic plants, which is lush and secluded. They spread out the soft, colorful blankets and the ample provisions among them.

Selina is the first to shed her layers and dip into the plunge pool. Her movement makes the water lilies and lotuses dance around her. As if she needed their help to look any more like a garden nymph—lithe and graceful.

Earlier, she stole him away for a private chat about how much she enjoys Villa Meraviglia and how handsome he is. She laid it on thick, but he sensed some sincerity behind the smoke-and-mirrors of her well-practiced flirtation.

"Who tailors your clothes?" she'd asked.

"My dear friend Gabriele Vitale. He is the best," said Dario. Gabriele was the only person he trusted to make him look dapper and professional. Too often, people mistook his lack of height for a lack of power. Gabriele made sure that with the right lift of his shoes and the perfect hem of his trousers, Dario could conquer the world.

"I simply must meet him. I look divine in menswear," she said with a bat of her long, natural lashes. "Imagine the looks we could pull out together. We could show up to galas and awards dinners all suave and elegant." She stroked her stylish nails down his lapel.

"Indeed, we would make quite the pair," he said through a thick swallow. Her beauty made him nervous and excited.

"I have to admit when I caught you and Charlie kissing last night, I got very jealous," she said, coming in so close that her breath wisped across his mouth like a tease for what was to come. "I've been wanting to kiss you since I arrived."

"Is that so?" he asked, feeling sweat start to dew above his upper lip. Nothing about her attitude when she arrived made her seem hot-and-bothered from the jump, but he was just a man after all. How could he resist her?

"It is so," she said, wiping away his feeble worry. "So?"

He nodded his assent. With the travertine wall pressed to his back, she kissed him with more tongue than he was expecting. She was an expert at passion, and that's what worried him most. Passion was a torch in the woods, liable to blow out with a bad gust of wind. Companionship, however, was a limitlessly fueled lantern in the dark forest, always ready to guide you home.

Head still reeling from the confident kiss, he rejoined the group and saw Charlie, which only complicated matters further. He is supposed to be entertaining all connections, but how is that possible when some are growing faster than others?

Charlie sits on a rock not far from the group. A violet baseball hat is tugged down over his head, obscuring his eyes. In his hand, a pencil scratches away on a fresh page of his sketchbook. It is clear the native plants with their interesting shapes and colors have inspired him.

An hour passes, the sandwiches disappear, and everyone dries off by baking themselves in the sun. Once they've all crisped up, they head back to the beach where they pack the boat for their return voyage.

Selina points out the time. "The day is still young. Can we swing up to Isola Maggiore?"

All the bliss and relaxation Dario gathered over the hours seeps out the soles of his boat shoes. Maggiore is the last place he wants to be today. The island is smaller despite its name and, in the summer months, always crawling with tourists eager to visit the locally famous lace museum, quirky shops and fine restaurants.

Beau pulls up an image search. They all gather around, except Dario who has been there, seen it, suffered *a panic attack* outside its historic church. But he can't very well announce that to the group.

When he first started dating as a teenager, his mother sat him down and handed him several pages of sheet music for a Handel aria. "Dating is like reading music. Once you know the basics, you can only get better from there."

Dario squinted at the sheet and read aloud, "Da tempeste il legno infranto—"

"No." She stopped him, covering the text with her hand. "Not the lyrics. The music. Look at the way it's written. This—" she pointed to the top "—is the A section. That is the melody, and the part of the aria where the singer sets forth the subject and mood. Think of this like the 'who are you' phase," she said. "The basics. The beauty of you.

"Then comes the B section, in a minor key, with contrast and different text. This is where your mess comes out. The prickly bits." She tapped her finger to a phrase above the staff farther in the song. "What's this say?"

"Da capo," he said. "From the head?" Blow jobs were the first thing that sprang to mind—weren't they always at that age?—so he laughed a little to himself.

"From the *beginning*. From the *top*. Con piacere. *With plea-sure*. Now that we've gone through the emotional turn of part B, we can return to part A and find new shades of meaning and understanding," she said, sounding as worldly as a well-traveled scholar. "If you started with part B, you might scare off the listener. Invite them in with the melody in your heart, then share with them the minor key of your soul. If they stick around for the da capo, then they are a true match."

This week is part A. It is about riding the beautiful melody, the same way his boat rides the wind toward Isola Maggiore. His anxiety flaps in his gut like the sail overhead. He is hit with motion sickness like never before. It grows rowdier and rougher the closer they get to the docking point.

The biggest problem with Isola Maggiore is that the pier feeds right into Via Guglielmi, the island's main street. On those narrow blocks, stuck inside a slow-moving crowd, Dario would end up gasping for air, red in the face and ready to faint. If he caught a glimpse of the church where his grandfather's funeral was held, he might even break down. That is not the early impression he wants to make on his future spouse.

As the others disembark, Dario pops open an umbrella and affixes it to the rail to provide him shade and solace. Beneath the polyester shell, he will be able to breathe. He cracks open a book, in which he's using Cosimo Sr.'s latest, unread letter as a bookmark.

"You're not coming with us?" Charlie asks. The others trot ahead.

"No. I have seen it all before," Dario says, trying to hide his wheezing. Anxiety has a way of stopping up his words like he's swallowed a handful of coarse sand from the beach.

"Are you sure?" Charlie asks, appearing concerned.

"Quite," Dario croaks. "I am comfortable here."

Charlie glances over his shoulder. Only Michelle has hung back to wait. "Would you like me to keep you company?" he asks.

Far be it from Dario to stand in the way of Charlie seeing the famous bronze statue of Saint Francis, shopping for scarves and souvenirs along the strip, and smelling all the fragrant, flowering wisteria that is certainly in bloom right now.

"No, grazie. Go and enjoy," Dario says, heartened by the gesture but unwilling to accept.

Charlie hesitates for another moment before relenting with a quick goodbye, jogging after Michelle.

A loneliness creeps off the beach and into his boat, which he combats by opening the latest letter. He imagines his nonno there beside him, like he had been many times before. Out on Lake Trasimeno was the only time Cosimo Sr. refused to talk business.

Caro Tesorino,
You excel at command.

Whether on the factory floor or behind the helm of La Anima sailing Lake Trasimeno, you shine brightest when you are in control.

I take it, however, that this excursion will have a detour or two. Such is the way when a group of strangers converge in a new, exciting place. How will you handle the changing winds— the whims and wants of others? How will you adapt to what's outside your grasp?

My nonna and nonno always said there was a third person in their marriage—the work. Their love of chocolate and Amorina elevated the brand to new echelons. This came with its own challenges. Juggling two great loves takes a lot of energy, faith and trust.

There is no one in the world I trust Amorina to more than you, Tesorino, but I worry you do not trust yourself.

The world is an uncertain place. People can be dishonest. But being the head and, by virtue, the face of a global chocolate brand, you cannot live in fear of the unknown.

Go forth and surprise yourself today.
Overcome and reap the reward.

Unlike with the other letters, a surging sense of sentimentality does not flourish through him. Instead, resentment clunks down in his gut like he swallowed a monstrous, rotten piece of fruit whole.

Overcoming is not that simple.

Mental illnesses don't just go away because you wish them to.

Sometimes, he wishes he grew up in a country where talk of anxiety wasn't so taboo. Maybe in a different place, born into a less visible family, he could reach out for support and find strength in community. Instead, he battles silently and alone, sitting on a bobbing boat on a lake beside an island where beautiful people who want to marry him frolic and drink and take photos.

He would love to reap the reward.

But he fears the greatest one of all—inheriting Amorina Chocolates—is slowly slipping from his grasp with each passing minute that agoraphobia claims the better of him.

Thirteen

CHARLIE

The vibrant red sunset over Lake Trasimeno caresses the top of the rolling Umbrian landscape. It is the most spectacular sight Charlie's ever seen.

The second most spectacular sight is Dario's face lit up with the proximal glow.

Gone is the clenched jaw and deep groove between his brows from earlier when he declined to step off the boat at Isola Maggiore. Questions about that circulate in Charlie's brain. Surely Dario had seen Isola Polvese before they hiked it as well. Why was that the excuse he gave for not touring Maggiore with them? What was he feeling but not saying?

The whole time Charlie trekked the gorgeous, more touristy island, he missed having Dario around to spout facts and share snacks with.

As soon as they were alone, Michelle stopped at a café, ordered a glass of wine, and popped in her earbuds and cued up a *Luxurious Ladies of Provence* recap podcast since she missed this week's episode. Beau unpacked his guitar case on a street corner and busked for the passersby. When Charlie asked why he'd perform for free like that, Beau said, "Best way to test out new songs is to play them for an unsuspecting audience and see how many people stop to listen."

Now, Beau has everyone listening as he gets up to give Dario a gift. From his bag, he pulls out a pack of olive oil–infused lip balms.

"These smelled really good. Thought you might like them," Beau says. Charlie had gone into that shop and had sticker shock from everything on the shelves. Beau must've used the money he earned from his performances to afford them.

"Thank you," Dario says, cheeks pinkening.

"Definitely a better taste than that olive from earlier," Beau says. Charlie imagines Dario trying out the lip balm and then kissing Beau, which causes his stomach to harden.

Michelle clucks. "You do not eat lip balm." Everybody looks at her with concerned expressions. "The idea makes me have to—" She runs for the bathroom once more. Poor thing. Everyone can hear her retch, so Charlie turns up the music.

Selina pulls a bottle of expensive bubbly wine from a bag. She shows the vintage off to everyone, as if Beau's gesture were a direct challenge to her that she could not back down from.

"I got you a little something as well," she says, already reaching for the wine cork on the nearby bench seat.

Conveniently, there are only two clean glasses left on the boat, so Selina claims them for herself and Dario.

Pop! She pours them both flutes while Beau slinks back to his seat.

"¡Arriba, abajo, al centro y pa' dentro!" Selina shouts, glass raised in cheers, but to what, exactly? Charlie shrugs to himself.

Unable to watch from the sidelines as Dario gets wooed

away by money and beauty he can't compete with, Charlie ducks downstairs to hold Michelle's hair back.

Later that night, when there is a knock at his bedroom door, Charlie expects Dario, so he quickly makes himself presentable, but Beau stands at the threshold instead.

"Have you seen Dario?" Beau asks.

"Not since dinner," Charlie says.

"I knocked on the barn house door and there was no answer."

"I think he said something about going for a walk after dessert."

Beau purses his lips and then holds a folded piece of paper out to Charlie. "Can you give this to him when he gets back?"

"Of course," Charlie says, taking it. "Wait, what is it?"

"A note," Beau says.

"Why can't you give it to him yourself?" Charlie asks, noticing Beau's crossbody bag with his passport sticking out from an unzipped pocket.

He clears his throat. "I'm gonna dip."

"For the night?" Charlie asks.

"Nah, for the rest of the trip," he says, shrugging. "I didn't want to say anything back on the boat, but I met a couple musicians out on Maggiore while I was busking. They're a blues band, out here to perform at this cool festival down in Castiglione del Lago in a few weeks. One of their guitarists had a family emergency and had to fly home short notice. They said they liked my vibe, and if I wanted to do a gig, they could use my talent. I've never played the blues before, so…"

"It's a new challenge for you," Charlie fills in.

"Exactly," Beau says, shooting him with finger guns.

Charlie squints at him. "What about Dario and the contest? Was this just another challenge for you?"

"At first, marriage was the challenge, but Dario's a cool guy. Weird, and definitely shorter than I expected, but cool. I just don't think we're on the same wavelength, you know? I explain it all to him in the note." Beau points his nose down at the paper Charlie still holds. "And no offense here, but I think Selina's already got this on lock. I saw her kissing Dario on Polvese."

"So? You saw me kissing Dario in the pool," Charlie says.

Beau appears as if he doesn't remember that. "Right, yeah. That's true…"

Charlie gets the impression that whatever Beau saw transpire between Dario and Selina was hotter and more substantial.

Charlie sighs. A touch of him wonders how the five of them were selected from what must have been hundreds of thousands of applications. They are an odd, disjointed bunch.

"I just don't want to waste anybody's time. Not Dario's and not my own," Beau says.

"Sure, but don't you think you should still stick around until you can give this to Dario yourself?" Charlie asks, not wanting to be the bearer of bad news. What if Dario really liked Beau?

"Yeah, uh," Beau says, swiping a hand at the back of his neck. "The band is already outside in their van waiting for me. I timed this so if things got awkward, I could leave quick." Beau's phone beeps in his bag. "That's them. Can you just give that to Dario for me and tell the others I said bye?"

"For sure," Charlie says before biting the inside of his cheek. "Have fun."

The air has cooled significantly by the time Charlie ventures outside after Beau's departure. A light steam billows off the heated pool. Charlie rests on a cushioned chair beneath the striped awning that drapes down from the villa. He faces the distant shadow of the lake with Beau's note shaking in his hands while he waits for Dario to come back.

At the first squeak of the side gate, Charlie bolts up. Angelo, off-leash, comes bounding toward him, letting out several small barks.

"Angelo, cosa fai?" Dario asks from around the corner. He appears right as Angelo flops onto his back, exposing his belly for Charlie to pet. "Oh, ciao, Charlie. Were you waiting for me?"

"Sort of," Charlie says, standing again. "I'm here to give you this."

Dario accepts the paper. "Did I drop this? Is this one of my grandfather's letters?" he asks in a rush.

"What? No, this is from Beau," Charlie says, trying to soften his words in hope it might cushion the blow.

"More song lyrics?" Dario asks. "He's been slipping them under my door. They're very sweet, but if I don't get to them before Angelo, they end up slobbered upon, torn up and unreadable."

Charlie gives a small, pained smile. "I don't think this is a song."

Dario's brow furrows. "I don't understand."

"I'm not sure I do either, but Beau left a little while ago," Charlie says.

"It's late. When will he be back?" Dario asks.

"Uh, never?" Charlie says, then cringes realizing how indelicate that sounded.

Dario stops unfolding the paper, clearly embarrassed now. Charlie really wishes he hadn't been put in this position. He hates the weighted frown on Dario's face. "I see," Dario says.

Now Charlie understands why Beau wanted to make such a quick getaway. The awkwardness of this encounter is torture, and he's not even the one rejecting Dario. "How do you say 'I'm sorry' in Italian?" Charlie asks.

"Mi dispiace."

"Mi dispiace," Charlie echoes.

"Right on the first try," Dario says, a soft encouragement.

"It was bound to happen eventually," Charlie says with a slight laugh, then holds up his hands. "I meant about me saying Italian words correctly, not Beau—"

Dario shakes his head. "I understood you, Charlie. You don't have anything to be sorry for."

Charlie shoves his hands in his pockets. "Buona notte."

"Two for two," Dario says with a weakish smile.

"I'm going to quit while I'm ahead," Charlie says, turning back to the villa.

"Sogni d'oro," Dario whispers to Charlie's retreating form.

Back in his room, Charlie tries his best to type the Italian words into his translator app.

Common meaning, *sweet dreams*. Literal meaning, *dreams of gold*.

Charlie burrows himself in the blankets and considers the silly image he first had when he saw Dario's net worth, of a swimming pool full of gold coins.

Funny to think that now Dario's heart seems a far greater treasure than any fortune.

Fourteen

DARIO

At breakfast the next morning, Dario's three remaining suitors sit around the covered outdoor table picking at fresh fruit and sipping from tiny white espresso mugs. There are more empty chairs than claimed ones at this point.

Last night, reading Beau's note, which was as poetic as his lyrics, caused rejection to swarm Dario like hornets with their stingers at the ready. In the morning light, however, when he read the note again—the reasoning, the apology, the desire to be friends—he realized Beau had paid him a kindness. Instead of sticking around, making a good show of it, and potentially allowing Dario to fall for him, he bowed out as soon as he realized it wasn't going to work.

So Dario faces the option to stew and curse the blues band that stole Beau away from his villa, or to focus on the positive. Now he only had to divide his attention three ways!

He chooses to carry on, and carry on he shall. Keep calm, however, as the Brits say? Not as likely.

"Anyone up for a bike ride around Lake Trasimeno?" Dario asks. The shed is full up with bikes of all sizes and sport speeds. Bicycles are how the Cotognas got around the village most days in childhood. It was the one form of family exercise they could all agree was fun and enjoyable.

Michelle pulls off her round sunglasses and shrugs her wrap down off her shoulders. Her skin is as red as a freshly caught lobster. "I forgot to reapply."

"I have some aloe in my bag if you need it," Charlie offers. His tiredness is visible in the slouch of his shoulders.

Michelle covers up again. "I am okay. I have some. But I do not want to hurt any more than I already do, so I will stay back from the bike ride if that is all right."

"Me, too," Selina says. "Not because I hurt but because I don't want to. Bicycle seats are extremely uncomfortable, and I was hoping to steal you away, Dario, to Solomeo for the day to visit Cucinelli's hamlet and boutique. I am in desperate need of some quality cashmere."

Acidic anxiety coats Dario's throat, thwarting any type of response. While many people travel far and wide to the charming hamlet that billionaire fashion mogul Brunello Cucinelli rebuilt to house his empire and revitalize craftsmanship, Dario has never been, even though it's so nearby. He adores menswear and admires Cucinelli for his factory practices and his "humanistic capitalism" but new places ratchet up Dario's agoraphobia, so he would much rather stick to his predetermined schedule.

Bike ride. The lake. No more deviations.

"You two won't mind if I take Dario for the afternoon?" Selina asks, barreling on, uncaring of any answers. "I would invite you both, but Cucinelli's pieces are expensive. I would not want either of you to feel pressured or out of place."

"I know about Cucinelli," Michelle says. "I am a fashion student."

"Do you think you can pull off beiges, grays and browns in your present condition?" Selina asks.

"I guess not." Michelle raises her wrap and slinks back in her seat, clearly unwilling to argue more.

"I would still be down for the bike ride," says Charlie. "Maybe it will pep me up. The espresso doesn't seem to be working." He tap-tap-taps the side of his mug with his pointer finger. "Is this thing on?" he jokes.

"Excelente. Charlie will ride, Michelle will stay here, and we will shop," Selina says, racing a long nail up Dario's silky tie. He swallows, and it sounds like a gunshot in his own ears.

Solomeo is a tourist destination, and Cucinelli's enterprise and factory employ hundreds. Going there is another recipe for a panic attack. God, how he wishes he weren't such a prisoner to his own thoughts.

"I would prefer to stick close to the villa today," Dario says, even though what he should really say is *every day*.

Selina's catlike eyes narrow, obviously not used to being told no in any form. "Solomeo is not far. I checked. It is only fifteen minutes by car."

"I know," Dario says, sensing his pits start to sweat. "Truly, I only wear Gabriele's creations these days. A visit to Cucinelli's boutique would be a waste for me."

"Could you not use a little variety in your wardrobe?" Selina casts her disapproving gaze over him. She must be tired of his five-piece, colorful suits, but it's what he feels best in. If she can't accept that, then she's probably not the person for him. Right? Or are his resistance to change and his anxiety going to be the death knell to his tenure as the head of Amorina?

He feels like he's tied to three separate horses who have been sent running in different directions.

Dario withholds a flinch and takes charge of the day the only way he knows how, with logistics. "I'll arrange a car to take you to Solomeo. Michelle, is there anything I can do for you?"

Her eyes flick toward the TV mounted on the wall inside the propped open doors. "Leave the streaming passwords?"

"Done deal," he says.

Selina, looking pissed, retreats to her room to get ready.

Dario hopes he has made the right decision.

A little while later, with helmets on and bikes rolling at their sides, Dario and Charlie arrive at the marked trail in Torricella Peligna. In Charlie's bike basket, he has water bottles and protein bars. Dario turns his into a doggie bed for Angelo who appears thrilled to be away from the villa.

The sun is blazing, but the sweat is welcome as soon as they take off. Dario's muscles relish the push and stretch of sole to pedal after being stitched up with worry last night over Beau's departure.

As they pass vegetable gardens and small beaches, he keeps a slower pace than usual, so he and Charlie remain side by side.

"Sorry if I was awkward last night," Dario says, sounding sheepish.

"Oh no, *I'm* sorry that Beau didn't tell you himself. I shouldn't have agreed to get in the middle of it," Charlie says.

Dario shakes his head. "You were only doing what was asked of you. There's no harm in that."

Charlie's eyes flick his way. "You're not upset Beau's gone, then?"

"I'm quite the opposite. I'm happy he was honest." Dario

pedals a little harder, enjoying the breeze on his cheeks. "Honesty is not a quality I've come to expect given my history."

Their tires crunch on the gravel, kicking up rocks as they go.

"Are you talking about Preston Browborn?" Charlie asks.

That name makes every muscle in Dario's body cramp up. An overgrown olive tree hanging into the path nearly topples him off his bike.

"Sorry," Charlie says. "I googled you."

"You have no reason to be sorry. I'm the one who made a fool of himself in front of the entirety of Amorina and all our competitors," Dario says. The aftermath of the situation is a halting set of chains wrapped around his bike tires, slowing him down and causing him to struggle for breath.

"I'm sure it wasn't that bad," says Charlie.

"Oh, it was," Dario says, thankful they hit a slight downhill slope so he can coast for a second. "I pushed for my grandfather to sponsor a special chocolate festival in Castiglione del Lago with a focus on fair trade and sustainability efforts. I knew if he did so, many of our competitors would invest as well. It would be a sign that the chocolate industry was listening, and a way to tell the world that we care about our effect on the planet."

"That's really admirable," says Charlie.

"I knew for my grandfather it was about optics, but for me, it was part of my vision for Amorina and my overall mission," Dario says. "The mission I shared with Preston. I met him when we were classmates at the University of Perugia where we both studied Food & Sustainability. After two years of dating, I thought we shared much more than a mission. I was very wrong."

Dario pulls over when they reach Sualzo Beach. They park their bikes to the side of the path and venture out into the sand.

The heads of swimmers wobble in the lake water. A few red pedal boats cruise along the surface. Birds squawk overhead.

"I know there is this stereotype of Italian men being suave and charming, but my brother inherited all of those qualities. I'm confident in business, but not so much in love," Dario says.

"I'd beg to differ," Charlie says, sitting beside him in the sand beneath a pre-stationed umbrella. He hands Dario one of the water bottles, which he cracks open. Angelo trots ahead, splashes into the water.

"You've only known me for a matter of days," Dario says.

"Yeah, but you're juggling and entertaining five potential spouses in your gorgeous villa. What's more suave and charming than that?" Charlie asks.

"One lied to me, and one just wants to be friends. It's not going so well. I would've never done this on my own," he says.

"But look at you! You're doing it." Charlie smiles, and it's enough fuel for him to share more.

"I suppose that's true. I wasn't sure when or if I'd be ready to get back out there after Preston," Dario says.

"He must've really hurt you," Charlie says.

"Preston and I were together for almost two years when the festival came up. By that time, I think we all knew my grandfather wasn't going to live much longer, so I got this idea in my head that I'd propose to Preston at the festival after giving the big keynote speech. I knew it was almost like my audition to be the face of Amorina, and I nailed it. I was rehearsed and confident and clear-voiced. Everything went perfectly, up until I called Preston onto the stage, got down on one knee, and he rejected me in front of the huge crowd. There was shock and laughter. I was humiliated," Dario says.

"Couldn't he at least have pretended for the audience? I'm sorry it went down like that," Charlie says, clearly hanging on every word.

"Offstage, Preston told me he'd been having doubts about us for a while, and that he wished he'd said so sooner, that it hadn't come to this, but that he couldn't go on pretending that he saw a future for us," Dario recounts, the memory racing to the surface of his skin like a poison pushing its way out. "He didn't even stay for the rest of the festival. He left me there, alone. I suffered such a debilitating panic attack that my mom found me sometime later sat in an alley with my knees to my chest staring into space. I didn't even remember how I'd gotten there."

"Oh, Dario," Charlie says.

"It was a big, foolish mistake," says Dario.

"Mistakes are part of being human. Placing your trust in someone is always a gamble even when you think you know them inside and out. Even your own family, sometimes," Charlie says, sounding beaten down by a situation outside his control.

"Has someone in your family hurt you?" Dario asks, hoping Charlie lets him in.

"You know how I told you about my grandpa's injury? My uncle was the one who pushed him to file a lawsuit against the company who manufactured the crane that malfunctioned and caused him to lose his foot. My grandpa was really hesitant at first, claiming the company he worked for had been good to him, especially with the workmen's comp. But eventually, my uncle wore him down and Grandpa won his case. The settlement was massive. Maybe not by global chocolate company standards, but for us? Where we come from, it was life-changing money."

"Your lives didn't change?" Dario asks.

"They did for a brief time. I was a kid. But even then, I could tell. My parents seemed less stressed. I got more toys that Christmas. My grandpa set up an appointment with a prosthetist and got his first prosthetic foot. He got up and walking again and we all thought the universe was finally rewarding the Moore family." Charlie's expression darkens; cheeks slacken. "Then sometime the following spring, I woke up to hear my grandparents and parents whispering in the kitchen. Nobody was even touching the French toast Dad had made, which is saying something because that is his specialty. I knew better than to interrupt grown-up talk, so I hung back and listened. My uncle had disappeared and the bank account they'd put the settlement money into had been drained."

Dario's heart grows arms that seek to reach from his chest and wrap Charlie up in a hug so fierce and protective that Charlie may never experience hurt again. "That is terrible. I am sorry. Did they track him down and recover the money?"

"His name was also on the bank account. Legally, he was entitled to it. Without that money, we couldn't hire anyone to get that money back. A bit of a catch-22 there," he says.

"I sincerely wish that had not happened to you," Dario says.

"It's okay. I never had a strong relationship with Uncle Buck, so that part didn't sting so much, but my grandparents had to sell their house and move in with us. My grandparents got the main bedroom, my parents moved into my room, and the living room was where I had to sleep, watch TV, do homework."

Villa Meraviglia—a word that translates loosely to "wonder"—lost its luster for Dario long ago. It is the place where he sleeps, feeds his dog and does his work. It is not a place he *lives in* beyond the literal sense. Because *living* requires a zest for the world that Dario doesn't know how to get back. The sort of zest he sees sparkling in Charlie Moore's eyes each time he looks at him.

Charlie Moore deserves *more*.

Damn, Dario Cotogna wants to give it to him.

"That must've been tough," Dario says, his privilege flocking around him like vicious gulls to a spilled meal.

"The only tough part was how emotionally destroyed my family was. One selfish person made them all guarded. Hope left our house that day," Charlie says. "I don't even mean, like, they all got mean and pessimistic. Far from that, actually. My family is goofy and loud and a hoot to be around, but more, that day, they stopped dreaming."

"You are here," Dario says around a ball of emotion stopping up his throat. "You must still dream."

Charlie's pensive expression shatters, making way for a bright smile that puts the luminous sun to shame. "I've been dreaming enough for all five of us," he says, gaze cast out over the lake like a fishing line hoping for the biggest catch.

Is that him? Is Dario the prize fish he's hoping to haul in?

"I would like to kiss you," Dario says, eyes trained on that mouth. Those perfectly imperfect teeth glistening between melon-colored lips.

"What's stopping you?" Charlie asks, an air of sweet cockiness cropping up in his voice.

Dario does not share the confidence Selina had at the fortress or the cheekiness Charlie had in the pool. Preston took any "moves" Dario may have had when he blindsided him a year ago, leaving Dario to question if any of it was ever real and if he possessed any lovable parts at all.

Those fears bury themselves in the sand as Dario inches into Charlie, someone he's only known for days but already makes him feel safe. With Charlie, he senses that he doesn't need confidence or cheekiness. He only needs what he has to offer. That all he is and all he will be is enough for Charlie Moore.

Dario's hand runs over Charlie's blue buzz cut as he stares into Charlie's eyes before gently tugging him in. Their lips meet, and the kiss is unrushed and salty from their mixed sweat and the olive oil lip balm. Nobody is coming to interrupt them this time, and Dario is thankful for that.

Kisses are like colors; each shade tells a different story.

If their kiss in the pool was a lustful scarlet, this kiss is a warm burgundy. Richer and deeper. A true display of comfort and care.

When they break apart, Charlie smiles, bites his lip, then points across the pier at a nearby field that is dotted with tall, sandstone columns. "What's that?"

"Campo del Sole," Dario says, still waking up from the kiss. "It is a statue garden."

Charlie climbs to his feet before Dario has even finished speaking.

The green grassy plot houses tan-colored art pieces that rise from the ground in concentric circles with a fountain at their center. Some are round and wavy, while others are brutal and jagged.

"It's like a more modern Stonehenge," Charlie says as they venture through.

"It's said to be a monument," Dario says.

"To what?"

"Anything. Anyone. As I am aware, it is untethered to any history. Maybe it is about the future? I guess it can be about whatever you desire," he says while he stares up at the art. His eyes trace the curves in the stone and he wonders about the dexterous hands that must have cramped as they sculpted for hours on end in search of underlying beauty.

"What if we say it's a monument to us?" Charlie asks, crushing the space between them with clear intent.

"I like that idea," Dario says, hope dispensing through his body.

They kiss again, and this time it's a whimsical raspberry. Vivid, youthful, and bursting with ripe possibility.

Fifteen

DARIO

Villa Meraviglia is a host of unfamiliar noises when they re-turn from the bike ride.

For once, Dario does not begrudge the theft of his solitude and silence. The warmth and life crackling inside are wel-come, especially after the glorious day he spent with Charlie, who hightails it outside and up the stairs to catch a shower.

The final glimpse of Charlie's pert ass in his shiny athletic shorts is enough to send Dario chasing after him, but he reins in that impulse. It's one thing to kiss Charlie out on the beach while they're alone. It's another to fuck Charlie silly while his other guests sit downstairs. Nothing in this villa is soundproof.

From another room, laughs and clanking glasses emanate.

Dario's knees are gelatinous from the exertion and the ooey-gooey emotions jiggling inside him, so it takes him some time to find the source.

In the living room, Michelle—slathered in colorful lotion—

watches *The Luxurious Ladies of Provence*. He stops for a moment as the scene on the TV plays out. Three women sit around a glass table on an outside terrace speaking in French. Their nails and hair are long and glossy. Their outfits and voices are loud. The tensions are high.

"You are back!" Michelle says, pausing the show.

Dario nods. "What have you been up to?"

Defying all logic, her face grows redder. "This. Just this."

"Sounds like a relaxing afternoon," he says. "Is Selina back yet?"

"She arrived about an hour ago asking for dinner. I think she is in the kitchen with Paola," she says.

Dario thanks her and leaves Michelle to her ladies. He wonders how he would feel about the rescripting of his life by some producer in an editing bay. His skin crawls. Cameras of any kind would never be welcome in his space.

In the kitchen, a feminine robot speaks in broken Italian. When Dario pokes his head in, Selina—wearing what looks suspiciously like one of Dario's suits, except tailored to her figure—has Paola cornered by the pasta crank. She holds up the speaker side of her phone where the voice crackles out.

"I'm sure I can double whatever Dario pays you," Selina says. On the island behind her, a plate sits scraped clean of food. Red sauce clings to the edges. After a few seconds, the robot voice echoes her sentiment in Italian.

Paola's face is a crumpled ball of confusion. "Ma perché?"

The keyboard on Selina's phone makes loud, obnoxious clacks. Anger flows hot through Dario's veins, but he holds himself back before jumping to conclusions and announcing himself. Maybe he has the wrong impression. He doesn't want a repeat of what happened with Ansel.

Selina's phone spits out garbled words that make no sense. With a groan, she slaps it face down on the counter. "You—"

she points "—come work for me—" she points the other way "—in Mexico when this is all over."

Now, that was impossible to misconstrue. He enters the room, footsteps echoing like thunderclaps. "What's going on here?"

Selina whirls around. Paola appears rattled. Fury burns hot on Dario's cheeks.

"Paola and I were just discussing her culinary training," says Selina in the boldest of fashions. Paola swirls her fingers around her temples as if to suggest Selina is out of her mind. Dario feels out of his mind too, except with rage that practically turns his vision red.

"I heard what you were discussing, and how dare you," he bellows. The sounds of the TV cut out in the background. The pitter-patter of the shower running stops, too. An audience is about to amass as his diatribe mounts behind his lips. "Paola is my family, and you're trying to hire her out from under me. Why?"

Selina rolls her eyes, clearly caught red-handed. "Because she's the best, and I want the best."

Flashes of yesterday in the ruins flood his head. Did that mean nothing to her? Did that mean— "What about me?"

She tilts her head and widens her eyes. "Please tell me you don't think there's anything romantic between us."

His eyes skip to Paola's, thankful for once that she isn't fluent in English, so she doesn't judge what he's about to say. "That kiss yesterday, it was… I thought it was nice."

She clucks. "You don't build a life on nice, Dario. You're Italian, dios mio. Drama, you have covered, but passion? You're missing it."

Dario breathes in sharply. "I have passion," he rebuts, though it comes out watery, weak.

"For chocolate making, maybe, but not for love. Not for

life. I tried to pull you out of your shell today, and you crawled right back in. I want adventure, late nights, wind-in-my-hair kind of love. I've known you—what?—five days, and I can already tell you live by the book. You can't give me that," she says before stepping closer and gesturing between them. "I want heat and all I feel here is warmth at best."

As she moves closer, the sharp angles of her face and her impeccable makeup come into focus. So too do the crisp lines and perfect seams of her menswear. "Did Gabriele make that suit for you?"

"I may have paid him a visit today," she says.

"You never went to Solomeo?" he asks.

She shakes her head. "I never made it." His upset must be caked across his face, because she adds, "We would have never made it either."

Dario senses Charlie and Michelle at his back. Their presence only magnifies his mortification.

"This has been fun and you are as sweet as can be, but I have friends waiting on me in Florence, so I think it is time like Beau I make my exit," she says. To add insult to injury, she whips a business card from her breast pocket and hands it to a still-quaking Paola. "If circumstances change." She struts from the room, head held high.

The fashions of love have clearly changed since Dario last walked its treacherous catwalk, because she wanted his life, but she didn't want him.

The flat-out rejection infiltrates his nerves. Powers off his fight response. Flight kicks in as soon as he turns to face the other two still standing. The other two who certainly have a lesser view of him now that he's been chewed up and spit out by Selina Velasco, one of the hottest queer models in the whole wide world.

"Scusi," he says as if this were his own personal catchphrase.

Angelo greets him at the door of the barn house. His wagging tail and happy yaps do nothing to lift Dario's spirits. His spirits are crumpled up in the compost bin with the food scraps back in the kitchen.

For the second time this week, he flops down face-first on the bed and screams into the sheets. How had a lovely day spoiled so fast?

Angelo uses his doggie stairs to tramp up onto the bed. Between his teeth is an envelope with Cosimo Sr.'s handwriting on it. It must have fallen from Dario's pocket as he raced inside, embarrassment hot on his tail.

He tears into the envelope and unfolds the letter.

Caro Tesorino,
Are you ready to give up yet?
  My sincerest hope is that your answer is no.
  My best guess is that true intentions have been revealed, unfit matches have departed, and feelings have blossomed between you and at least one of your guests. The romance of Italy is hard to fight, and you are a Cotogna man, you carry grace and handsomeness in your DNA.

Dario stops to chuff. Angelo barks in response.

He is not his brother. He does not have a debonair bone in his body. Selina made sure he knew how subpar he was. She must've imagined a playboy type, scoring sex left and right. City by city. Conquests on conquests.

His is a quiet, contained life. His heart is a fractured, sheltered thing.

Confidence, like Rome, isn't built overnight.

He continues reading:

Being a Cotogna also means you have access and assets at your fingertips. Access and assets other people will want to get their hands on. I know you know this because you've learned the lesson the hard way.

But learning a hard lesson does not mean you must harden your heart.

In truth, there was a time when I thought to wall off my heart as well.

Before your grandma—which was about as arranged as a marriage got in those days—I fell in love with one of the young girls who worked in my parents' factory. Her name was Giulia. She had auburn hair, bright green eyes, and a smattering of charming freckles that showed clearest in the summer.

She had not a penny to her name, yet we had so much in common. We both enjoyed pistachio gelato and the films of Fellini. We preferred the country to the city, and bike rides over car rides. She kissed me like she could breathe fresh life into me.

When I told my parents I had met the girl I was going to marry, they were aghast. They remained dead set against it. They said they would disinherit me if I went through with it. But like any teenage boy with too much money to burn and too much confidence to spare, I took what little I had of my own and Giulia by the hand with our sights set on Capri.

It wasn't until I made a stop off at the city hall that the haze of our love lifted.

"Why are we stopping?" she asked.

"To legally marry," I said, smiling from ear to ear.

She looked confused. "I thought we were to marry in Capri. You said you'd tell your family. I thought we were going to choose a location to wed."

I shook my head. "I wanted to wait until we got to Capri so as to not spoil our trip. My parents do not want any part of our marriage. They say that if we wed, they'll disinherit me. I say,

I'm too in love to care." I reached in to hold her. She shirked my advance. "Giulia, what's wrong?"

She grew cold, arms folded. "Take me home."

"What? Why?"

There were tears in her eyes. At first, I thought they were tears of sadness over my parents' disapproval. But then I looked closer at her wild, downturned eyebrows and realized she was upset at me. "I want to go home," she said again.

"You loved me not even an hour ago. What changed?" I asked, still young and foolish. Still imagining us as the innamorati in the commedia dell'arte, but then she spoke again, and I realized that I was Arlecchino all along.

"An hour ago, you were Cosimo Cotogna, heir to Amorina Chocolates. You could give me a real life, master of the world. Now you are, who? Cosimo Cotogna, heir to nothing, master of none. What can you give me now?" she asked. Her words were daggers, and I was strapped to a wooden, spinning wheel as she flung them at me.

My hands shook as they reached out to her. "I can give you my love."

She well and truly turned up her nose. "Take me home."

I drove her back to Perugia, and I never heard from her again.

As I write this, the tears come again, not because I think Giulia is the one that got away, but because I wish I had shared this story with you sooner. I wish I had told it to your mother.

When your father brought home April—a poor opera singer getting by on a per diem—I warned him against pursuing her. I told him he would regret it. I threatened to disinherit him. My, how we all become our fathers one day!

Your father was older and wiser, though. He knew what he wanted, and he found a life partner in April. That union gave us all many happy years and added two fine young men to our *family. April proved me wrong, changed my tune, and exposed my heart again.*

My words must not be mistaken. I loved your nonna dearly. Ours was a love that started small and grew over time. Time is what it took for me to let her in. A long time. Too long a time, considering it now.

I held my feelings close. I barely let her know me. I spoke in riddles and changed my mind a million times about whether we should marry. I think I drove her wild. I drove everyone wild. Perhaps if I hadn't spent so many years steeling my heart, I wouldn't have had such a hellish time letting down my guard.

Remember there is more bravery in shedding your armor than there is in drawing your weapon.

Con affetto,
Nonno

Dario clutches the letter to his chest as if the words might melt off the page and soak into his skin like tattoo ink. If only he could embody these sentiments. Time and experience have warped him.

Preston was deceitful, Ansel was opportunistic, Beau was adventuresome, and Selina was self-assured. Dario was…

Dario is…

He has no clue.

Dario lost his sense of self, and if he has to marry, he needs a partner that will roll out the map, retrace his steps and help him find it again.

There is a knock at the barn house entrance that stirs him out of his stupor.

Leaving the letter on the bed, he rises with little enthusiasm until he is met with Charlie's smiling face on the other side of the door, looking a lot like an explorer willing to excavate Dario again.

Sixteen

CHARLIE

"I hope I'm not bothering you," Charlie says.

"You could never," Dario says, looking at him in such a funny sort of way.

"I came to check and see how you were doing." Anxious energy shoots down to his feet, causing him to rock back and forth.

As soon as he heard the commotion down in the kitchen when he stepped out of the shower earlier, he raced to see what was wrong. His gut sank at the uncomfortable scene he stumbled upon.

The way Selina spoke to Dario lit a fire beneath Charlie's skin. The urge to protect Dario flamed up, fierce and immediate. While he commended Selina for her directness, he wishes she'd been gentler about it.

"Va bene," Dario says, one hand still clutching the wood of the door. He looks one wind gust away from toppling over.

"Didn't seem *va bene* back there," says Charlie. "Selina's left, if that matters to you." Selfishly, he is glad of this. One less person in the villa means one less person to compete with for Dario's hand.

"Va—" Dario clears his throat. "Thank you for letting me know."

They stumble through a long silence. "I can go," Charlie says, afraid he has made a wrong move by coming out here. Maybe Dario is someone who prefers to sit with his feelings in silence.

"I would rather you didn't," Dario says, opening the door wider. An offering.

Charlie steps inside.

"Make yourself comfortable," Dario says.

The chair he sat on to video-chat with his family a few days ago is piled high with work papers, so he takes a hesitant seat on the edge of the bed. He swipes his hands along the silken quilt that is both homey and high-quality.

"Can I get you anything?" Dario moves to the mini fridge that buzzes beneath the window.

"I'm okay," Charlie says. Tries for more: "Are you? Okay, I mean."

A can of San Pellegrino hisses as Dario opens it. It sweats in his palm, the way Charlie sweats with nerves on the bed. "I am. I think I am."

"You think?" Charlie's hands bunch up in the quilt as Dario leans his backside against the reclaimed wood counter behind him. For such a short man, he has a big presence and, it seems, even bigger emotions.

"I've faced worse. I'm more upset that this is the cap to our lovely day together," he says. A refreshing *ahh* follows his first sip. The sound makes Charlie's toes wiggle.

"It doesn't have to be the cap. The night is still young," Charlie says. The clock on the wall is in plain sight. It is slightly after 8:00 p.m. "Plenty of time to turn this night around."

He waits patiently for Dario's eyes to light up with recognition. Is he being too coy? He is slightly out of practice in the subtle art of seduction. Half his sexual encounters back in Pennsylvania involve endless app conversations and quickies in the back seats of cars. There's not much conversation or eye contact before the zippers rake down in search of frantic release.

This is a different kind of encounter. Far more about showing Dario that he's here, that he cares, that he's attracted to him. Who needs Selina when they could make a life together? A beautiful life if it remained anything like today.

"Whatever you have in mind sounds better than wallowing," says Dario. "I am being too dramatic."

Charlie stands and catches Dario's drooping chin between his fingers. Lifts his gaze so they are eye to eye. He's not sure where this confidence came from, but he peers into those limitless hazel eyes that seem to morph with each passing second like a fast-moving storm. "Where you see dramatics, I see conviction," Charlie says.

"Selina didn't think so," Dario says, sounding downtrodden.

"Let's not talk about her anymore," says Charlie. He drops his hand. "If she doesn't see your passion for sustainability, kindness and connection, that's her loss."

"But your gain?" Dario asks, slipping his palm into the hand Charlie dropped.

"Yeah." Charlie slams the space between them shut. Their chests graze.

"Charlie Moore…" Dario gasps. "Did you come here to make me feel better with *sex*?"

Charlie shyly smirks and shrugs, playing up his small-town innocence. "If sex would make you feel better, then yes, that's what I came here to do. But if that's not what you need, I'm happy to snuggle and listen or leave or…"

In his head, this went smoother. But this is somehow…better? More honest, at least. Their fingertips trace tepid lines up each other's forearms. A tickling, sensual gesture that makes his breath hitch.

"That's very kind of you," says Dario, cupping his hands around Charlie's wrists.

"My grandma always says, 'Kindness is key,'" Charlie says, then cringes. "I can't believe I just brought up my grandma. There's nothing more unsexy than somebody's grandma."

"I'm sure your grandma was very sexy in her day," Dario says without thought. Charlie gapes at him. "I made it so much worse, didn't I?"

"So, so much worse!" Charlie shakes his head as his incredulous smile blooms.

"The moment is gone," Dario says ruefully.

"We can get it back. Let's try to get it back," Charlie says, remaining positive. He didn't break out his manscaper for nothing.

"How should we do that?" Dario asks, sounding as if he would go to the ends of the earth if that's what Charlie told him it took. But he's not here to make Dario work for it. He's here to make Dario feel good, valued. To build him back up after Selina's dressing-down.

"What if we listed things about each other that turn us on?" Charlie asks. Talking about sex always ratchets up his desire in any given situation. "You go first."

Dario laughs awkwardly. "Putting the pressure on me here."

"You're the one who said my grandma was very sexy in her day without any photographic evidence!" Charlie points out.

"Would photographic evidence have made it *better*?" Dario asks with raised eyebrows. A laugh blasts out of him. "You're the one who brought up your grandma in the first place!"

"Okay," Charlie concedes through a fit of his own laughs. "We're getting nowhere. I'll go first. Your eyes." He takes a calming breath and really looks at Dario. "God, your eyes are sexy. So open and searching. You have these big, basset hound eyes."

"First grandmas, and now dogs?" Dario cries. Charlie drops his face into his hands. "Speaking of dogs. Angelo, vai a giocare in giardino."

Angelo trots from his bed and out through the doggy door. His tiny *arfs* puncture the night.

The sultry darkness swells in through the half-open windows. They laugh again. Stilted and uncertain.

"I'll also see myself out through the doggie door," Charlie jokes. He's no more than two steps away from the door when Dario grabs him by the forearm and reels him back in.

"You will do no such thing." His palms graze Charlie's cheeks before he pulls him in by the back of the neck and kisses him.

The kiss is so spectacular that it ruins Charlie for all future kisses. What other experience could ever compare to kissing Dario Cotogna in his bedroom in his historic Italian villa?

This is Charlie's pinnacle. He's lightheaded as he finds himself at this unexpected romantic summit.

They topple onto the bed together. "Aside from my basset hound eyes," Dario says teasingly, "what else about me do you find sexy?"

"Your hair," Charlie says as he rakes a hand through the glossy strands. Charlie imagines what the top of Dario's head might look like while his face is buried between his thighs. "It frames your handsome face so well."

"I'm handsome?" Dario asks with earnestness. He truly doesn't know, can't see it himself. How does one look in a mirror and not see obvious beauty?

"You're handsome," Charlie confirms before planting a kiss

on the back of Dario's hand. "Your intelligence only makes you handsomer. You know and honor your family history. When you gave the tour in the museum, my heart raced. I was kinda turned on."

"Si?" Dario asks. "So my grandma is sexy, too?"

"Shut it, Candy Man," Charlie says, quieting Dario with a kiss.

The time for joking is over. His hands grip Dario's lapel tightly as if he is afraid to lose control of this situation again. "And you have an impeccable sense of style. Most people wear clothes. You, I don't know, *don* them or some shit."

Dario laughs. "That's all Gabriele's doing."

"Is Gabriele the one putting the clothes on and parading around in them?" Charlie asks, raking his eyes down Dario's body, which sprawls across the bed.

"No," he says, fiddling with the top button on his shirt.

"My point made," Charlie says, allowing lust to turn his voice smoky. "You won't be wearing them for much longer either if I'm lucky."

Dario seems to still with unspoken emotion under his touch.

"I would like to keep my clothes on," Dario says, eyes falling to the foot of the bed.

Charlie moves back in confusion. "Uh, okay? Do you not want to do this?"

Dario sighs. "I do want to do this, but first, please let me explain."

DARIO

A confession bubbles up and out. "These clothes that Gabriele makes for me are what I feel most confident in. When I'm naked, I worry about the position I'm in or the way the light-ing makes me look, whether my skin is clear of blemishes, or I missed a spot while trimming."

"I don't care about any of that stuff," Charlie says, deep sincerity sprinkled over his words.

Dario pushes up onto his forearms. "It is my anxiety. I get stuck in my head and cannot enjoy myself. Clothed, I know I am representing myself. Maybe I am not making any sense. I know it is not what everyone wants."

Charlie shakes his head, pauses for a moment. "I want what you want, Dario. I think I get it. It's like me with my tattoos. I like being naked because my tattoos represent me. They make me feel confident, so showing them all off heightens that confidence. Your fashion sense represents you. Sex is about showing up as your authentic self. This—" Charlie gestures at his covered body "—represents you. Very well, I might add."

"Grazie." His whole body blushes. "My ex was not so ac-commodating. It was exciting to him at first. He thought I got off on the rush of needing him right away, that I was too turned on to shuck all my clothes before getting down to it, but it was never that for me. For now, I am my truest self in these clothes."

"I think that makes total sense, Candy Man," Charlie says. The pet name causes Dario's dick to swell against his satiny briefs. "Only one question. What do you do about the, uh, mess?"

"I go to a very talented, very discreet dry cleaner who does not ask questions," says Dario before biting his lip.

"Sweet. I'll be much less worried about cleanup, then." Charlie's eyebrows hike up suggestively.

"I don't want you to worry about anything at all when you're with me." Dario's heart dances.

Charlie runs his hands over Dario, seemingly luxuriating

in the feel of the expensive fabrics against his palms. The front of his shorts tents out with anticipation.

"Why don't you get more comfortable?" Dario suggests.

Charlie preens at the idea. He stands, grabs the bottom hem of his shirt and whips it up over his head. His shorts and checkered boxers hit the floor. He stands there in his glory, a breathing, sexy storybook to be read cover to cover.

Dario's heart nearly quits from all the blood rushing straight to his cock.

Dario scoots forward, tongue outstretched and salivating. Slowly, he tastes the compliant American all fucking over. From tattoo to tattoo, he plays a long game of sensual connect-the-dots. When his tongue hits particularly sensitive spots—his hip bone, below his armpit, the dip beneath his left ear—Charlie shudders.

Dario runs a tender hand along Charlie's jaw. "Sei stupenda."

"I'm stupendous?" Charlie asks.

"Gorgeous. You are gorgeous." Dario claims Charlie's mouth with his own.

Charlie presses into him, tipping them both backward. The feel of Charlie's hot, supple, naked body against his fully clothed one makes his dick punch against his zipper. He beckons Charlie higher until Charlie's hands are splayed above the headboard and his rigid cock is right at Dario's mouth.

Spit builds before he wraps his lips around Charlie. He takes his time working the impressive length down his throat and back up again. A single taste is all he wanted. A pure tease.

He wipes his mouth on the back of his hand, and inches up on the bed. Charlie whimpers as Dario's zipper glides across the underside of Charlie's swollen cock.

Their slightly dewy foreheads press together as they look down at the second contact point between them. A sticky, wet mess forms as Dario leaks through two layers of clothes.

Charlie's precum links to the dark spot on the front of Dario's trousers, creating a spiderweb of sexual need. They are helplessly trapped in the gluey silk of it.

Dario hooks his hands under Charlie and swipes his thumbs across his already-erect nipples. They are two pink stars in the milky white galaxy of soft skin. Charlie quivers each time, as if his body got set to vibrate.

It hurts in the best way, how hard Dario is inside his pants. Gently, he guides the heel of Charlie's hand to the notable bulge in his slacks. Rolling his hips up and up and up, he writhes against Charlie's opposing strength while grabbing the exposed globes of Charlie's pert, hair-dusted ass. The friction is terrific and causes powerful jolts through his pelvis.

Dario delights in the expression on Charlie's face, totally contorted with indulgence. It's the same look he had when he taste-tested all those chocolates back at the factory.

"How do you say 'feed me' in Italian?" Charlie asks, fingers toying with the zipper on Dario's slacks.

"Nutrimi," Dario says.

"Nutrimi," Charlie parrots with near-perfect Italian pronunciation. Dario could come from the sweet sound of it.

Dario nods, so Charlie drags out Dario's firm, veiny, uncut cock and hefty, shaven balls. "When I saw the outline of this package inside your swimsuit, I knew I had to have it." Charlie's tongue dips beneath his foreskin.

"It's all yours," Dario says, voice cracking a bit from the explosive sensations.

Charlie wastes no time creating a steady pull and draw with his mouth. Dario can barely gasp in enough breath to stay conscious at how good it feels. Nobody has ever blown him like this. Made it feel like he's being worshipped.

Charlie uses one hand as backup for his mouth while the other toys with Dario's balls, which hike up with each passing slurp.

"I can't hold out much longer," Dario grunts through a tense jaw. It's been too long since he's been with another person, and the mounting pleasure quickly becomes all-consuming.

"Nutrimi," Charlie says again, gazing up at him. Those hooded eyes grow darker and more intense. "Feed me, Candy Man."

Dario plunges back into the heaven that is the blue-haired American's mouth. Such a hot, pliable entry that makes his dick ecstatic. He spills his cream down Charlie's throat. With his head flung back, he yelps in ecstasy, the sound echoing into the night.

Cum specks the corners of Charlie's rosy, ravaged mouth. Dario wipes at it with his pointer finger. All too happy, Charlie laps at it while pumping himself between his legs. "That might be sweeter than anything you make at your factory."

Dario chuckles. His muscles have unwound to the point of depletion. All he does now is flip his tie up and over his shoulder. Charlie crawls upwards on his knees. He hikes himself over Dario's still-proudly-standing erection. The slick, exposed head grazes the cleft of Charlie's ass, and Dario fantasizes about fucking the tantalizing tattooed hunk in his lap, feeling that tight, American hole stretch around his thick cock. Oddio, he feels he could come again already from the simple reverie.

Charlie must sense this, because he rubs his cheeks against Dario's length as he continues to stroke himself.

"Sei bello," Dario muses, roving his hand along Charlie's heaving torso. He can't take his eyes off Charlie, a complete smokeshow. "Sei molto, molto bello."

In seconds, Dario's finely pressed white shirt becomes a cum canvas for Charlie's spectacular load.

Charlie collapses over into the puddle of his own making, and Dario holds him close as their slowing breaths sync up.

Seventeen

DARIO

"How was your night?" Michelle asks, sitting down across from Dario at the patio table for breakfast the next morning.

The rising sun scorches the lawn already with temperatures set to reach thirty-two degrees Celsius. Over an untouched spread of orange slices, a hardboiled egg and a cappuccino, Dario cools himself with an artisanal fan decorated in a paisley pattern that was once his mother's prop in an opera, the name of which he's entirely forgotten. As a boy, sitting in the darkened auditorium watching his mother perform, he became infatuated with it, and on closing night, his mother gave it to him as a gift. "A fan for my number one fan," she said with a kiss on his forehead.

When she's touring—which she often is—he misses his mother with a childish fervor.

"Va bene," Dario says, avoiding direct eye contact with Michelle, who carries a yogurt parfait to the table. He worries that she will see in his eyes that he and Charlie had sex last night. Once again, has he crossed an unconscionable line?

Rather than discussing that moral conundrum, they trade pleasantries, such as "How did you sleep?" and "It's going to be a hot one." It is a delicate dance of a conversation through which Dario doesn't want to divulge too much for fear of upset or judgment.

After a while, Michelle pulls a sketchbook, not dissimilar to Charlie's, out of a bag. She flips past hundreds of designs for gowns. Faceless women wear various corsets and veils. Some have long trains and others show a lot of leg. They whirl by in blurs of peach and pewter and eggshell until she stops on a page with the barest bones of what appears to be a wedding dress on a not-so-faceless figure. This individual is Michelle, and the hint she's giving is unsubtle.

"That is astounding," he says. Because despite how obvious she's being, her designs are some of the most beautiful wedding gowns he's ever seen, and he's seen *a lot* of them. Many of the operas his mother has starred in featured big wedding scenes. Even the work of top costume designers couldn't compare to the work in Michelle's book.

The illustrated Michelle on the page wears a jumpsuit with a train. The neckline plunges deep with an impeccably tailored waist from the back of which a tulle train fans out and flows to the floor. There are notes in the margins about velvet fabric and fuchsia accents.

"Thanks." She smiles. "Ow." Her still-healing sunburn crisps up a little more with her furious blush.

"I'll try not to make you smile anymore today," Dario says.

"That is impossible," says Michelle with a laugh that rolls into a snort. She blushes harder. She ows louder. It is all painfully—pun intended—adorable!

Dario stands and comes around the table to claim the seat

beside Michelle. "May I see more? How long have you been doing this?" he asks when she slides the book toward him, which feels like her first act of true vulnerability with him. He leisurely pages through.

"Since I was a girl. My mother was a seamstress, and her mother before her. My mother jokes I learned to sew before I learned to write properly. C'est probablement vrai." Another laugh-snort combo comes out.

"Did they design clothes as well?" he asks.

"Non." She shakes her head and some of her auburn hair falls out of her loose bun. "This was my, um, how do you say, secret?"

"You kept all of this to yourself?" Dario asks, disbelieving. Her pencil strokes are confident and create sensuous motion on the page. They are a far cry from the person Michelle presents herself to be. Perhaps on the page she releases her inhibitions.

She bites the end of her pencil, then says, "I came from a poor village and an even poorer family. Dreams like designing were not entertained. The seamstress business was good, steady work. I was told to stick to what I was good at."

Dario stops on a dramatic design in a classical style with lace latticework up the clavicle. "You are very good at this."

"I am working to be better," she says. Her midnight blue eyes flitter over the page. A crinkle appears between her plucked brows. Her pencil taps the table as if itching to get back to it. "I am a bit of a slow crafter. I blame my upbringing. I would steal fabric scraps of dresses we'd hemmed and hand-sew them together late at night in my room trying to create something lovely."

Her methodology reminds him of how he's trying to utilize more of the cocoa fruit in his chocolate production. They have similar business minds.

"Surely you had sewing machines at your disposal," Dario says.

"They were old and loud. I did not want to wake my parents. I couldn't have them know. I submitted one of those scrap dresses to design school. That along with my story got me in and some financial assistance. I am still a long way from making any of this my career." She knocks her knuckle against the side of her sturdy book.

Dario's heart goes out to her, and her story mule-kicks some much-needed perspective into his head. All he has to do is marry someone to reap his life's purpose, while Michelle and Charlie could use a financial boost to reach their potential. Sure, he doesn't want the only reason someone marries him to be his money, but he's not naive enough to believe it won't be part of it. What good is wealth if it can't be used *for* good? Maybe Michelle would go on to design costumes for operas and join April Cotogna on the road. It would be an interesting melding of worlds.

"How much longer do you have?" he asks.

"One more year of school and then I am on my own. Then I will have to make this work…somehow," she says. He flips back to the work-in-progress page. A vision of her walking down the wedding aisle toward him in this striking number loops through his imagination. Any man would be lucky to entertain that fantasy.

But his stomach does not flip. Nor does his heart flutter. No curlicue emotions tower high in his throat.

Could those feelings come with time?

Time is in such short supply.

Monday is two days away. Thirty-two—his inheritance deadline—is fast approaching. So too is Charlie Moore, out from the villa, fresh and clean. All red cheeks and blue hair. An American dream in a six-foot-two frame.

Except he had vanished like a ghost come first light.

"Good morning," Charlie says. He appears to clock Dario's closeness to Michelle. Dario squirms beneath the scrutiny. A clap of jealousy seems to cross Charlie's features, so Dario shifts a bit. But not too much, so as to not offend Michelle.

Charlie asks, "What are we looking at?"

"Oh, nothing," Michelle says, slamming her book shut.

"Michelle's wedding dress designs," Dario says at the same time, unaware these were secret.

Charlie sits across from them. Several boiled eggs almost roll off into the grass for Angelo to gobble up. "You design wedding dresses?"

"I want to," Michelle says, sliding her book off the table and back into her bag.

Charlie nods while peeling an egg. "Cool. What's on the agenda today?"

Dario falters for a moment, both from the question and the coolness with which Charlie carries himself this morning. Dario's grandfather told him to drop his armor, but he fears sword fighting with Charlie might've been an act of self-sabotage. That empty bed this morning, it plagues him.

"Yes, what are we to do today?" Michelle asks, sounding less enthused but interested, nonetheless.

Dario pushes his plate away. "We were set for another chocolate lesson back at the factory, but I fear with just the three of us it might be a little dull. Do either of you have any ideas for what you might like to do?"

Charlie jumps in right away. "Since we only have two full days left, I was sort of hoping to explore the city of Perugia. I love it out here in the country, but I'd love to experience a little more Italian culture up close. I hear they have an incredible art museum."

Dario freezes at the thought, then cramps even worse under

Charlie's bright, hopeful gaze. It is like the Selina and Solomeo situation all over again. Can they see the hives cropping up beneath his collar?

Strolling the commercial streets of Perugia and visiting galleries to escape the heat would be a pleasant way to pass the time, but the presumed crowd levels stop him from agreeing.

Luckily, Michelle shirks the idea first. "I do not think I could spend the whole day out in this sun and heat in my condition still." She peels in unseemly places.

Charlie's expression falls. "I have SPF 100 sunscreen back in my room, and I'm sure we could get you a big hat and a parasol or something to carry around."

"I am still not sure it is a good idea," Michelle says, eyelashes fluttering. At once, she reminds Dario of a wedding gown—delicate, diaphanous fabrics stitched together with strong construction. Fragile yet lasting with the right upkeep. She is most certainly the kind of creative, attractive, well-spoken person the Cotogna family wants for him.

But still, what does he want for himself? A firm answer evades him.

"Dario?" Charlie asks, voice peppered with anticipation.

His fan hand can't keep up with the speed at which he sweats. "If Michelle stays here, perhaps I should as well."

Charlie's lips tighten into a frown. "Okay, that's fine."

"Do not let us stop you," Michelle says, sounding pleased. "Is today the day you sit down and watch *The Ladies* with me?"

"Of course," Dario says, aware of Charlie's disappointment steeping on the far side of the table. Last night had been heady and wonderful, but he should give Michelle a chance to spur some sparks, too. She came all this way. It's only fair.

Without touching the rest of his plate, Charlie says, "Then I guess I'll make an early start of it." He stands, casting a long shadow over their table.

"Allow me to call my driver for you," Dario says.

"I'd rather bike to the train station if it's all the same to you."

There is no malice in the words, but Dario's stomach sinks regardless. Sending Charlie off alone is not sitting right with him. "If you are sure," Dario says.

"I am," Charlie says with the weakest smile imaginable. "Stay cool today!"

Somewhere during hour three of watching *The Luxurious Ladies of Provence*, the front door to the villa flies open. Emilio's voice penetrates the otherwise calm house. Michelle perks up, while Dario groans to himself.

At least it provides a break from what might well be the inanest show he has ever had the displeasure of watching. Not that he gets that many hours to watch TV anyway with his busy work life, but still, if he and Michelle were to wed, on their Venn diagram of shared interests, this show would not sit in the middle oval.

In the entryway, Emilio stands in front of a man in baggy pants and a backwards hat who holds a large camera. Emilio talks a mile a minute about how he grew up in Villa Meraviglia and runs through all the great times he had there.

"What's going on right now?" Dario asks, forgoing a greeting.

The cameraman swings the lens toward Dario. He shields his eyes from the searing spotlight strapped to the front. Without being able to see her, Dario senses Michelle straighten and hears her step forward to join him, peacocking once she does.

Emilio continues talking as if Dario hadn't spoken. "This is my brother—mio fratello—Dario. He is the loner, homebody type. And who is this lovely lady?"

Michelle fawns as Emilio leans in to kiss her on both cheeks. "Michelle Trottier from France."

"Pleasure to meet you, Michelle Trottier from France. You're one of Dario's little contest winners?" he asks. The snideness causes Dario's skin to crawl.

"I guess so," Michelle says.

"Didn't think you'd catch any cuties, Dar," Emilio says, jutting an elbow into Dario's stomach. He grunts both from the impact and the annoyance of having to deal with his brother in his space. Emilio skipped university, married young, and moved out right away. Dario couldn't have been happier about it all.

"Can you point that away from me?" Dario asks. When the guy in the hat makes no move to comply, Dario shoves the camera out of his face. His patience runs thin when Emilio is around.

Emilio rolls his eyes. "Craig, fine, stop rolling."

From behind Craig and the bulbous piece of recording equipment, Dario's mom appears. April Cotogna seems as flabbergasted by her youngest son as Dario is. Dario rushes in to hug her.

"What are you doing here?" Dario asks, relieved to see her.

"I have a few nights off from the tour, so I flew in to see how you were doing with the contest. I told your brother it would be nice if he came along for support. I found Craig with him when I picked him up at his place," April explains.

"Craig goes where I go," Emilio says, leaning up against a wall with one arm. He talks to Michelle with a closeness that is unbecoming of a married man.

"Who is Craig?" Dario asks, needing to find a foothold in this conversation.

Craig speaks for himself, "I'm an American filmmaker and producer dipping my toe into the reality TV space. I reached out a year ago about doing a documentary on how Amorina is one of the leading chocolate manufacturers in sustainability and global initiatives, but schedules never aligned with Cosimo Sr. and documentary funding is slim. Right after your grandfather's passing, Emilio messaged saying he had a great idea for a reality show."

Michelle interjects, "Did you say reality show?"

"He did, bella," Emilio says while clapping Craig on the back.

"We are pitching this package as *Succession* meets *The Real Housewives*. My producing partners back in the US loved the idea, so I hopped on the first flight I could to get out here and start shooting for a fiery pilot episode," he says.

Dario shakes his head. "Did you know about this?" he asks his mother.

"Only as much as they told me in the car ride over," she says, holding up her hands in presumed innocence.

A headache builds slowly at the base of his neck and grows stronger as he speaks. "I do not consent to having any part in this."

"We'll just blur out your face then," Emilio says, unfazed and with oodles of little-brother defiance.

"Everyone will obviously know it's me," Dario contests.

"Fine, then consent and it won't matter." Emilio smirks beneath his patchy mustache.

"You're not even inheriting Amorina. You know I have until my thirty-second birthday to marry before it passes on to you. My birthday is still three months away," Dario says.

Craig hoists the camera back up into position and starts rolling again. Dario refuses to look like a yowling monster in whatever nonsense this footage inevitably becomes, so he refrains from making any bigger scene.

Emilio looks about the villa. "I'm not seeing many suitors left, Dario, and as far as I can tell Mademoiselle Trottier isn't wearing an engagement ring." He hooks her hand in his, and she leans into the forward gesture.

"I still have time," says Dario feebly.

"Tick, tock. If I were you, I wouldn't waste any of it before snatching up this beautiful woman," Emilio says in a near sickening singsong.

"You're forgetting you have a wife," says Dario pointedly. "Where is she, by the way?"

"She is in Greece visiting her family. Must you be such a buzzkill?" Emilio asks.

"Must you be such a nuisance?" Dario retorts.

"Must you—"

"Boys!" April shouts. "You fought less when you were children. Act like the grown men you are."

"One of us is not grown," Dario says under his breath.

"One of us is hardly a man," Emilio says, then shoulder-checks Dario. Hard enough that he stumbles back into a table displaying a clay vase that has been in the family for centuries.

Unable to stop himself and unwilling to let Emilio waltz in here and do whatever he pleases, Dario shoves back. That shove turns into a push and the push escalates into a frenzied tangle of arms and legs. Before he knows it, Dario is red-faced and reaching for his brother, slapping at empty air.

"You are such a prick," Dario says, heat making his skin itchy beneath his many layers.

"Boys! Both of you. Take a walk and cool off," April demands, stepping between her sons with hands outstretched.

Dario lets out a loud, bullish exhale before straightening his suit and tie.

Emilio, seemingly sensing a weak spot, lunges in, but April is too fast for him to outsmart her. "Walk it out. Cool off. Now!"

Mama's boys through and through, Dario and Emilio splinter off in separate directions. Craig never stops rolling, even for a second.

Eighteen

CHARLIE

After exiting the train in Perugia, which is the capital city of the province with the same name, Charlie boards a mini metro. It is a single, silver, futuristic-looking car. As he glides along a high track, the city tunnels past him at an exciting speed, with its yellow, orange and rust-colored roofs.

Used to being alone, Charlie is unbothered by the prospect of exploring the city by himself. What does bother him is the thought of Michelle cozying up to Dario on the couch all day while they watch a show and craft inside jokes.

The green monster of jealousy must be conducting this mini metro, because the higher the car climbs, the harder Charlie finds it to shake the image of Michelle and Dario making out.

Charlie has slept with his fair share of men and never has he spent the whole next morning obsessing over their possible feelings for him. Granted, he has never been in a five-way competition for the hand of the heir to a chocolate empire before either—who has?—so he supposes he should not be so surprised to find himself in uncharted territory.

He is in Italy, for God's sake. An unfamiliar country where the customs delight him and the language evades him and the world feels both beautiful and scary.

Scary because maybe, despite telling himself not to, he has developed a genuine liking for the cloistered chocolate maker with a tender heart and knack for business.

Now not only might he lose his family home should Dario choose Michelle or neither of them, but he might win a broken heart to boot.

Taking a moment, he searches for a positive spin.

This solo trip to Perugia might be super well-timed, at least. Several years ago, his parents went through a rough patch. His father lost his job, and his mother felt the strain. One day, she came home from work and set her bonus check down in front of his father and said, "Take a fishing trip to the cabin."

His father looked up from the online job application he was filling out, disbelief running all through his features. "No way. Not with your hard-earned bonus."

"I've thought about it. I want you to go to the cabin," she said.

When his father left—duffel bag and fishing rod in hand—Charlie squared with his mother. "Why'd you do that?"

His mother smiled. "Because, Charlie, sometimes you need to give the people you love a chance to miss you."

He scoffed. "If you wanted him to miss you, wouldn't you be the one going on a trip?"

"No, Charlie. That would be a punishment. I love your father. This is a treat that will go much farther," she said, pulling the car keys off the hook by the door. "My treat is taking you to the movies, so go on and grab your shoes."

A day with Michelle is a weekend at the cabin for Dario.

★ ★ ★

The trickling sounds of Fontana Maggiore lure Charlie into the main piazza. Life throws itself all around him. Fashionable people sit at café tables nursing midday coffees and cigarettes. Tour groups traverse into the looming, Gothic palazzo with cameras around their necks. Sea green statues of a lion and a Pegasus guard the door with open mouths. Birds waddle and squawk at his feet, searching for food scraps to feast on.

Sweat starts in the small of his back as he weaves through cobbled alleys and summits the city's many medieval steps. Flowers burst from hanging boxes out second-story windows. Their fragrance floats down around him. He snaps a million pictures he will show to his family.

Stopping for lunch, Charlie devours a buffalo mozzarella pizza while people-watching. In two days' time, he will be on a plane back to Pennsylvania. He needs to soak up as much culture as possible before then. Who knows if he'll ever leave Slatington again after this?

To walk off the pizza, Charlie ventures into the National Gallery and gets lost in the art and frescos. He stops before statues and sketches them in his notebook with pithy speech bubbles hanging over their heads. He imagines what these models might think about modern times. Some of them end up being good enough to consider getting tattooed, even if he is slowly running out of pages in his sketchbook and prime real estate on his body.

So enraptured, he wanders there until closing, wishing his family was there to share in the beauty. Exiting into a gorgeous sunset, he goes in search of a café with internet where he can post up and call his family to fill them in on all that has happened.

Well, maybe not *all*.

He will keep last night to himself.

A half an hour later, the faces of the four people he cares about most in the world pop up on his phone screen. Unbothered by the grainy quality of the video, he chats excitedly about all the sights he's seen and facts he's learned since arriving.

"Why are you still on the phone with us?" Grandpa asks no more than fifteen minutes later. "You should be out exploring. When in Rome!"

"I'm in Perugia," Charlie says with a laugh.

"Make a new saying then. Don't be a lose-a in Perugia!"

Mom and Dad barely let out a chuckle. "Is everything okay?" Charlie asks. You don't spend twenty-eight years under the same roof with people and not catch on to their moods.

A grim energy seeps through the screen. "Of course," Dad says, but Charlie pings the lie right away.

"Mmm-hmm," Mom agrees.

"What aren't you telling me?" Charlie asks.

"It's nothing to bother about," Grandpa says with a huff directed at Charlie's parents. "They're worried. We had a visitor yesterday. Someone from the bank. He said we failed to respond to a letter they sent. We told him we didn't get any sorta letter and that shut him right up."

Charlie swallows hard. "A letter about what?" he asks, unsure why he is playing ignorant. The letter in question is tucked inside his duffel bag back at the villa—a pointy, paper time bomb that's nearing explosion.

"It was about the mortgage," Dad says, notes of embarrassment mixed into his words.

Charlie wishes he could reach through the screen and hug him. From what he read online about timelines, there should not have been any follow-up from the bank until he returned. He had meant to shield his family from the burden of this. "What about it?"

"Don't worry about it, kiddo," Dad says. "We will handle it. We always do."

"I know, but maybe I can help," Charlie says, still running with this act. Dario's wealth is a slow-knitting safety net beneath them.

"You can help by enjoying yourself," says Grandma.

Mom stays silent even though she's usually a chatterbox.

A pang of guilt for not being home while this is happening weaves through him. Eviction hangs over the house on Cemetery Street, and here he is carbo-loaded and wine-flushed in a European city.

Sure, he's chasing a chocolate heir who might be the key to keeping their lives status quo, but he can't say that to them to ring a bell of false hope.

At this point, he has no engagement ring, no insurance policy, no nothing.

"Okay, if you're sure," Charlie says, bulldozing over his one moment to come clean. Because there is far too much to say, and he knows he will mess it up. "Miss you all. Be back soon."

"But not too soon," Grandma says. "Plenty of time to make more memories!"

And secure a wealthy husband, Charlie thinks.

"Leave us old farts be. Buon giorno!" Grandpa says.

"That's good morning," Charlie informs. "Say, ciao!"

"Ciao," they all say before the call concludes.

Frustrated, Charlie follows the remains of the Roman aqueducts back toward the metro station. Trotting alongside the structure, he contemplates how they carried so much water uphill without motorization. If the Etruscans could innovate and do the impossible, so can he!

He stumbles upon a sign for Pozzo Etrusco—an old well. He has just enough time before his train to make a pit stop if he's quick about it.

Down, down, down, he descends into an ancient water reservoir. The steps are narrow, and the walls are close. He presses his hands into the cool, rough stone to keep from losing his balance. When he reaches the rectangular window that looks down upon the well, he surges with a sense of adventure, feeling like a poor man's Indiana Jones.

Leaning over the ledge, the darkness seems to go on and on. His breath gets taken away by how much history can be hidden in a place like this. He only wishes he were sharing this experience with someone. Dario's face bounces through his mind.

A little farther down, a plexiglass bridge connects one side of the well to the other. There are signs posted written in red lettering. He can't read the Italian words, so he shrugs and steps out.

On the bridge, he records a video on his phone. Awe and gratitude catch in his chest.

What he doesn't catch, however, is his phone slipping out from between his oily, sweaty fingers. The iPhone bangs on the side of the plexiglass, hits the stone wall of the well and—plop!—falls into the water burbling way down below.

"Fuck!" Charlie cries. "No, no, no. What am I supposed to do now?"

The question echoes back at him like several slaps to the face.

There goes a thousand dollars and any chance of getting back to the villa. His digital train ticket was on there. Dario's phone number was on there. Any sort of translator app he might need to communicate what just happened is on there.

For the first and only time since arriving, he wishes he'd never left the dreary safety of Slatington.

DARIO

Dario's temper cools off with the summer day.

As the sun sinks, so too does Dario's ire toward his imposing brother. While he can choose a spouse, he has no choice in his blood relations. Emilio is and always has been a pebble stuck in his proverbial shoe.

His mother appears while he sits in solitude out on the veranda, watching the full reflection of the moon shimmering on the still lake water.

"You didn't eat dinner," April says. She holds a small plate out to him.

His stomach, which has been in knots all day, lurches toward the meal, so he accepts it. Forkful by forkful, Paola's cooking revives him. Pollo alla diavola, an herbaceous dish that brings back memories of long family dinners filled with laughter and spilt sauce on his shirt, satiates his stalled-out appetite.

Between bites, he finally says, "I should probably go and apologize to Michelle for being such a bad host today."

"I would say you should probably apologize to your brother, too," she begins, "but he's been a bit too good of a host to Michelle today, so I'm still debating on that one."

Dario groans and his voice boomerangs against the side of the barn house.

"Don't be so hard on yourself," his mother says, kicking her bare feet up on the low-standing coffee table.

"Three-fifths of my suitors are gone. One was married and only wanted a free vacation, one only wanted the challenge of winning me over, one thought I was not passionate or adventurous enough, and one is inside doing who knows what with my brother," he details. "The common failing denominator must be me."

His mother sighs. "I miss your softness. I miss the boy who threw himself headfirst into the lake and drew mustaches on his face with chocolate just to make me laugh. Where is that Dario?"

"CEOs of major chocolate empires don't get to be soft," he says while picking a peppercorn out of his teeth.

"Truffles have hard shells and soft centers." Her eyebrows lift as if daring him to contradict her. "That Dario wouldn't be yelling and shoving his brother, no matter his intrusions. You were the calm one, like your father."

Dario knows his calm is a mask for his anxiety. A way to wall off the storm inside from breaking out. He wonders if his father experienced something similar. He saddens with the weight of never getting to ask.

When Preston rebuffed him at the chocolate festival over a year ago and his mother found him mid-panic attack, he had a chance to tell her what he was feeling and struggling with, but it was impossible when he didn't understand it fully himself.

Dario goes to say *he started it about Emilio* but stops himself. As a man of nearly thirty-two, he knows it's time to put petty excuses behind him. "You're right. This whole punishment has been making me angsty and keeping me on edge."

"Come over here."

He squishes onto the couch beside her. She pats her lap. He lays his head there like he did as a boy. She strokes his hair and asks a hard question, "Why do you call it a punishment? I admit, your nonno's ways are extremely unconventional, but there are worse fates than hosting five beautiful, international guests at your home with an eye for marrying one of them."

She massages his scalp, and he closes his eyes. He would

be in heaven if he were not so hell-bent. "Nonno has forced me into a corner!"

"Nobody has forced you into anything. You can easily rescind," his mother says with an air of knowing full well there would be nothing easy about that.

"You want Emilio to run Amorina into the ground?" Dario asks, chest hiccuping, voice rising.

Her hand presses more firmly while she lets out a gentle *shh*. "I want my boys to be in harmony and be happy. You used to look after him like a proper big brother. You two used to kick the ball around in the yard, go on long bike rides and swim races against one another until you were prunes and blue in the lips. Then your father died. Some deaths bond people more deeply together. His tore you and Emilio apart right before your teenage years. I thought Cosimo Sr. passing might bring you back together. I wish you two would talk it out finally."

"There is no talking with him. There are texts and snarky voice notes and now camera crews, but there's no real talking," he says, eyes snapping open.

His mother laughs, a light chuff. "I used to be like that, too. I lived for the show and the dramatics. I was acting everywhere that I went. Acting like I deserved the best roles. Acting like I deserved your father's affections. Acting like nothing and no one could touch me. I thought it was a gift—this ability to turn my personality on in a split second—but it was a curse. A curse your father broke."

"What do you mean?" Dario asks, sitting up. It has been years since they've talked deeply and openly about his father. Losing him was like having their mouths sewn shut. If they kept his name from infiltrating their home, maybe they could all tiptoe around and pretend he was still going to walk through the door at any moment with a booming, jovial greeting and a Vespa helmet under his arm.

"Before he told your grandparents we were to be engaged, he took me out on the boat and we drifted on Lake Trasimeno beneath that parfait sky and he said to me, 'April, I love you. I love you *for you*.'" She paused for a moment with a fond look in her eyes. "He said, 'When you're on stage, you shine, but you don't need to shine all the time, around everyone. Save your brightness so you don't burn out. Let my parents see you for the you that I know. April Cotogna is not a role.' Just by him saying that aloud to me, the idea lost its usefulness and its power."

"That's all it took?" Dario asks. Positivity springs up into his throat like a flower poking through a crack in the cement. On her nod, he blurts out words he has been meaning to say for far too long, "I am agoraphobic."

He waits for this impressive weight to be lifted off him, but he only feels marginally lighter from having admitted this.

Confusion crisscrosses her brows. "Say again?"

"I have agoraphobia. My therapist diagnosed me earlier this year. The reason I've not gone beyond the villa, the lake or the factory in over a year is because I have this deep anxiety that if I go anywhere too unknown or too crowded, something bad will happen. I get these panic attacks that feel like someone is choking the life out of me."

"Oh, Dario," she says. "Is that what happened outside Nonno's funeral?"

Dario nods, unable to say more on that topic for fear the memory will immobilize him.

"I assume that's what was happening when I found you at the chocolate festival as well. After Preston…" She cuts off that sentence. "I'm sorry you're struggling with that. Why didn't you say something sooner?" she asks, oozing concern.

"Nonno got sicker, you got the role of a lifetime, and Emilio was being Emilio. I did not think I could afford to be heartbroken or unstable when everyone else needed me to be strong," he says, feeling anything but. "Especially without Dad here. I had to hold down the fort."

"Wants and needs? Dario, what about yours? I'm your mother. Your wants and needs are my wants and needs." She takes his hands in hers, rubbing her thumbs back and forth across his shaking knuckles. "I would've never taken the touring role if I had known you were suffering."

He snatches his hands back, heart caught up in his throat. "That's exactly what I didn't want you to do."

"If I had known, I could've at least offered support in other ways." She scoots closer, undeterred by his posture.

His feet are turned away, ready to run from the discomfort of this conversation, but then he stares into her eyes, though his own are watery. "I want to get better. For myself, for Amorina, for—" Charlie's handsome face flashes through his mind.

He was fooling himself entertaining Michelle today. She is beautiful and talented and right for the Cotogna name, but not right *for him*.

"For?" his mother prompts.

"For the fifth suitor. For Charlie Moore," he says. His heart sings. Charlie Moore rearranges itself into Charlie Cotogna in his mind. What a lovely name that would look perfect on a marriage license.

It is not love he feels for Charlie. Not yet. But he, like the Olmec people in Mesoamerica who first thought to domesticate the cacao tree, knows a good thing when he tastes it. Oddio, did Charlie Moore taste sweet.

His mother smiles for the first time all conversation. "Where is Charlie?" she asks.

Dario realizes Charlie missed dinner and he has not called since he left for the train earlier this morning. Worry sprouts in his stomach. "That's a very good question."

Together, they go into the house and inquire after him. Paola, who is cleaning up, hasn't seen him. Michelle and Emilio, who are sitting a little too closely on one of the couches, haven't heard anyone come in—as if they could over the blaring TV. Out front smoking a cigarette and scrolling on his phone, Craig says nobody has come up the drive since he's been standing there.

Panicked, he calls Charlie's phone, and it immediately goes to voice mail.

Up in Charlie's room, he searches for evidence that Charlie has been there since this morning, but this feels more like snooping than anything. At least Charlie's clothes and toiletries are still spread around. He hasn't snuck off for good.

"No sign of him?" his mom asks. He shakes his head. "Where did you say he went today?"

"Perugia. By himself."

"Does he speak Italian?"

"Not at all." Whatever lightness he had felt out on the veranda is gone.

"I'll call the driver." She wraps him in a hug. "Don't worry. We'll find him."

Nineteen

CHARLIE

The cab driver outside the train station has never heard of Villa Meraviglia, which is just Charlie's luck. And "Charlie's luck" means *not any*.

What was the village's name? It was on his phone, which is now at the bottom of a well. Much like his hopes of getting back tonight. Alongside his hopes of marrying Dario Cotogna.

The train back left forty minutes ago because he read the schedule wrong—damn that twenty-four-hour clock—and he does not remember the name of the station he parked Dario's bike at. It was nice to spend a day in a less touristy city, but he's sure in Florence or Rome he would've found an English-speaking person to assist him by now.

A brilliant idea occurs to him. "Amorina Factory?"

The mustachioed cab driver curls his lips. "Si."

"We can go there?" Charlie asks.

The driver brushes his hands together. "Non è aperto."

"Uh, what?" Charlie asks at a total loss.

The driver mimes doors opening, closing, and then locking. "Oh, yes. I know it's not open. I still, uh, need to go there?"

The driver throws up his hands as if he's going to drive away. Charlie tries to win him over with what little euros he has left.

Only trouble is, he pats every pocket and none of them contain his wallet. "What the—?"

He has his passport holder, but not his wallet. He scours the ground at his feet, squinting in the dark. Someone, somewhere in the city must've stolen it.

The enchantment of Italy fades more by the second. So caught up in the beauty of this place, he let his guard down and now look at him. Guileless and penniless in the street of a city where he can't speak the language. He doesn't belong here any more than he belongs with Dario Cotogna.

An Italian woman and her small child weasel between Charlie and the idling cab. She gives clear, concise instructions to the driver, leaving Charlie coughing on a cloud of exhaust.

Around him, hotels advertise on massive, light-up signs. But without cash or cards, he is hard-pressed to find even a hostel that would take him in for the night.

Unsure what else to do, he takes shelter on an uncomfortable bench inside the bustling train station.

An hour passes as arrivals and departures are announced over a loudspeaker. There is no gloomier place in the world than a train station when you can't go anywhere.

In the distance, two police officers chitchat with one another while passengers pile through to catch their trains.

"It's fine. I'm fine. I'm safe. Someone will come find me," Charlie says softly to himself to keep panic at bay. "Someone at the villa will obviously notice how long I've been gone and come looking for me,"

Though it felt like Dario barely noticed him at all over breakfast. He was too distracted by Michelle and her designs.

Not that he blames Dario, even if a rowdy jealousy ran through him then like a streaker across a football field.

"They wouldn't let me languish out here all night," Charlie murmurs more meager reassurance. "Imagine the lawsuit against the contest and Amorina. Violetta wouldn't allow it." Much to his dismay, he's thinking like his disowned, selfish uncle Buck. He shudders at the mental comparisons. "Well, I couldn't afford a lawyer anyway!"

The wood of the bench is rough, scratching at his back as he slumps down like his splintering thoughts are sticking into him, turning him into a porcupine of regret.

Is he any better than his uncle?

Didn't he come out here to marry up and out of a terrible situation?

It wasn't romance he was after, no matter what he feels for Dario now.

He came to Italy for his family. For the house on Cemetery Street with its sagging foundation and wind-scraped windows and in-need-of-a-replacement hot water heater. For his parents and grandparents who've worked to the bone to keep the roof over their heads and the food on their table.

But do plentiful reasons beget dishonest intentions?

An image of talented, caring Dario rolls through his mind. Remorse rages in his gut.

Being stranded here all alone is perhaps what he deserves for being a dirty, rotten gold-digger.

DARIO

At the Magione train station, shiny red trains with blazing headlights barrel by. Charlie's bike is chained outside, but

Charlie is nowhere to be found. Nobody disembarking looks anything like the tattooed American he is in search of. Concern clutches his heart in gnarled knuckles.

Back in the car, not only is Dario fearful for what's become of Charlie, but he's panicking over where he must go to find him.

As Fabrizio speeds toward Perugia—the only other place Dario can think to look—Dario taps on the overhead light. Instead of obsessing about the strength of the panic attack that awaits him at the end of this car ride, he reads his nonno's next letter.

Caro Tesorino,
The true mark of a person is how they act in a crisis.

In business and in love, extreme situations arise without warning, and you have to trust that the people around you are ready to rise to the challenge.

Observe who steps up and who shies away from the difficulties the universe throws at you.

Life, at times, can be hard to swallow. Look for the ones who fill up a water glass for you to make the big gulp easier. Investigate if you would do the same for them.

Many people think finding their life partner is about looking outside themselves for the perfect person. Alas, if only it were that simple. Choosing a mate often means turning inward and inspecting the parts of yourself you would rather not address.

It is unfair to ask your partner to be brave for themselves and to be brave for you, too. While there is give-and-take, that leans heavily toward the latter. To have a balanced union, you must have equal measures of both. You must have harmony— just ask your mother.

You have shown your courage by agreeing to my unorthodox

*plan to find you a partner, but passively going along with this
to inherit Amorina will not lead to the outcome most wanted.*

*I beseech you, Tesorino, to dig deep and live boldly. The right
spouse for you will emerge once you take the leap.*
Con affetto,
Nonno

Closing his eyes, Dario visualizes the ideal outcome, like
his therapist taught him to. In his head, Charlie, entirely un-
harmed and happy, stands outside of the American-owned bar
right off Piazza IV Novembre. A sweating, light beer rests in
his hand as he talks with a group of coeds who are taking a
summer study abroad. The nightlife swells around him. People
ask about his tattoos, and he talks of his time in the Amorina
Factory and at Villa Meraviglia.

The fantasy fades out right as they crest into the lot outside
Fontivegge with its high-arched entryways.

At first sight of the mobs of travelers waiting on pickups
outside the station, all the adrenaline leaks from his body. The
very idea of stepping toward that crowd makes his skin itchy
all over, and his chest collapses inward.

He snaps his eyes shut again and attempts to summon Charlie as if he were a patron saint of strength. His racing heart
shouts messages at his head, "Run! Hide! Go home!"

This vicious anxiety! How he wishes he could spoon it out
of himself and serve it up to Angelo who would scarf it down
without tasting it.

Fabrizio opens the car door and Dario captures enough
bravery to stick a leg out, but that's as far as his body will allow.

As soon as the summer breeze crests across his blazing
cheeks, he slams the door shut, and clutches the seat belt for
safety even though the car is in Park.

Fabrizio pokes his head back in the driver door. "Stai andando dentro?" *Are you going inside?*

Out of the corner of his eye, he notices a raincoat he must have left back here during the last storm. It's no suit of armor and it does not match his outfit, but it will have to do. He tugs it on, throws up its hood and heads into the fray.

The outside air is oppressive, especially with the thick coat fabric taut around his face. The beep of the car locking behind him is a whip at his backside, speeding him up so he can return to safety soon.

Please find Charlie here. Please find Charlie here. Please find Charlie here.

It's a prayer, an incantation, a plea. A call to his father, his grandfather. Anyone who can hear his thoughts and act on his behalf.

One foot after another, he gulps in a breath and focuses on what he sees in front of him.

An arrivals board. A luggage area. A train pulling in. A blue-haired man on a bench. A dog running off its leash. A suitcase spilling open.

He glances back, thrilled he has not imagined it. There Charlie is, in the flesh! Near the far platform, Charlie stares down at his shoes while clutching his passport in antsy hands.

Dario whizzes through the throngs to get to Charlie, who looks up just in time. Dario slides across the bench and crushes Charlie with the world's most relieved hug. All the anxious energy pounds on top of his skin like an extra layer, donned and zipped and suffocating.

"Grazie a Dio! You are okay." Dario takes a sharp inhale of Charlie's scent. That sunscreen fragrance lingers beneath a day's worth of sweat. It's a weak balm for his frazzled nerves.

"Oh, good. I thought I was imagining you," Charlie says,

while sagging against him, as if he trusts Dario enough to hold him up when he's not strong enough to do it himself.

"I am here." Dario reassures Charlie. But it's hard to reassure someone when a stampede of anxiety elephants clomps through his chest.

"Are you okay? You're shaking." Charlie's hands splay strong against Dario's back.

Overwhelmed, he buries his head in the crook of Charlie's neck and shuts his eyes against the world. His fingers claw at the fabric of Charlie's shirt, needing to ground himself in this moment, which is impossible when it feels like the bench is sliding out from under him, little by little.

"Dario, I'm here. I'm okay. We're okay." Charlie's voice sounds a million miles away, stuck behind several panes of glass. It's like he's missing all over again even though he sits right there, has his arms around him. Why must his brain play tricks like this?

Charlie takes him by the elbow to the nearby, single-stall bathroom. Dario barely registers as he gives Charlie a euro to pop in the lock and twist.

The tile floor is grimy, and the lights are an off-putting yellow, making the white walls look like bruised banana peels. But this room with its four walls and its lock is like an oasis. And Charlie Moore is a beautiful mirage in the mist of a gurgling waterfall.

Except there's no waterfall and Charlie is flesh and blood, leading him to the porcelain sink where cold, tap water plunks out. Dario splashes his face. The temperature shock settles him the slightest bit.

Charlie's right hand lands on his upper back where he rubs slow, gentle circles. His left hand gathers Dario's hair back, so it doesn't get wet. Dario appreciates that because every other time he has been hit with a panic attack over the past year, he has muscled through it by himself.

Talking to his mom tonight made him realize that maybe there are people out there who understand and want to help. He just needs to give them the chance to.

"Should I call someone?" Charlie asks. "Like a doctor?"

Dario closes his eyes, steadying himself with the edge of the sink. He takes several breaths. "No, grazie. It is a panic attack. It will pass. Eventually. I get them often…"

"I didn't realize," Charlie says.

"I have something called agoraphobia," Dario stutters, the word still feeling foreign in his mouth the way "grazie" felt foreign to Charlie on the first day they met.

"Isn't that a fear of spiders?" Charlie asks.

"It's a fear of open places. When I go to places I've never been or crowded places, I get intense anxiety and panic attacks. It's debilitating." He thinks momentarily about what they left outside this bathroom. The crushing crowds. The swell of noises. The speeding trains. As much as he wishes he could spend forever in this bathroom with Charlie Moore, he'll have to face his triggers again and soon. The acrid smell of this room is starting to wither in his nose.

"What about Isola Polvese and the factory?" Charlie asks.

"Those are places I go often. They are in my comfort circle. I haven't been past the factory in over a year," he says. A swarm of shame engulfs him. His hands shake harder.

"Is it rude of me to ask what caused it?" Charlie's eyes are beseeching and sweet. "I'm just trying to understand."

"I am still trying to understand it myself." Dario sighs, wishing explaining himself could be as easy as running a board meeting or wooing distributors. But he's learned the hard way that he can't treat his mental health like a business. If he could, he would've sold off his agoraphobia a long time ago, even if it came at a loss to his bottom line. The human brain is far more complicated than candy.

"Take your time," Charlie says, meaning it. Obviously unperturbed.

"You see, it's like this. My brain plays tricks on me. It tells me I'm not safe even when there's not a specific threat. My anxiety started when I was young and my father died. He was there one morning and gone by the time I got home from school, and suddenly the world was terrifying. I worked through that," Dario says, tracing back his struggles on a timeline of his life as if it were an exhibit in the Amorina museum. "Once everything happened with Preston, the panic attacks started up again. They got sharper and more frequent, until I broke down very publicly at my nonno's funeral and have avoided crowds since."

"So that's why you didn't want to go to Isola Maggiore?" Charlie says.

Dario nods. "My grandfather's funeral was held at the Church of Buon Gesù on the island. You may have seen it while you were there. It's a tall, orange-and-green historic building with these fading frescoes on the inside walls. It's exactly where I'd have expected my grandfather to want to have his last service. But it's also tiny. It was originally an oratory, so it was not meant to house hundreds upon hundreds of family members, friends and candy lovers. As soon as I saw the number of people in and outside the building, I froze and shut down," he says, reliving that awful day over again. "I haven't been back since." He stops for a long breath. "Scusi, I'm ashamed to talk about this."

"Why are you ashamed?" Charlie asks.

"Here, it isn't like in America. We don't talk about mental health. It is taboo. I only just told my mother tonight. I suffered alone for so long." Dario stares down at his hands, which have calmed a bit.

"Hey," Charlie says, stepping nearer. He pulls Dario close. "You're not alone. I'm here. I want to be here for you. Tell me what to do to help." Charlie squeezes tighter.

"You being here already helps," Dario says. "Exposure therapy is supposed to help, too."

"What's that?" Charlie asks.

"It's a form of therapy where I confront my fears. I go to places I haven't been or have been and had a panic attack before, allow the anxiety to come, and try to push through." Dario takes another ragged, much-needed inhale. His brain thanks him by quieting a little.

His therapist introduced exposure therapy to him not long after his failed proposal. He made sure Dario knew how important it was to choose recovery so he could live a full life.

Dario was praised when he went sailing again for the first time, and his therapist almost cheered when he went back to the factory. But then his grandfather got sicker, and Dario remembered that the world was a scary place that took more than it gave.

He pushed recovery to the back of his mind and focused on learning everything he needed to know before his grandfather passed.

"Exposure therapy sounds uncomfortable," Charlie says, as if he'd battle away every discomfort in the universe for Dario if he asked. But he couldn't. He *wouldn't* because...

"I miss the world, Charlie," Dario says through an unmistakable break in his voice. It's not a break of defeat, though; it's emotional defiance. He does not want to let his sometimes-traitorous brain run the show any longer. "Coming inside this train station a week ago would have been unmanageable, but I want to get better, and I had to find you. I was so worried that you were gone or hurt or worse. I..." He clutches tight to Charlie's soft shirt. "I like you, Charlie. More than I expected to like anyone who showed up through this wild stunt my nonno concocted, yet here you are, and I can't deny how I feel."

"I like you, too," Charlie says. He clings closer, yet he looks away. A divot forms in his brow.

"What's wrong?" Dario asks.

Charlie steps away so swiftly Dario nearly tears the shirt right off Charlie's back.

"You shouldn't like me," Charlie announces.

"Who says?" Dario asks.

"I say."

"How come?"

"Because... I've been dishonest," Charlie says. He backs up to the door, knocks his head against it, glistening eyes cast up at the ceiling.

"Dishonest how?" Dario asks, stomach shriveling up with nerves. Ansel proved they did not do their due diligence when it came to background checks.

"The bank is going to foreclose on my house," Charlie says.

Between the noxiously humming fan overhead and the pounding of his heart in his ears, it takes Dario a moment to connect what Charlie has said with the situation. "Your family home?"

Charlie nods. Then shakes his head. Then nods again. "The day I found out was the day I saw the call for contest entries. When I noticed your net worth, I thought, 'That's the kind of money that could save us.' Without that house, we would have nowhere to go. Before six days ago, you were just a dollar sign to me, a blank check, and that was wrong. You deserve better than that."

"Charlie..." Dario's mind flings to Nonno's letter about

his first love. A tightness takes up in his chest. But he can't forget about his earlier thoughts of helping Michelle start a fashion line. He has money, and marriage would mean he'd share it with his spouse. Charlie should not feel guilty for needing help.

Maybe he and Charlie are alike in that giving voice to their anxieties does not come naturally. But perhaps that's a good thing. Something they can work on together.

"No, please. I can't put that on you." Charlie berates himself. "I had plenty of time to think while I was stuck here, and I realized I've behaved badly. My parents work so hard and my grandparents have been through so much that I wanted to take this burden on for them and shield them from any fallout. But the bank came knocking and now they're panicked. And I'm falling for you. I like you too much to ask you to take on our problems when you have your own."

"Thank you for your honesty," Dario says, unsure what to think or how to feel. Today has been a cyclone of conflicting emotions, but he wants to see the bright side. There *is* a golden light at the end of this, he can sense it. "I think it would be best if we continued this discussion tomorrow, once we've rested. We have both had hard days. You must be exhausted. We can come back to this fresh."

Charlie hesitates, then nods. "That sounds good."

Dario grabs Charlie by the hand, and they exit the bathroom.

Twenty

CHARLIE

One day left in Villa Meraviglia, and today is the day Charlie gets his heart broken.

That's the one thing he is certain of as he stands in his room in only his boxers and opens the curtains. The Italian sunlight dances in for the penultimate time. Tomorrow, he gets on his cramped plane back to America and faces the music of his miscalculations, possibly loses his family home.

Last night, in the train station, sewn up with worry, he berated himself for his senselessness on all counts. First, for boarding flights of fancy. Second, for losing his phone. Third, for dragging Dario into his boneheaded scheme.

That's what it was. A scheme. To luck his way into a fix for his family whom he withheld the truth from, which makes him no better than his uncle and no good for Dario Cotogna. Apologies are in order and packing needs to be done, so he better get to it before he starts crying.

As he relishes one of his last showers in a private bathroom, a scintillating moan of pleasure seeps through the shower wall. For a moment, Charlie thinks he let it out himself, but then it reprises, and his voice hasn't gone that high since puberty.

Is that…Michelle?

He shuts off the water, dries himself and dresses. He tries to make as few noises as possible, catching what bits he can.

The moans don't stop. They grow stronger. A masculine voice enters the mix. Whispered words are muddled by the wall, but there's an unmistakable Italian accent there.

If Michelle's not alone, does that mean…

Maybe when Dario went looking for him last night, Michelle went out, picked up a guy and brought him back here. It's a long-shot theory, given Michelle's general character, but that has to be the explanation, right?

The sex sounds paint a picture in Charlie's head that borders on voyeuristic, so he tears the metaphorical canvas and goes down to breakfast.

The back doors are flung open. Morning air traipses through the gauzy curtains like a welcome guest. Dew still clings to the blades of grass in the garden. It would all be peaceful if Charlie weren't so curious about his neighbor's escapades.

Upon first bite of burnt toast—mind too preoccupied to pay close attention to the timer—he hears two sets of footsteps creak on the stairs. From his vantage point, Charlie can only see the backs of heads.

Michelle's hair is unruly. The man she's with has a hand on her back. He is short and has shoulder-length, chestnut brown hair.

A torpedo of possessiveness zooms through his gut, until the pair turns the corner. While the man Michelle is with bears a striking resemblance to Dario, he has a rounder face, bushier eyebrows and a stouter figure with no shirt on. Still, he walks with far more directness and panache than Dario, a man who wears five-piece suits on the regular.

As soon as Michelle sees Charlie at the table, she steps away from the man. "Good morning," she says, shyly brushing a hair behind her ear.

"Morning," Charlie says through a big bite of toast. His appetite balloons, with the certainty that Dario wasn't the person keeping Michelle company in the shower.

"Which one are you?" the man asks with an impolite point.

Charlie wipes his mouth before answering. "Excuse me?"

"Which contest winner? There was the model, the musician, the salesman, the French bombshell—" he nibbles on Michelle's exposed shoulder, which is still red, so she swats him away "—and…you?"

"The American, I guess?" Charlie says.

"I thought the musician was American."

"The *other* American, then?"

The man snaps his fingers. "The gas station one."

Charlie goes to correct him but decides it's not worth the breath. It's not like he's an astronaut or an engineer. It's not like he's going to be Dario Cotogna's husband either. What's the point?

"You are?" Charlie asks.

"I see my reputation doesn't precede me," he says, extending a hand to Charlie. "Emilio Cotogna, future head of Amorina Chocolates."

A door opens behind Charlie. He turns expecting Dario, but it's another man he's never seen before. This man is carrying a camera, and is trailed by a tall, lithe woman with porcelain skin and blond hair. Where had all these people come from? What had he missed yesterday?

"Why aren't you rolling? We need as much footage as we can get," Emilio says.

Michelle backs up. "I should probably change and put my makeup on." She wears an oversize, stark red shirt, the collar of which is stretched out and askew, making it appear one wrong move away from slipping right off.

"What are you filming for?" Charlie asks. At no point did he sign a release to be filmed. The vibe in Villa Meraviglia is drastically different this morning, and he doesn't like it one bit.

His question is drowned out by Emilio saying, "Stay. You look sexy right now." He lets out a purr-growl that makes Charlie uncomfortable.

The woman who recently arrived rushes up to Charlie at the table. "You made it back! Thank goodness. We were worried about you last night. Charlie, right?" She has a musical, American accent that reminds Charlie of home.

"That's me," he says.

Paola enters and upon seeing the crowd gathered at the table, turns on her heel and slips back into the kitchen. Charlie wishes he could join her.

"I'm April, Dario's mom. I've heard such wonderful things about you," she says before quickly switching topics and asking him about his tattoos.

The sound of the doors slamming scares them all into silence.

Dario stands in his swimsuit and a swim cap. Pool water drips all over the floor. "What's going on in here?" He scans the room and reddens. "Ah, Charlie, I see you've met my family."

Charlie nods as Michelle returns. Still pantless. Still in Emilio's shirt. "Emilio, have you seen my—" She stops in her tracks when she locks eyes with Dario. Charlie holds his breath.

Dario's piercing glare skips like a hastily tossed stone over to his brother. "Real nice, Emilio."

"Ma dai! As if you were ever going to make a move," Emilio says, fight in his words.

"As if you were ever going to be faithful to your wife," Dario shoots back.

April intercedes. "Boys! Oddio! Basta! Who raised you?"

"Voi," Paola says, ever the quick wit as she clears the breakfast spread.

Dario and Emilio snicker at Paola's remark.

"Grazie, Paola. Very helpful. I did my best!" April calls after Paola's retreating figure. "Can you two be in a room together more than a minute without fighting?"

Charlie grew up in want of a sibling, but this dynamic seems toxic enough to change his mind. The men glare at each other across the room, fire burning in their eyes.

Dario tears off his swim cap and says, "We wouldn't be fighting if he didn't have sex with one of my contest winners!"

Charlie cringes at Dario's word choice.

Michelle, shocking everyone, says with a fierceness, "I am not *yours*." It's like she's miraculously transformed into one of her favorite reality TV starlets. Charlie half imagines the gaudy dangling earrings and designer heels, the wineglass in her hand and the plastic plumpness of her cheeks.

Dario flushes cherry red while visibly fighting for words. "Si. No. Of course you are not mine. I didn't mean it the way— You see, he…" Dario points his finger, voice falling off his breath. It's obvious his brother brings out the worst in him.

"He, what? He spent the day with me. He was kind to me," Michelle says. "I can have sex with anyone I choose." Charlie would cheer for Michelle standing up for herself if it weren't at Dario's expense.

"Yeah!" Emilio chimes in. "She can have sex with anyone she chooses, and she chose me."

"You are not helping," Michelle says. "My decisions do not need your conditions." Her hand sassily sits on her hip.

It rings like a clunky catchphrase meant to be turned into a meme, but still, good on her.

Dario opens his mouth, but after a moment of speechlessness, makes the wise choice of not extending this conflict any farther. The tension in the room is already gooey mozzarella strung to its limit.

"This is my house, and I would like you all to leave," Dario says, slow yet firm.

"It's Mom's house actually," Emilio says.

April pinches the bridge of her nose, crosses the room to her son. "Emilio, let me help you find a shirt that isn't already spoken for so we can get out of Dario's hair. We've overstayed our welcome."

"But—"

April waggles a finger in his face and points at the stairs. The three of them exit without further protest.

Uncertain, Charlie follows the crowd.

"Not you," Dario says. "Please stay. If you want to. I want to finish our conversation from last night."

Charlie turns back. Dario's still soaking wet, and now he's shaking, partly from the cold and probably partly from the emotions running through him.

Despite the scene, Charlie wraps him in a towel he grabs from the lounger outside. "You good?" Charlie asks.

"Better now," Dario says, stepping in for a hug that confuses Charlie. Isn't this the part where Dario lets him down easy? Tells him he has no room in his life for gold-diggers?

"You didn't tell me your family was here," Charlie says,

holding Dario, wondering if this might be one of the last times he does so.

"Between finding you and my panic attack, I am surprised I told you anything. It is all a big blur," Dario says into the meat of his chest.

"All of it?" Charlie asks.

Dario nuzzles his head, and Charlie's heart frustratingly flutters. "The part where I told you that I like you is still there, I promise."

Charlie waits for the inevitable *but...*

When it doesn't come, Charlie says, "I leave tomorrow, as per the contest rules," stating the obvious.

"I don't care about the contest anymore," Dario says. "I care about you, and I want you to stay."

Wrapped in the oversize towel, Dario looks small. He sounds small, too. As if his vulnerability has shrunken him down. Charlie could practically pick him up and stick him in his pocket, carry him around and protect him forever.

"I care about you, too, but I need to get back to my family soon," Charlie says. "We have...stuff to figure out."

Charlie can't name it again. Can't bring himself to think about the house on Cemetery Street, and how selfish he was for using Dario as his salvation.

"I think we have stuff to figure out, too," Dario says, pulling back and looking Charlie in the eyes. "Like where I can deliver the check to save your house and what kind of engagement ring you might like."

Charlie widens his eyes. "Wait, what? You can't do that. It's too much."

"It's not too much. It's never too much when you have more than enough like I do," Dario explains. "I thought about what you said last night, and I appreciate you being honest with me.

But let's face it, whoever I marry was always going to need something from me."

"But isn't that wrong?" Charlie asks. "To take like that?"

"I'm taking, too. A marriage means I get Amorina. It was always going to be an exchange. Marriage is an exchange. It's business. Love is the part that's personal," he says with a thrilling intensity in his expression. "I see that now."

Charlie remains speechless for a moment. His brain is one long-looping *daaaaaaamn*. He didn't know what to expect upon meeting Dario Cotogna, but the man's maturity and perceptiveness are beyond anything he could've prepared for. Somebody better find a crash mat and quick, because Charlie Moore is certain he's falling even harder for the chocolate maker.

"I guess I hadn't considered that," Charlie finally says.

"Stay another week," Dario says, eyes crystalline, voice a sparkler of faith. "Let me show you what this life can be like, just the two of us without the intrusions or the dramatics."

"You're not just saying this because I'm the last one left?" Charlie asks, feeling unsteady on his feet. He woke up resolved to be brave in the face of heartbreak. Now he doesn't know what to do with his fiddling hands and somersaulting heart.

"I would be saying this if there were a million people in this room, because you're the only one I have eyes for," Dario says, sincere as can be.

Charlie is a chocolate bar in heat. "You're sweet. If it was only me to think of, it would be a yes, but my family needs me. It was a hassle to lose me for one week, let alone more."

"They did not approve of you coming here?" Dario asks.

"It's not that," Charlie says, a little cagily. "They need me around more than they'd ever admit. For all intents and purposes, I'm my grandparents' primary caretaker."

"I meant to ask, do they pay you for that?"

Charlie raises an eyebrow. "Of course not. As you know, they can't even afford the mortgage. But they're family."

"How many hours a day do you look after them?" Dario asks.

"My parents leave for work around six forty-five in the morning and get back around six in the evening, and my shifts at the liquor store start at seven, so…eleven hours?"

"That's a full-time job, Charlie," Dario says.

"A job I'm happy to do." He is grateful for everything he has and everyone in his life. It's wonderful that Dario wants to give him more, but judging by the way his fellow contest winners and Dario's brother acted, maybe more isn't always better.

"Labor is labor even if it's a labor of love," Dario says. "Think of all you could accomplish if you had eleven hours more to yourself every day." Dario gives a small smile. "You could finally apprentice for a tattoo artist. You said you're the family dreamer. Why aren't any of those dreams just for you, Charlie?"

Back in Charlie's bedroom at home, there is a bookshelf full of completed sketchbooks. Each one shows Charlie's growth, creativity and style as they have flourished over the years. He knows he has the artistic talent, but he doesn't know if he can hack the rest. He doesn't fully believe he deserves to find out.

"If you stayed here with me, we can find you an English-speaking tattoo artist to train under. We can get you the equipment and sanitation tools you need to practice here. The possibilities are endless." Dario's words push open several locked doors in Charlie's mind that he never thought he'd be able to walk through.

"Let me talk to my parents about staying longer," he says, queasy already over what they might say. He pats his pocket before he remembers yesterday. "Can I borrow your phone to call them?"

"Of course. My bedroom awaits you," Dario says, gesturing toward the door. His face flushes. "I mean for making the call."

"Right," Charlie says, sporting a playful smirk as he goes. "I'm sure that's *exactly* what you meant, Candy Man."

Twenty-One

CHARLIE

"I have some news," Charlie says. His headphones are in. Angelo is curled up in his lap, looking like a well-packed snowball. On Dario's phone screen, Charlie's family questions him, confused about why he is calling from an unknown number. "Oh, I lost my phone in a well." He laughs this time, the comedy of it hitting harder.

"That's the news?" Grandma asks.

"No," Charlie says.

"We can't afford to help you get a new one," Dad says, sounding concerned.

"I know. It's all right. Dario is taking care of it." Charlie wouldn't be surprised if there was a new phone ready to unwrap when he got off this call.

"How will you pay him back?" Mom asks. "I can wire you a little something, if you need to get rolling."

"That's okay. He wouldn't take the money if I offered," Charlie says.

"There's no such thing as a free phone, Charlie." Dad sounds like a poorly rewritten economics textbook.

"Sure, but generosity is free, and Dario is really generous and caring," Charlie says. "I can't go a whole week in a foreign country without a phone."

"A whole week? We thought you were coming home tomorrow," Dad says.

Oops. Charlie jumped the gun and now his cheeks are aflame. "About that…"

"We started making you a welcome home banner!" says Grandpa.

"That's really kind. You might just have to hang it up a little later. See, 'cause Dario invited me to stay one more week… here…with him…" Mom and Dad's faces fall almost immediately. Grandma, however, looks more excited than when she sees the tree on Christmas morning.

"Charlie, that is wonderful! My, he must really be generous to extend all of your stays like that."

"Not all. Just mine. Just me." Charlie lets out a shaky yet excited breath. "Dario wants to marry me. I think you remember that this whole contest was a bid to find a spouse to help him head up Amorina."

"That was serious?" Dad asks.

"Why wouldn't it have been serious?" Charlie asks.

Mom says, "It did sound a bit outlandish. We thought maybe it was a cheesy gimmick."

"What do you mean?" Charlie asks.

"You know, like a cheesy gimmick to sell more of those fancy-shmancy chocolate bars," Dad says.

"No, it—it was real," Charlie says, stumbling over his words a bit. "We've really connected, and you know I've never really been the romantic type, but he's incredibly smart, well-spoken, not to mention well-dressed. I…like him."

Grandma nearly explodes with elation. This is the happiest he's seen her in a long time. "Charlie! Oh, Charlie! How exciting! A wedding! We've always wanted to be around when you married. Haven't we, Grandpa?"

"You betcha." Grandpa beams alongside her. "What wonderful news!"

Charlie can't focus on his grandparents' delight when it's being overshadowed by his parents' evident skepticism.

Mom shakes her head. "He's known you for a week. How could he possibly know he wants to marry you?"

"Charlie's a catch!" Grandma says, coming to his defense.

"Grandma and I got engaged after only a few weeks. When you know, you know!" Grandpa exclaims.

Dad sets down his coffee mug. "Today's world isn't like it was back then."

"I'm not prehistoric," Grandpa chides.

"What does he want from you?" Dad asks, ignoring Grandpa.

"Companionship and love! What else could he want?" Grandma says.

"I think your dad is asking about logistics here. It's one thing to win a contest and a free trip. It's another to accept an engagement from a stranger," his mom relays in a much calmer manner.

"He hasn't asked, and I haven't accepted yet. He's only requested I stay longer so we can figure out whether we could get married and build a life together." Angelo stirs in his lap. Charlie pets him between the ears to give his fidgeting fingers something to do.

"Well, good," Dad says with a huff. "I don't care how smart or well-dressed he is. Call me old-fashioned, but I think it's a man's duty to meet the father and ask for his blessing before he proposes. That's what I did."

"Dad, this isn't some Austen novel. You don't need to give him a dowry or some sh—stuff." He hates cursing in front of his grandparents. He can have the blue hair and the tattoos and the piercings, but he draws the line at that. His rebellion has its hard limits.

Is one of those limits not marrying someone his family disapproves of?

"Still, we should meet the man in person if he wants to be a Moore!" Dad says.

"Maybe we can arrange to have you all come out here?" Charlie says, confidence dimming.

"And miss work?" Mom asks.

"I'm not sure I'm well enough for a nine-hour flight," says Grandma, losing some of her sparkle.

"We're about to lose our house, Charlie." Tears speckle Dad's eyes. In twenty-eight years, his father has never shown this much emotion before. It frightens him a bit.

"I know…" Charlie's voice is as thin as a chocolate wafer. His breath shortens.

"Do you?" Dad asks, really laying into the words.

"I do because I'm the one who got the letter from the bank." They all go ghostly white at the confession. Charlie wishes relief came along with his words, but the hurt he's inflicted on his family registers deeper than before. His guilt is a mallet plunking him on the head. "I'm sorry I didn't tell you. I know you're all under a lot of stress right now with your jobs and your health, and I wanted to step up and handle this for us. Originally, that was the reason I came out here. Dario must marry to inherit Amorina, and he is very rich."

"Marrying him doesn't make it your money, Charlie. Don't you think you'd have to sign a prenup?" Mom asks.

"You were using him for his money?" Grandma asks, concerned and perhaps a tad disappointed.

"No, I mean, well, at first I…" Hadn't he already worked through this? Hadn't Dario confirmed that Charlie's need did not outweigh his feelings? That he would write the Moore family a check to save their house, no questions asked, because he *liked* Charlie.

"Sounds like *he's* using *you*," Dad says.

"It's not like that," Charlie protests, trying and failing to cling to his optimism. His usual refrain of *we get on just fine* reveals itself to have been more of a defense mechanism than a long-held truth.

"You just said he has to marry or else he loses his big, cushy corporate job," Dad says.

"It's not a big, cushy, corporate job. He's managing one of Italy's largest chocolate production operations. He's trying to make it more sustainable and help it thrive. He can explain it all better than I can." Charlie's head hurts, and his thoughts scramble together.

"Then Dario should come here and shake my hand and tell me himself," Dad says.

Charlie sags in his chair. "I… I'm not sure that's possible."

"Why not?" Dad asks in challenge.

Charlie won't share Dario's diagnosis. It's not his place. So all he says is: "I just don't think he can."

"If he's too busy or too good to come out here and do the gentlemanly thing, then he's not good enough for you, kiddo," Dad says. "End of discussion."

"No. Not 'end of discussion.' I'm not a 'kiddo' anymore. I'm twenty-eight years old. I contribute to our household as much as anyone else. I wanted to do what I could to fix this for us," Charlie says as his voice and eyes grow watery. Even adults need to let their emotions out sometimes. "I really care about this guy, and he wants to help us fix this. Why would we turn away from that?"

"We're not in the market for charity," Dad says, seemingly already dead set against this. Charlie wants to take him by the shoulders and shake some reason into him.

"Help and charity are not the same thing! It's not charity when it's family," Charlie protests.

"He has a point," Grandpa says.

Dad shakes his head. "If he can't come here to meet us and make his intentions known, then I want absolutely no part of this," Dad says with a note of finality. He stands and exits the room.

The phone shakes. Charlie calls after him but he doesn't come back.

Mom sighs after several seconds that feel like hours. "Maybe it's best you stay another week. It'll give him time to cool off and—who knows—maybe come around. If that's what you want. I love you, Char." She gets up and follows Dad, disappearing around the corner.

The tears percolate but they don't fall. Charlie is more stunned than anything else. His mouth hangs open, barely any words left.

"I don't mean to pour salt in the wound, but you should have at least told *us* about the letter when you got it," Grandpa says, sounding a bit hurt. His cheeks sag more than they already do.

"I know. I'm sorry," Charlie says. Because he betrayed his grandparents' trust when they've never given him a reason to be dishonest. They've always been there for him. Theirs were the smiling faces he saw each day when he got home from a long day at school. Theirs were the shoulders he cried on when he came home soaked through with rain from Max's house after being outed and dumped. Theirs were the hands he squeezed for luck when he opened the email to see if he'd won the Amorina contest.

His grandparents have given him so much his parents couldn't that he didn't waste a second thought when he turned eighteen, graduated high school and took over as their full-time caretaker.

He just wanted to do this one thing alone for the good of them all. Now regret is a clamp around his heart, cutting off his blood flow.

"You probably should've eased your father into this a little more, too. You know he doesn't take kindly to change," Grandpa adds.

"I know." Charlie hangs his head as a tear slides down his cheek.

"Despite that, we're very excited for you," Grandpa concludes, happiness playing softly behind his words.

"I know." Charlie feels like a broken record, but he looks up and smiles through the tears.

"Really, truly, over-the-moon excited for you, Charlie," Grandma says, hands pressed to her chest.

"Thank you." Charlie hiccups. "Will you two be okay for another week?"

"Who, us?" Grandpa asks. "We have been A-okay for eighty-plus years. We plan to stay that way. Don't you worry 'bout us."

"I do worry about you guys, though," Charlie says. He would've never gone through all this if he didn't. And despite his dad's dismissal, he still thinks he was right to be reckless this once. If he hadn't been, he'd have never met Dario Cotogna, and that would've been a tragedy.

"Don't let worry get in the way of living your life," Grandma says. Her eyes beam a million hugs through the phone screen.

"Que sera, sera," Grandpa says.

"Huh?" Charlie reaches for a tissue from the box on Dario's bedside table.

Grandma starts to sing in her shaky, sweet voice the Doris Day song she taught him a long time ago. They'd sing it every time they did the dishes together. Standing at the kitchen sink as she washed and he dried, their voices floated higher than the soap bubbles.

He wipes away the last of his tears, joins in for the last line and internalizes the lyrics about accepting the future, whatever it may hold.

DARIO

At the front gate of Villa Meraviglia, the town car idles. The last of Dario's guests are fumbling about behind him, making sure nothing is forgotten. Zippers rise and wheels rattle.

Dario takes a moment to open the last letter from his grandfather.

Caro Tesorino,

I have no more stories to tell, advice to share, or lessons to impart.

As with all good mentorships, eventually, the student becomes the teacher. It seems as if I blinked one day, and you surpassed me in knowledge and skill.

Each one of these letters has been a reminder for your head of something you already knew in your heart.

You have a good heart. It won't steer you wrong.

Ti amo, tesorino.

Until we meet again.
Con affetto,
Nonno

Dario turns the paper over again in his hands.

That's it?

There has to be more. This can't be the last—

His guests pile through the door behind him—except Craig who hangs back, still recording. As if Dario's life weren't already an embarrassing display. He withers, wondering how he'll be portrayed in whatever heinous edit comes out of this footage.

Before it got that far, would Violetta help him sue Emilio even though she's also his lawyer? No, that's too messy and too time-consuming. Time is a commodity he swears not to waste anymore.

Emilio slides inside the car without a glance back at Dario, which is fine for now. Theirs is not the kind of strain that can be healed in an afternoon.

Before Michelle can pass, though, Dario stops her to say, "I am deeply sorry for my behavior earlier. It has been a privilege getting to know you. I hope you will take only fond memories with you as you go."

Michelle nods, not quite meeting his eyes. "I am sorry to have hurt your feelings. It was not my intention. Your brother, he is—"

"I know," Dario says, hurt feelings nowhere to be found. His brother is charming. He is sweet when he wants to be. He is winning. He always has been. Facts are facts are facts. "Apology accepted. Safe travels."

"Before I go…" She rips a page out of her design book. It is the one with the nontraditional wedding outfit she was showing him yesterday over breakfast with the tuxedo detailing. "I want you to have this."

"Are you sure?" Dario asks, taken aback and somewhat confused. She added beading to the vest and a veil to match the train.

"Sometimes, when I am designing, I put myself in the shoes of the woman who would wear that dress. I pretend I am her. I think like she would think and do like she would do to create the most perfect dress I can come up with that will make her feel beautiful." She brushes stray hair from her face. "I think, this week, while I was drawing this, I was walking around as 'woman you would marry.' It was not until I finished the illustration this morning that I realized, she is not me. Maybe 'she' is a 'he' or a 'they.' Maybe you can use parts of it. Maybe you should throw it away. J'sais pas. It is a gift, to you."

Dario holds the paper to his chest, understanding flitting between them. "Thank you."

"Au revoir." She rolls her purple suitcase down the front walk.

Dario's mom steps out with a bag on her arm. "That Charlie is not at all what I expected."

"How do you mean?" Dario asks.

"The tattoos and the hair and the optimism in his eyes like your father had," she says, a happy-sad smile on her face. "He surprised me."

"He surprised me, too," Dario says. "In a good way." He smiles to himself, thinking about his blue-haired boy back in the barn house talking to his family about their inevitable engagement.

"Absolutely, in a good way." She takes his face in her hands. "Now remember, the world is never as cruel as our minds convince us it is. Be kind to yourself and don't forget to *be* yourself."

"I'll take the note," Dario says, borrowing the language they use in the opera world when the director gives a fix.

"When you need me, please call. You're never too old to need your mother. No role is more important than you, sweet Dario. Always know that. Ti amo."

"Ti amo, Mamma." He kisses both of her cheeks before closing the car door behind her.

As soon as the black car rolls away, a swelling sense of relief hits Dario, which only escalates when he turns back and discovers Charlie standing barefoot at the gate.

Dario rushes to his blue-haired American and poorly attempts to lift him up and spin him around. "All went well?" he asks, setting Charlie down before they tumble into the garden and ruin their clothes in the mud.

"All went, but I'm not sure I would say well." Charlie nervously toys with Dario's tie.

"What happened?" He stills Charlie's hands with his own. They shake slightly.

Charlie sighs out the weight of the world. "My dad wasn't very receptive. I think, after everything that went down with my uncle, he is leery when it comes to windfalls and people with money. He won't accept it. At least not right now."

"Why don't I get him on the phone? I would be happy to talk with him and make my intentions known." Dario is undeterred. In the boardroom, he learned by example from his grandfather how to crack even the toughest nut. Whether through flattery or mastery, everybody could be charmed. Maybe he wasn't all that dissimilar from Emilio in that way.

Charlie bites his lip, shakes his head. "That's just it. He does want to meet you. He just wants to meet you…in person. On their turf."

The sandcastle of Dario's hopes and dreams gets swept away by the rising tide. "My birthday is in three months," he says.

They should be ring shopping and setting a date and figuring out how to turn the Amorina museum into a ceremony space, the Tasting Room into a banquet hall.

"I know, but my dad said he'd have no part in our marriage if he didn't meet you in person." Charlie's gaze falls to the grass. "My family means the world to me. I can't go through with this without their blessing, and I can't get married without them present." In the light, Charlie's hair almost takes on a deeper, sadder shade of blue, an ocean that Dario could drown himself in.

"I would never ask you to." Dario imagines a frowning Charlie on their wedding day, looking to his side of seats and not seeing anyone there. He knows how he would feel if his mom missed his big day.

Aside from his mother, Paola, Gabriele and, begrudgingly, Emilio, who else would he invite? Violetta and her family, of course, but he wouldn't say they were close. There are business associates and press people who will attend at the behest of Amorina executives, but he doesn't count them among his own.

The Moores may be his key to *more*. More loved ones, more family, more people to entrust and care for and look after. The way Charlie has described them, he will take to them easily, just as he's taken to Charlie. He shivers to think of what impression he has already made on them given this elaborate ruse to find him a spouse.

"Did you tell them about my agoraphobia?" Dario asks.

"Of course not," Charlie says. "I wouldn't tell something that personal without your permission first. And I would never ask you to fly an ocean away when I know you're not feeling up to it."

"Right." The impasse sizzles hot between them. Was this week all for nothing?

"I still have my ticket home for tomorrow. I can go. It's no trouble," Charlie says with leaden voice, "I'm sorry if I wasted your time."

Dario reaches out for him, imploring. "No time with you will ever be wasted, Charlie Moore."

Charlie, teary-eyed, kisses him. In that kiss, he scrounges up the strength to rebuild the sandcastle. His great-great-grandmother never gave up on Amorina despite all the many setbacks. He refuses to give in, to back down. He will fight this. Even if the thing he is fighting is himself.

"I will find a way to get there," he says, determined. "After this week, I've been reminded that the world is big, and if I continue to let my life get small, I will fail Amorina and I will fail myself. I've been meaning to get to America sooner rather than later anyway."

"Dario." His name from Charlie's mouth is loaded beyond belief. A projectile soaring through the air that he deflects.

"Charlie," he says, letting Charlie's name morph into a butterfly flitting on the breeze. "I am going to go to Pennsylvania and meet your family. I don't know how, but I know when—before my birthday—and I know why—because…" He hovers over the words that sit sugar-cube-sweet on his tongue before ultimately deciding to trust himself. "I'm falling for you, Charlie, and I want this to work."

"You do?" Charlie asks, mouth agape, eyes alight.

"Si." He tugs Charlie closer. "Without the noise of the others around, I hear a future with you so clearly."

"You're amazing, Dario." Charlie kisses him again. Is it possible that this one is even fiercer than the last? It nearly knocks Dario sideways from a headrush of hormones and hope.

"You think so?" Dario asks.

"I know so. And my family is going to think so, too, once they get to know you. The real you."

Wasn't that what his mother had told him his father had said to her? Wasn't that her advice right before she left Villa Meraviglia?

She had to have been at least partially right. The world could not be as cruel as he imagined, because the world had brought him Charlie Moore, and Charlie Moore is a miracle.

Twenty-Two

DARIO

Under the guidance of Dario's therapist, they come up a with a plan of action.

Rolling out Dario's date book, they schedule outings to places where Dario can expose himself to triggers safely. They detail escape routes and identify coping tactics to get him centered should the anxiety overwhelm him and a panic attack come on. Dario refills his as-needed anxiety medication to calm him when all else fails.

Early in the morning on Monday, they sail across Lake Trasimeno to Castiglione del Lago, the site of his proposal-gone-wrong and where the annual blues festival—a tourist attraction he would usually give a wide berth to—is already underway. The festival, where they will watch Beau perform, is the final test of Dario's exposure. He worries a week may not be enough to overcome such debilitating fear, but for Charlie, he feels like he could move mountains, so he has to try.

The sail is smooth, and the sky is clear, which are normally good things, except today where Dario searches for any reason to turn this boat around. But Charlie smiles at him, and he doesn't veer the helm off course. He trains his eye on the horizon and visualizes the ideal outcome.

When they dock in the bustling marina, they have no intentions of getting out. Small steps lead to bigger results. Rather than trotting around the city, they picnic beneath the sail and people-watch from a comfortable distance.

Dario eases through the worst of his panic, letting the acidic burn come and taper off with breathing and time and ample amounts of sunshine.

"Did you sail a lot with your dad?" Charlie asks, clearly hoping conversation will quell some of the fear. Some of the fear *of fear*. Isn't that strange? Brains can be such fickle beasts.

"Every week we would bike down to the lake as a family and sail for hours, Emilio and I trading off roles as skippers," Dario says.

"What was your dad like?" Charlie asks, stealing another slice of cheese from their charcuterie board.

"He was a total adventurer. I swear nothing scared him. He sailed, he drove a Vespa, he rock climbed and cliff dove. I think sometimes when you grow up as well-off as he did and have as many experiences as he did when he was young, you become addicted to chasing adrenaline," Dario says. A memory book of his father flips fast through his mind. The unfilled pages at the end remind him that some lives get cut too short. "I don't know if that's true. I never got a chance to ask him. There's a lot I never got the chance to ask him."

"If you had the opportunity to ask him one more question," Charlie says, "what would it be?"

"I'd ask him if he ever wanted to take over Amorina," Dario says, eyes cast on the few white clouds charging overhead. "It was always in the background in the way I imagine princes in a monarchy are aware of the line of succession but if they think too hard about it, they might combust from the stress of what's to come. After my dad died, my brother kept saying that he acted with such reckless abandon because he never wanted to be a corporate suit. But that's never been what Amorina was like. I think Emilio was projecting. That couldn't be what my dad was thinking."

"What's your theory?" Charlie asks curiously.

"That he was fearless for so much of my childhood because he knew that, as soon as he took over Amorina, he would love it so much he wouldn't want to retire. Like my grandfather, he would spearhead it until he passed. I think he did it right. He did retirement *before* claiming his career," Dario says, wistfully. "I know that's extremely privileged. I'm not saying it would work for anyone else, but for him? He was just as happy captaining this boat as he was discussing business with my nonno."

Charlie soaks this in. "Would you have done it that way, if you could have?"

Pondering the could-haves has always been hard for Dario. When his father died, he learned very young that he had to make peace with what was. There was time for grieving, and then there was a time for looking ahead. If he dwelled, he risked slipping on the banana peel of pity and never getting up again.

"Amorina is at my fingertips much earlier than I anticipated, but I have to roll with it. I would need more balance anyway," Dario says. "All play and no work would leave me a little adrift. All work and no play..."

"I'll make sure there's play," Charlie says. He raises his eyebrows suggestively while running his bare foot under the hem of Dario's boating trousers.

"Can I hold you to that?" Dario asks, scooting closer.

"You can hold me any way you'd like, Candy Man," Charlie says.

Dario leans in, hauls him to standing, and confidently kisses him.

On Tuesday, they take their exploration further. After a session with his therapist, Dario gathers up Charlie from the pool and they board the boat again to make the trek across the lake. This time, when they tie up, they disembark.

Dario's never had sea legs in his life given all his experiences out on the water, but today as they venture into the fray of tourists in town for the big music festival, he wobbles all over the place. Charlie's arm linked in his steadies him some.

For an hour, they wander in and out of shops, sticking to the sidewalks and trying their best to keep a slow, even pace.

Eventually, as Dario knew it would, the overwhelm catches up to him. His mind becomes a timer blinking up the seconds he's been away from home, then a film reel of worst-case scenarios that won't stop.

When his breathing grows labored, Charlie pulls him into the least crowded storefront they come across.

To both of their surprise, it is a desolate tattoo parlor. The walls are a smorgasbord of designs big and small. In the next room, there's a comfy-looking chair with supplies on a rolling tray beside it. A woman with jet-black hair pulled up in a high ponytail comes out from the back asking if they had an appointment.

"What did she say?" Charlie asks.

"She says if we don't plan to get a tattoo then we can't loiter here." Dario grips his chest.

"You just need a place to reset. Can't we tell her that?" Charlie asks.

Through the haze of his anxiety, he gets a better idea. After a brief exchange and a flashing of some cash, the artist ushers them back to the chair with little fanfare.

"What's happening?" Charlie asks as Dario takes a seat.

"We are getting tattoos," Dario says as he breathes in the sanitized leather of the chair.

"Of what?" Charlie asks.

"You tell me," Dario says. The panic attack subsides incrementally. While his heart still thrums, it does so with excitement. He had never thought about getting a tattoo before, but he likes the way they look on Charlie, and he wants to share this experience with him.

"You want us to get matching tattoos?" Charlie asks, seemingly stunned. The tattoo artist appears impatient beside him, since they've clearly disrupted a chill day in her studio.

Dario nods. "Something small to remember all of this by."

Confusion dovetails into enthusiasm. Charlie reaches for his sketchbook. The stool gives a soft *pfft* as he sits on it. "This is your first tattoo!" Glee widens Charlie's eyes. "Where do you want it? What do you want? Oh my God, this is going to be good."

Charlie's zeal laps over Dario in sonic waves. "I trust you to decide for me," he says.

"You know a tattoo means no sun or pool for a few months. Are you sure about this? It's permanent." While he understands the hesitation, he loves—*loves*—every inch of ink sketched across Charlie's body. Anything Charlie's beautiful imagination comes up with will delight him.

"I'm sure. Anything, anywhere," he says, placing his trust where it will be valued and honored.

"Anywhere?" Charlie's eyebrows go up. "Your lower back? Your dick?"

"Okay maybe not *anywhere*."

"I got you, Candy Man," Charlie says, and Dario wonders if he knows just how much he's *got him*.

Charlie sketches away. Dario uses this time to work through his deep-breathing exercises. Meditation should rid him of the tingle that still infects his toes from the abrupt onslaught of anxiousness that hit him. A performance from the festival must've gotten out. People spilled en masse into the street. His fight-or-flight responses kicked into overdrive.

Centered enough, he reopens his eyes and chats with the artist.

She watches over Charlie's shoulder as he works, angled away from Dario. "Lui è bravo."

"She says you're good," Dario translates for Charlie. He blushes, responds with a timid, "Grazie."

"È un artista?" *Is he an artist?*

He tells her that Charlie is self-taught and that his dream is to become a tattooist.

"È stato apprendista?"

"She's asking if you've been an apprentice before," Dario says to Charlie who is deep in a creative headspace. He comes out of it just enough to shake his head and get back to work.

"È americano?"

"Sì."

"Adesso vive qui?" *Does he live here now?*

Dario's heart speeds up. "Lo spero." *I hope.*

"What are you saying about me?" Charlie asks.

"Nothing bad," Dario reassures him as Charlie holds his sketchbook to his chest.

"Do you want to see what I've come up with?" Charlie asks.

Dario shakes his head. "I want to be surprised." He reaches out for Charlie's chin and gently tugs him in for a chaste kiss.

The tattoo artist—who eventually introduces herself as Marcella—finesses Charlie's sketch and properly sizes it. Once

Charlie is happy, they run it through a thermal imager to create the stencil that they will transfer to his skin. Dario was unaware of how many steps went into this process. Enough to make him second-guess this a few times over before reminding himself that Charlie knows what he's doing.

Dario strips down to his undershirt. Dirty thoughts practically float out the top of Charlie's head. Dario bites back a smirk.

"Va bene se ascolto musica?" Dario asks. Is it okay if I listen to music?

Marcella agrees as she opens a single-use razor pack and tenderly applies a light coating of shaving cream on the upper area of his bicep. Slow swipes of the razor remove any stray hairs that might get in the way of the needles. The cold alcohol wipe she uses has a pungent stench that burns Dario's nostrils.

From his phone's music library, Dario selects a recording of his mother singing various opera arias. Charlie immediately seems enchanted by the ebb and flow of the music. The instrumentation is lush, yet it's the athleticism of her voice that has always made Dario most proud.

"Your mother is very talented," Charlie says.

"I couldn't agree more." Dario misses watching his mother perform. If all goes well with his exposure therapy and the possible wedding, he'll be sitting front row with Charlie by his side the next chance he gets.

Marcella removes the needles and tubes from their sterile casing, and she sets the ink caps out. A bit of ointment is applied over the purplish stencil, which Dario refuses to look at.

The whir of the tattoo machine starting up scares him, so he turns the music up a little higher to drown it out.

"I bet she sang you some pretty epic lullabies when you were a kid," Charlie says. Dario sees this for what it is, a bid to distract him.

Dario dons a nostalgia-smeared smile. "My brother and I got whole concerts instead of bedtime stories. Divas never miss an opportunity to perform." As he runs down a whole setlist of songs performed before bed or at parties, he barely registers the pain of the first line being drawn on his skin.

Thirty minutes later, Marcella is done. Dario checks his first tattoo out in a handheld mirror.

The image is a partially unwrapped Amorina bar with a wide-open, cute Cyclops eye in the middle.

"Eye candy," Dario says, delighted. Charlie clearly knows his tastes enough to have drawn him a tattoo that he would cherish, which bolsters his already-flourishing feelings for him. Dario is also pleased with himself for choosing spontaneity over retreat. He could've forced them back to the boat as soon as Marcella said they couldn't stay in the parlor, but he opted to take a chance over falling back into old patterns.

"And?" Charlie asks. "Where's it placed?"

"My arm? Oh. Arm candy." He laughs.

"It's to remind you how sexy and delicious you are, Candy Man," Charlie says as Marcella sprays and gently wraps the piece. "Do you like it?"

"Of course I do." Dario *loves* it, but he worries about uttering that word too soon.

"You're not just saying that because it's now forever inked on your body?" Charlie asks.

Dario leans on his arm before wincing from soreness. "I'm saying that because it's exactly what I would've asked for had I known to ask for it. You read a part of my mind I've never even accessed before."

"Good, because it's my turn," Charlie says, helping Dario up so they can switch places.

Twenty-Three

DARIO

A full suitcase stands on its wheels at the doorway of Villa Meraviglia.

Tonight is the first night Dario sleeps somewhere other than the villa in almost a year.

He enlisted Paola's help in packing since he has nearly forgotten what one brings on an overnight trip. He'd packed underwear but no socks, toothpaste but no toothbrush.

In the midafternoon, he and Charlie check into the panoramic suite on the top floor of a boutique hotel that's only a stone's throw away from the action of the blues festival. It took some major string-pulling to score this reservation, given that the whole village is booked up for the duration. Luckily, the Cotogna name carries a lot of weight when he needs it to.

The king bed in the room is crisply done up in white sheets with a romantic, cream canopy floating above. It faces a floor-to-ceiling sliding glass door. Outside, a stone terrace offers

360 degree views of the glassy lake. A hot tub already turned on bubbles nearby.

"I can't wait to soak in that tonight," Dario says, stopping himself from trying to spot Villa Meraviglia all the way on the other side of the lake. Home is not calling to him as hard as it usually does or, if it is, he has closed his ears off to it.

"Not your arm, though. Your tattoo is still healing for the next two to three weeks," Charlie says. He has been slathering Dario with Aquaphor for the last twelve hours. "You have to avoid directly submerging it and keep it out of the sunlight, which I guess won't be a problem for you given you're always wearing your suit jacket."

Dario shrugs, which causes his raw skin to itch. He taps the tattoo through his shirt to assuage the niggling sensation. His eyes roam over Charlie, who leans against the hot tub, gaze trained on the view. The only view Dario cares about is the bulge in the front of Charlie's tan shorts. Tonight, he wants to take Charlie's cock inside him. He burns for the throb of that, the ache of it. It's the one thing that's going to get him through overcoming his agoraphobia and attending Beau's concert.

In town, they walk up the steep staircase to Rocca del Leone. Blues fans from all over the world are gathered, talking about the acts they have seen and drinking colorful cocktails and pale beers. Music floats on the air. Dario counts his steps instead of thinking too hard about how many people surround him.

They take dinner on the outskirts of the action, sitting at a café table as far away as possible. Over seafood and white wine, they talk of their favorite music genres. Dario doesn't want to come across as corny or pretentious, but he is afraid he sounds it as he talks even more about opera. Unlike his mother, he can't sing for his life, yet the arias have always lifted his spirits in a way no other song style can.

Rising from the plaza is a slow-moving, ginormous Ferris wheel. Instead of letting Charlie get lured in by the rhythmic sounds emanating from the medieval fortress where the festival's main stage is, Dario tugs him toward the ride. The two of them get strapped into the metal seat.

The cart hoists them back and up. They hold hands over the safety bar, and this sort of public display of affection already feels natural and helps to rewrite the romantic rejection Dario associates with this town. The simple act has Dario hardening in his slacks. Charlie Moore has reverted him back to the careless, hormonal nature of his teenage days.

"I used to be scared of heights," Charlie relays when they hit the apex.

They can see clear into the fortress from here. Listeners are packed in tight, swarmed up toward the lip of the stage. Dinner roils in Dario's stomach, and he wonders how he's going to ever survive in there.

"How did you get over it?" Dario asks.

"I guess like you. Exposure therapy." Charlie wraps an arm around Dario, obviously sensing his need for it. "There was this carnival every year in a town not too far from me. It happened at the end of the summer right around the start of school, so it was a big social thing. In the sixth grade, which was my first year of middle school, a bunch of us got driven over by someone's parents—I don't remember whose—and left on our own for the first time. Just up and handed some cash and a bunch of ride tickets while the adults went to drink by the petting zoo area. I was having an amazing time. We played games and ate cotton candy. Everything was going so well that I thought middle school was going to be a blast. In America, that's basically unheard of. But then this girl, Sandra, who I'd won a stuffed animal for, suggested we go on the Ferris wheel. I froze up when we got to the front of the line. I wouldn't hand over my ticket. I lied and said I had to use the bathroom and ran for the Porta-potties."

"Aw, Charlie," Dario says, understanding how embarrassing it must've felt back then, but still finding the story sweet.

"Nobody talked to me the whole ride home and come the first day of school, those kids didn't even look at me when they passed me in the hall," Charlie says. "The next year, when the carnival came around, I vowed to ride that Ferris wheel until I wasn't scared anymore."

"That worked?" Dario asks, amused.

Charlie nods. "I rode it for six whole loops. But I had downed two corn dogs and chili fries right before getting on. So I got so sick to my stomach that I ran off and immediately vomited into a trash can. The stomach sickness was worse than any fear over the ride ever was. From then on, heights didn't really faze me, but I never had a corn dog again."

"Is that a great loss?" Dario asks.

"Not if I'm getting a lifetime of Paola's cooking," Charlie says, wiggling his naked ring finger.

By the time they've swung back into the station, Dario is prepared to face the crowds.

They scan their tickets, pass through security and enter the festival. The boisterousness spooks Dario back a step. But only a step. One foot after another, he acknowledges his fear and confronts it anyway.

Music has the power to transport the listener, so Dario lets his ears take him on a journey while his body copes with the unwarranted stress.

As two bodies in a sweaty mass of them under the setting Umbrian sun, Dario and Charlie move together at the periphery of the crowd. Dario stands in front, Charlie right behind. Charlie's hands wrap around Dario's middle with a protective air. His embrace chases away intrusive thoughts.

The sensual sway of their bodies to the unexpected rhythms becomes hypnotic.

Dario Cotogna never gets to be just a face in the crowd, so he relishes this time together away from duties or title. Each anxious thought that hitchhikes beside the highways of his mind, he acknowledges and then drives right past. He is transcendental as fuck as he leans back into this tall, solid man who smells of sweat and tropical sunscreen and optimism.

The sun gives way to the moon, and they're still locked into the music. They grab alcoholic drinks and locate chairs to rest their tired feet before the headliner.

Around nine thirty, the final band takes the stage. Electricity runs through a structure that predates the very concept. Dario leads Charlie into the mob. Charlie's question of "Are you sure?" gets drowned out by the opening strum of a guitar. An older, full-bodied Black woman in an all-orange outfit emerges onto the scene as bright lights flare up. Bass and drums come together to buoy the night in joyous song. It's a far cry from opera, but it makes Dario jump up and down.

Beau is off to the side, bedecked in a fashionable linen suit while he plays the electric guitar. Dario moves over to get a better view of his former houseguest, who appears at home on stage in front of such a large crowd.

Dario reflects on the last two weeks. He sends subliminal thanks to Beau, who looks like a deity up there bathed in sweat under the roar of the audience. If not for Beau's honesty and his challenge-seeking behavior, Dario may not be here now with Charlie Moore, staring down his own challenges, daring to live a bigger life with his potential love.

He could say the same for each of the contest winners. While they all had their faults, they all taught him something as well. Ansel taught him to be honest upfront. Selina taught

him to be confident and direct. Michelle taught him to follow his heart and be himself.

And Charlie…

Charlie, whose eyes don't even leap to the stage. They fix
on Dario, who hasn't been this carefree in months. Or, frankly,
this aroused.

Charlie has taught him to see the world as new and exciting again.

Near the middle of the set, Dario inches up onto his tippy-
toes and says to Charlie, "Let's get out of here."

"Are you okay?" He holds an arm out, giving Dario space.

"Charlie!" Dario calls over the next song's intro. "I'm better
than I have been in ages. I just really want to get you alone."

Concern swaps for sultriness. Charlie bends down to kiss
Dario before carving them out of the crowd.

A bike cab idles at the curb outside the fortress. Charlie
hands the bored-looking rider a stack of euros and tells him
to step on it. He burns rubber all the way back to the hotel.

In the lobby, the ancient elevator takes its sweet time to descend. It clatters in its cage several stories above. Impatiently,
Dario heaves Charlie to the stairs, careless of how many flights
they need to climb to get to their penthouse.

The room door isn't even shut before Dario is tearing off
his suit. Gabriele will be mad that he was careless with such
luxe fabric, but his desire is practically scorching through the
threads anyway. Having conquered some of his agoraphobia,
he feels invincible, like he could bench-press a car or leap off
the terrace and fly.

But first— "Go soak for a bit while I freshen up," Dario
says. Under the sink, he left his toiletries. He plans to be
squeaky clean for the first time he takes all of Charlie Moore
inside him.

Charlie smirks at this, shucking his pants and striding toward the door. "Take your time, Candy Man." His cock is already rustling to attention. Growing longer by the second.

Dario shuts himself in the bathroom, looks himself over in the mirror, and takes a moment to pat himself on the back. He is here. In a new town. With a gorgeous man. And he did not have a single, full-blown panic attack. There were a couple close calls, but each time he stopped, took a few breaths and reminded himself that he was safe. Turns out, if he works with his mind instead of against it, sometimes it cooperates.

Twenty minutes later, Dario slides the back door open and steps out into the night in nothing but his birthday suit. Fitting, given that his birthday is approaching like a high-speed train. Only now it's one he's happy to ride, which is the same way he feels about riding Charlie Moore.

Charlie sits in the hot tub. His newly tattooed arm is resting on the edge. The bubbling water obscures the view of his lap, but there's no mistaking the small pull he does with his arm when he sees Dario naked. "Where's your suit?"

"I didn't pack it." Dario beams.

"I thought you preferred to be clothed."

"I thought I'd never spend the night outside Montecolognola again. Things change. You've changed me, Charlie. Now I want you to fuck me," he says, displaying confidence that rivals even Selina's.

The air thrums with music. In the distance, the festival rolls on. Drums pound and electric guitars wobble, then suddenly an entire horn section wails with pulsating abandon. All good sex needs a soundtrack.

Charlie pulls himself up. His body glistens with droplets of water. Some cling to the length of his astoundingly erect cock. Charlie reaches for his towel, but Dario stops him, drops to his knees on the tile, and licks the underside of Charlie's shaft.

"Out here?" Charlie asks, head swiveling around.

"Nobody can see us up here. It's the only panoramic view in the village, remember?" Dario says. "Is that okay with you?"

Charlie audibly swallows before saying, "Yeah, it's okay." Dario twirls his tongue around the shiny head of Charlie's cock. "Oh, it's *more* than okay, Candy Man."

The pet name causes Dario's dick to swell, and he initiates long licks up and down Charlie's impressive length. He doesn't even mind the chemical taste from the hot tub water. He's too focused on pleasing this man whose patience and kindness have helped him so much over the last several days.

Dario straightens up into the press of Charlie's fingers as they roam through his hair, moving it off his face and behind his ears.

A night breeze sweeps across Dario's blazing cheeks. His eyes tilt up to Charlie's face. He dissects each twitch of pleasure, each flicker of gratification. Bracketed in by Charlie's tattoo-speckled thighs, he lets himself go and engorges himself on every inch of Charlie's shaft. Given its slight downward curve, it eases past the back of his throat.

Dario ignores his triggered gag reflex and his watery eyes. He holds himself there, embracing the elasticity of his lips and the gentle tickle of Charlie's leg hair against his ears.

Once this trip ends, Charlie goes back to the States to talk with his family and give his job notice. Dario returns to the factory and to his interim duties before flying out to join Charlie and convince the Moores to be his in-laws.

The very idea of stepping foot on a plane, leaving Italy, should send him careening into a never-ending canyon of anxiety, but he pumps the brakes on that part of his brain. Tonight is about taking back his life.

Tonight is about taking Charlie Moore to the hilt.

He guides Charlie over to the lounger beside the hot tub.

Stepping over, Dario positions himself above Charlie, then looks down, ready for landing.

"Shouldn't we—" Charlie begins to ask. While he'd love to let Charlie toy around with his hole with his fingers and his tongue sometime, that's not what he needs right now. Right now, he wants to skip the aperitivo and get right to the main course.

"I'm ready for you," Dario says. He checked and double-checked in the bathroom with a toy and lube. His hole is wet, pliable, and more eager than ever before. Charlie's cock is slick with his spit. Slippery in all the right ways.

Like the abandoned hotel elevator from earlier, Dario's descent is a slow one. Not by design, but by necessity. Charlie holds the base of his cock firm and upright as Dario takes all the time he needs to line himself up just right. The mouth stretch was easy. The hole stretch takes more patience.

Little by little, his body acclimates to Charlie. Lets him in.

Wasn't this whole contest about letting people in?

Fuck. He nailed it.

And Charlie is going to nail him.

Charlie's micro gasps become background vocals to the jump blues singer belting an up-tempo swing number in the distance.

A joy bomb goes off in Dario's pelvis when he reaches the base. An utter explosion of sensation speeds through his body. He has done this before but never has it felt this way. Like someone realized the painted-over switch on the wall isn't just for show and flicked it on, powering up a second generator nobody knew about. Energy courses through Dario with unthinkable pace.

He places his palms on Charlie's bare chest, arches his back and starts to bounce.

Charlie clutches his hips. Nails dig into his flesh the way

the tattoo needle did. The pierce of them only incites him to ride harder.

Charlie goes to speak but Dario stops him with a finger that he slides between Charlie's teeth. Charlie closes his lips around that finger and sucks on it, pokes his tongue out and licks into the cleft. Every time he surprises Dario with more vigor, Dario adds another finger. Four fingers in, he curls over his knuckle and holds on to the back of Charlie's teeth as leverage, like they're reins, and he rolls his hips forward and back. The muscles of Charlie's stomach spasm.

Tightening his grip on Charlie's cock, he pitches forward, removes his hand and kisses Charlie hard on the mouth. There's a primal hunger in it, like they've both discovered something predestined in their DNA.

As Dario bucks back, Charlie rears up to meet the thrusts. The opposing forces slam Dario's prostate, filling his body with thousands of popping candies. *Snap. Bang. Pow.*

When he grows tired of standing on his feet, he rests his knees on the sagging fabric chair. Charlie sits up and scoops Dario into his arms. In a feat of impressive flexibility and strength, he rolls up and sets Dario on his back, cock never leaving its cozy burrow inside Dario's ass. The experience is dizzying, but he stays along for the ride.

Charlie tunnels down, pounding him out almost in time to the far-off, pulsating music. The stars twinkle above them. None are as bright or as alluring as Charlie's eyes.

Dario yelps in pleasure. Charlie hooks his elbows around Dario's knees, drawing him closer as he plunges away, which pushes Dario into total-bliss territory. Drunk with pleasure, Dario pulls the skin back on the head of his uncut cock and teases himself, picks up a drop of precum on his pointer finger and feeds it to Charlie as fuel for more fucking. Faster fucking. Full-of-feelings fucking.

Dario half wishes Craig were still around to capture this on his professional camera. They could direct and star in the world's most scintillating porno. A clip that would break the internet. A clip Dario would rewatch repeatedly when horny with a desire to step back inside of the memory. Instead, he'll have to settle on storing this away in his mind for rainy days with his right hand.

Charlie loses steam, wiping a sheen of sweat off his forehead. "I need a small break, Candy Man."

Dario feels the loss as soon as Charlie pulls out. His lube-slick cock shines in the light. "Take a break. I want to have you for the long haul."

As these words clear his mouth, he can't deny their validity, nor can he deny that they stand for more than just tonight, this session. Two weeks of Charlie Moore would never be enough. He wants his body to be Charlie's sexual outlet and second tattoo canvas. He wants his heart to be Charlie's place to call home. He wants his literal home, Villa Meraviglia, to hold Charlie's belongings. But not just his belongings—the sketchpads and Nike socks and hair dye. But also his laugh and his mischief and his stories. One day, potentially, his family members—should they be willing to move across the world.

The romance of it all is a lost Caravaggio masterpiece found in the dusty vault of Dario's heart set out on a museum display. He can see it so clearly now for both its light and its shadow.

"I need you inside me again," Dario says not even five minutes later. His erection rages on, and the beauty of his home country works its magic on him. Charlie smiles as he sets down his water glass and meets Dario over at the terrace ledge.

Dario turns to the railing, gazes out at the lake and bends slightly at the waist. Charlie enters him again. His gasp at the sudden impalement gets stolen by the night. He grips the warm iron bar as Charlie ramps back up to speed.

Charlie pulls him close by the sensitive underside of his neck then runs his tongue along the nape of it, tasting the sweat collecting there. Dario twists his head so they can kiss in the moonlight. Shadows cover half of Charlie's face, and still, it's the handsomest face he's ever beheld. The world blurs from the constant push and retreat of Charlie's cock in his ass.

"I want you to fill me, Charlie," Dario eggs on. "Leave me dripping. Unload inside me."

"Okay, Candy Man. Any second now you'll get your filling."

The silliest of sentences can be the sexiest when lost in the hedge maze of amazing sex. Dario's cheeks and Charlie's balls clap together, echoing in the night, like premature applause for a set that hasn't ended yet.

Dario jerks his own cock in his hand, tension mounting. "I'm right there," he whispers in exquisite agony.

"I'm right there with you." Charlie groans deep, plunges deeper.

Charlie crosses the finish line first. The hot expulsion rippling through Dario prompts an exceptional orgasm of his own. Quivering and legs nearly giving out, he spills all over the tile on the terrace as Charlie pumps one final time inside him.

The musicians playing at the fortress conclude their set to a thunderous reception. Cheers crackle through the night, giving way to chants of "Encore! Encore!" Charlie leans in and whispers, "If they insist…"

Dario bites his lip and gears up for another round.

Twenty-Four

CHARLIE

The house on Cemetery Street looks different after some time away and especially from the back of a hired town car. Dario wouldn't hear of Charlie making his family pick him up from the airport, just as he wouldn't hear of Charlie flying economy home. "My soon-to-be fiancé deserves the best," he had said.

Charlie was amazed how differently you could be treated on the front side of a flimsy curtain. Complimentary champagne, a spacious seat that reclined all the way back, an eye mask and slippers, and food that actually tasted good. He could get used to these kinds of amenities.

Now he halts in the back seat, peering through the tinted window at the overgrown grass and landscaping showcased in the weak light that spills from the peeling windowpanes.

Two weeks seems such a short time when looking at a calendar, but Charlie feels a seismic change inside himself. Will his family notice the difference?

As he ventures up the front walk, he wishes Dario were beside him. Their parting outside Villa Meraviglia was mostly wordless and as bittersweet as an Amorina Indulgence bar, their dark chocolate with orange bitters artisan selection. As much as he longed to stay in the celebratory safety of Dario's Italian hilltop villa, his family needs him too much, and of course he missed them dearly, so he steps through the door.

In the entryway, his family holds up a poster that says, Welcome home, Charlie!

His heart squirms a little. Somehow, the house on Cemetery Street doesn't quite feel like home anymore. As they pass through the hallway and into the kitchen where a BBQ dinner is already laid out to be eaten, something seems off, and it's not only his father's distant indifference. These people are still his people, but perhaps this place is no longer his place.

They gather around the table. While he loved Paola's cooking, he missed Dad's BBQ. Corn on the cob gets passed alongside baked beans and chuck burgers. Charlie slathers his with barbeque sauce and frizzled onions. The all-American flavors he didn't know he missed until now.

Sitting back at his usual chair, he can't help but feel he dreamed up the last two weeks. How could something so spectacular have happened to someone who comes from this? The wooden table they eat at has a wobbly leg and the plates they use are dollar-store paper. The chandelier overhead has a lightbulb that's been burnt out for several months. The windows are thrown open to let in a cross breeze because even in the evening the Pennsylvania humidity wreaks havoc that their ancient AC system can't mitigate.

Throughout the meal, he regales them with tales of Europe. In his sketchbook, he drew pictures of monuments and dishes he enjoyed. It's what he's got in place of photographs. He lost all of those to The Great Phone Fall at the well in Perugia. He never wanted to pay for cloud storage. Now he regrets it.

Though, in a way, the sketches are more indicative of his time in Umbria. His perspective shines through in every stroke of his pencil in a way his phone camera could've never captured.

"Is this the Cotogna boy?" Grandpa asks, tapping on a face within the pages.

It occurs to Charlie as his family flips through his doodles that he drew a lot of Dario. Dario captaining his boat. Dario lying out beside the swimming hole on Isola Polvese. Dario teaching chocolate making in that silly chef's hat. Dario Cotogna might be the muse of all muses.

"Yes," he says, trying not to be embarrassed.

"Quite the looker," Grandma says. "You can tell you really love him by the way you have captured him."

When the sketchbook is returned to him, he stares at the drawings and considers what Grandma said. He was willing to enter a loveless marriage for money because he'd never been in love before. It was an intangible idea hovering way out of reach. He didn't know what it felt like or how it changed you. But it's clear now by the drumming of his pulse and the racing of his heart that he's in love with Dario Cotogna, and that nothing will ever be the same.

Charlie smiles and doesn't negate the sentiment nor confirm it. The first time he uses the l-word should be with Dario. "I can't wait for you all to meet him."

"So he's coming, then?" Dad asks. Only the second thing he's said since "Hello, Charlie."

Charlie nods, heart abuzz. "In a couple weeks. He had some work to attend to, but once he has that settled, he will come out. He is really excited to meet you all." Over his half-eaten corncob, he adds, "I hope you'll give him a chance."

"Of course we will," Grandpa says, sounding light.

Dad gives a gruff, slow nod that's at least better than a "no way."

Behind the glass of the liquor store, Charlie sketches away. Italy inspired him to keep working on his craft.

Lost in a design, he barely notices his phone vibrating. He pops in one earbud and is surprised to hear Dario's dulcet voice. "It's two in the morning. What are you doing up?"

"I'm too excited to sleep." Dario arrives later this week. "I did it! I spent nine hours on the jet without a single panic attack. I slept, I did paperwork, I answered calls. I got my backup prescription filled just in case. I think this is all going to work."

Throughout the week, Charlie received updates. Photos pinged in of Dario packing a bag, driving to the tarmac and loading his luggage on the jet even though there was no pilot aboard. Dario's therapist told him to think of it like a rehearsal. The more prepared you are, the less the unexpected can faze you.

"Proud of you, Candy Man," Charlie says, smiling, knowing he shouldn't be taking a call while working, but he already put in his two weeks' notice to his boss. To say the least, he did not take it well, but Charlie couldn't care in the slightest.

"Grazie." He beams. "I'm proud of me, too."

He wishes he could crush Dario's handsome face with a kiss.

"How is your family?" Dario asks.

"My grandparents are thrilled to meet you, my dad is cagey about the whole thing, and my mom is holding the middle ground," he says.

Things in the house on Cemetery Street have been tense. The court sent a notice of the foreclosure proceedings. They have twenty days to contest or accept. Everyone tries to act normal and prepare for Dario's visit.

Grandma has been trying to clean. Charlie has been cleaning up after her attempts when she's not around. Dad has been pretending it's not happening. Mom has been inquiring after every one of Dario's food preferences, so the house is well-stocked because that's the best way she knows to show she cares.

"It is good to know what I'll be walking into," Dario says darkly.

"It's some ivory tower mentality bullshit that I know he'll get over once he meets you," Charlie says, and then a thought pops into his head. "Do you own clothes that aren't five-piece suits?"

"Of course… Somewhere…" On the screen, Dario peers around his bedroom.

"Just curious. Slatington is not the kind of place where formal wear is seen outside of funerals." Charlie witnessed a lot of those as a child from the upstairs windows. Hearses were more common on his street than ice cream trucks. "But come in what makes you feel good. I want you to be comfortable."

"You make me feel comfortable, Charlie. If jeans and boots will go over better, I'll get Gabriele on it right away," Dario says. "Getting there is the hard part, so once I'm there I don't want anything standing in the way of your family getting to know me."

A person stands in the light Charlie has been using to sketch and clears his throat. Charlie looks up from his page to see a veritable ghost from his past on the other side of the glass. Max has gotten taller. His face is rounder, and his dark brown hair is shaggier. A patchy beard takes up most of his face but there are red splotches that appear to be ingrown hairs, angry as if his face is rejecting the look.

They don't speak. Not at first. They're clearly both trying to figure out if they can pretend they don't know each other.

"Dario, I'm going to have to call you back. I have a customer. Get some sleep. Sweet dreams," he says.

"Buona notte."

The call clicking off in his earbud sends a chill down his spine.

"Hey, there, Charlie," Max says in a low, raspy voice that's unrecognizable from the one he had at eighteen. Slatington is a small town, so they've run into each other here and there, but they've always maintained a safe, unspeakable distance. "I didn't think you worked here anymore. Didn't I read somewhere you won a contest to stay with an Italian prince?"

"Still here and still working," Charlie says, unbothered with correcting him about the prince thing when he's this thrown off guard. His eyes track back down to the wedding band on Max's hand, slowly enough that Max catches it.

"You got married?" Charlie asks.

"Oh, ha, yeah." He waves his hand as if he forgot all about it. "Thought you might've seen it on Freida's social media."

"Was she in the wedding party?" Charlie asks. A self-consciousness he thought he once shed zips up around him. Makes him feel trapped.

Max's face turns a shade of red that camouflages his acne scars. "Oh, no, ah, she's my wife."

The news that his former friend and his former secret boyfriend are married and living back in Slatington lands with a splat. "I see. Congrats. When was this?"

"A year ago?" Max says, sounding nearly uncertain.

"Cool," Charlie says.

"Yeah."

Awkwardness pulses through the air.

"Could you grab me a vape refill from back there?" he asks, eyes trained beyond Charlie.

Charlie moves on autopilot, pulling down the pink lemonade flavor. He recalls Max downing icy cups full of the sugary drink during summer months as they loitered at the old quarry. Funny how a decade can pass, your attitude can change, and yet a single person can still fling you back like a computer retrograding through old operating systems.

The pinch of Charlie's shoulders and the sting in his sinuses makes him wonder if he ever quite shed the feeling of being eighteen alone on a porch hoping his best friend/secret boyfriend would tell him it's all been a big misunderstanding. Max standing here now is a symbol of everything Charlie couldn't move past while stuck in this one-horse town.

"Haven't had this flavor in a while," Max says, mouth curving up. Charlie wonders what else Max *hasn't had in a while.* His cheeks heat with the memory of school nights in the shed behind his house. What it felt like to finally kiss and connect with a boy.

For a few years after, Charlie convinced himself he imagined everything between them. That Freida had been right. That's how he sort of felt about his time in Italy, too. But that was easier to prove. All he needed to do was lift his shirtsleeve and see the tattoo there to know someone on the other side of the world was thinking of him and holding him in his heart.

"Your arm okay?" Max asks.

Charlie had not realized he was rubbing the spot where the eye candy tattoo is. "Yeah, all good. Cash or card?"

Max taps his credit card to the reader while Charlie bags up the beer and the vape juice. Questions swirl through his mind then disintegrate to mental dust. It is not his business if Max is living an authentic life married to Freida. It is not his concern if Max is happy.

In his head, he had imagined this moment countless times in those years following high school graduation. There were so many colorful and creative ways he could tell Max off for hurting him.

But he looks at Max now, shaky fingers punching in his pin number on the keypad, and all he sees is a scared boy in the body of a man. Saying any of those things, dredging up the junk from the basement, would only clutter Charlie's own mental space again.

He will not let the bank take his house, he will not let his dad take his happily-ever-after, and he will not let Max take his peace of mind.

"Take care of yourself," Charlie says, pushing the goods back through the window.

In a neater version of this situation, Max might have reached for the bag and then stopped himself, taken a breath, and acknowledged how he acted all those years ago. But not all love interests are heroes. Not all relationships get happy endings.

Charlie doesn't even get a "You, too."

All he receives is a head nod and a receipt with Max's signature on it.

For a moment, he stares at the still-childish scrawl of Max's script and wonders if like Slatington, Max has stilled in time.

The beating of Charlie's heart reminds him that he is anything but frozen. He is hot-blooded and running toward a brighter future with Dario Cotogna.

Twenty-Five

DARIO

The Cotogna family private jet sits fueled up on a tarmac ready to ferry Dario to America and into the waiting arms of Charlie Moore.

Dario Cotogna sits in the back of the idling town car with cement bricks for feet. He has made no move to exit the vehicle, even as Fabrizio shoots him questioning looks through the rearview mirror.

In his hand, he clutches his phone. On the screen, a text from Charlie reads: I can't wait to kiss you <3

Earlier, he received a text from his mom: Have a safe trip. Text me when you land. Give my love to Charlie and our soon-to-be family-in-law.

He counts his inhales but every one of them gets caught up in his throat. Every signal his brain sends his muscles to move is counteracted on by a second contradictory signal of DANGER! DANGER! DANGER!

He did everything his therapist told him to. He rehearsed. Every night before bed he meditated on the ideal outcome. He even dry-swallowed one of his as-needed anxiety pills.

He'd run through the same steps to attend the blues festival with Charlie.

Maybe therein lies the issue.

Charlie is not here.

Charlie is waiting on a different continent.

Charlie is going to be disappointed if he doesn't get his act together.

A cascade of anxiety drenches Dario in the back seat. His mind waterboards him with the worst thoughts it can stream. *You're not brave enough. You're not good enough. You're not well enough.*

That's the rub about recovery, it is not linear, and it can boomerang at the worst moments.

Before he fully registers what he is doing, he sends a text to Charlie with a simple I'm sorry.

His hands cramp as *sorry* slinks through his veins. He's sorry to Charlie, sorry to his nonno, sorry to Amorina. Most of all, he feels sorry for himself.

Right as he is about to instruct Fabrizio to take him home, a bright red sports car speeds onto the tarmac. It screeches to a halt and the driver steps out.

Squinting against the sun, Dario can just make out the shape of Emilio hurtling toward the car. Is he imagining this? The wrap of Emilio's knuckle against the window tells him he's not.

Dario opens the window a crack and asks, "What are you doing here?"

"Saving your ass. Get out of the car," Emilio says.

His muscles clench. "I—I can't."

"What do you mean you can't?" Emilio asks, some of his impatience steaming off.

"I can't. I just can't, okay?" Dario whips his head away. He doesn't want his brother to see his flaming cheeks or his watery eyes. It was one thing to talk to his mom and Charlie about his agoraphobia. It's another thing to tell Emilio. He wouldn't understand. Emilio might even use his diagnosis against him to petition the Amorina board for control on the grounds that Dario is unfit to run the family business.

Emilio lets out an audible huff. "Slide over."

"What?"

"Slide. Over."

Begrudgingly, Dario does, even though he does not trust his brother's intentions in the least. These are the closest quarters he has shared with Emilio in a long while.

When he finally musters the courage to turn back, he hip-checks a designer duffel bag strewn on the seat between them. "What's that?"

"My stuff," Emilio says.

"Your stuff for what?" Dario asks.

"For the trip." Emilio stares at the rising partition that separates Fabrizio from them.

"What trip? You knew I was using the jet today," Dario says, running defensive as he always does with his brother.

"Oh, cazzo!" Emilio bangs his head back into his seat. "Can't you see I'm here to go with you? Fabrizio texted that you'd been sitting out here not moving for over an hour. The jet crew is ready to go. We're already screwing the environment by flying private. Let's not end up on one of those hit-list social media feeds for billionaire fuckwads that are escalating global warming. You of all people should care about that!"

Dario screws up his face in skepticism. "What's in America for you? Is this some plot to screw me over and get your mitts on Amorina?"

"Don't make me regret coming here," Emilio says, a tinge of genuine hurt in his words.

"Why *did* you come here?" Dario asks. His brain can only supply nefarious reasons.

"Because I figured you were scared! That Mom's touring and Dad's gone and Nonno and Nonna are gone and maybe you needed someone! Our ranks are fucking dwindling, and I don't know, I thought we could stick together for once but—oddio!—if you'd rather sit here boiling in this hot car alone all day and let your one chance at happiness and owning Amorina run off, then be my fucking guest," Emilio says, crossing his arms.

Despite Emilio's tone and the curse words, Dario is inordinately touched. His breathing slows, and his mind calms. This is almost definitely the most vulnerable his brother has been with him in...a decade?

While he has every reason to be wary of Emilio's dramatic behavior shift, he can't deny that Emilio's right. If Dario doesn't board that jet and soon, everything he's ever strived for—success, love, balance—will be lost for good. Dario had been wishing for a travel companion, and Emilio's offer is the best he's going to get.

Dario doesn't know what else to say, so all that comes out is, "Andiamo." Let's go.

Post-takeoff, sitting across from his brother in the tan leather reclining chairs, Dario gives in to the temptation of real conversation. He grips the armrests and asks, "Did you mean what you said back there about us sticking together?"

Emilio's gaze stays trained out the window. "Obviously."

"I didn't think it fazed you," Dario confesses as the flight attendant comes by with trays, meals and drinks for them.

"Just because I don't show it doesn't mean it doesn't faze me." He illustrates the sentiment when he finally meets Dario's eyes. There is an apathetic calm spread over his face—a stoic, masculine mask—but Dario sees a crack in it now.

Antagonism always seemed easier in the mired face of their differences.

"Mom told me about the…the…the thing you have. The anxiety thing. I don't remember the name. I called her before I drove over," Emilio says.

While Dario doesn't love that his mother shared this without his permission, sometimes, needs must. He gets that. "That was nice of you."

"I can be nice," he says. As if to prove his point, he gives Dario first dibs on the plate of bruschetta.

Dario picks a caper off his chicken and says, "What happened with Michelle?"

"We spent some time together and then she flew back to France. She's really sweet. Talented, too," Emilio says. Stripped of his usual bravado, he comes across as genuine.

"And Daniella…?" Dario asks, even though it might bungle the easy rhythm they seem to be falling into.

Emilio downs half his chicken in one bite. He chews, clearly stewing over this. "I want a divorce, but Daniella won't give me one."

Dario's head might explode from the news. "Che?"

"I know you and Mom don't want to hear this because you love her, but she's been cheating on me since we got married. I realized pretty quickly that she'd married me because she thought Nonno left me a lot in the will," Emilio says, wearing a pensive expression.

Dario refrains from saying that that doesn't sound like her because, what does he know? He's been absent from his brother's life for a while now. Social media posts and occasional text threads don't amount to the character of a person.

"That sounds tough," Dario says.

"It didn't bother me much at first, telling myself it was slip-ups because I wasn't around a lot or because we'd been to-gether a long time and I wasn't keeping it fresh, but then it continued happening, and I realized that maybe it was always about the money," he says. "I'm not stupid. I know our wealth is half the reason some women want to get with me. I didn't get Dad's looks like you did."

"What are you talking about?" Dario asks.

"Vaffanculo!" Emilio says with no bite. He even laughs a little. "Take the compliment. All I'm saying is that when I re-alized she was never going to change or be with me the way I want her to be, I told her I wanted a divorce, and she refused. Anything I inherit from Nonno once everything is cleared can be put in our joint account, which means she gets half if I were to leave her," Emilio says. "If I inherit Amorina, that half goes way up, but fuck that."

"Merda. That's awful. I'm sorry, Em," he says, wishing he'd been there for his younger brother earlier. "When you showed up at the villa with Craig, you made it seem like you wanted Amorina."

"I did that to piss you off. If you haven't noticed, I'm good at that," he says with a self-aware laugh. "I figured if I riled you up enough, you'd kick your ass into gear and get the fuck married. Saying it now, I know that it was selfish of me but I don't want to run Amorina. I've never wanted to run Amo-rina. I just pretended to so Daniella would get off my back and you'd get hitched."

"A devious plan but," Dario says, "I think it kind of worked?"

"I have good ideas every now and again."

"Coming here was a good idea. Thank you for that. I'm getting better, but I think I tried to rush it by going alone. You saved me back there. I appreciate it," he says. At over 31,000 feet in the air, having listened to his brother's woes, his problems down on the ground feel tiny in comparison.

"Don't mention it. You should probably get some sleep before we land. You look like shit," Emilio says, slapping his knee. "You need the energy to woo Charlie and his family."

Dario darts for his phone. "Charlie! Right before you showed up, I texted him. He probably thinks I'm not coming. He's probably a wreck." He frantically drafts a text that won't send. Airplane mode. He tries to switch to the Wi-Fi but it won't work. The flight attendant informs him that it's out of service and that they weren't able to fix it before takeoff.

Dario flops back in his chair. "Damn."

"Maybe Charlie is a big fan of surprises," Emilio offers.

Dario prays for that to be true.

Twenty-Six

CHARLIE

I'm sorry.

That's all the text says.

Charlie is sorry, too. Sorry for getting his hopes up. Sorry for believing love and change were possible for a guy like him. Sorry for telling his family when nothing was set in stone.

Every response text fails to send. Every voice call goes un-rung.

Is he being ghosted by a world-famous chocolate maker?

He fails not to look devastated over breakfast, which he barely touches. He stares into his watery Keurig coffee, watching as the creamer separates into clumps. His heart mirrors them, glopping off into tiny bits floating through the vacuous nothing of his body. On they swirl until—

"Charlie?" Mom asks.

"Huh?"

"The syrup. Can you pass the syrup?" she repeats.

He wakes up enough to perform the simple task that feels Herculean. What did they put in the bottle, cement?

Mom made pancakes. Dad griddled bacon. They both took paid days off from work to prepare the house for Dario's arrival tomorrow morning. Grandma and Grandpa were too excited not to be up, showered, dressed and ready to be wheeled to the kitchen table to share a rare morning meal together. It's a full house for the denouement, though it seems this isn't the comedy that ends in a wedding they all hoped it would be.

Charlie slaps a pad of butter in the center of his pancake stack. It melts and oozes off the sides.

Mom opens a window to dissipate the overwhelming scent of frying grease that the barely functioning stovetop fan couldn't handle. The early-morning air carries in the first traces of autumn—a nip and an earthy wetness. It mixes with the nearly tangible anticipation crowding the kitchen.

"Dario isn't coming anymore," Charlie says, unable to hold back for another second.

The room quiets save for Loretta Lynn crooning over the radio, a mid-tempo ditty about being a coal miner's daughter.

"What's happened, Charlie?" Grandpa asks.

Grandma clasps her hands together. "Is he in good health? Has something happened to Amorina?"

"I think so, and I don't think so, and I don't know what to think." His brain is as fried as the bacon.

"What did he say?" Mom asks, standing beside the sink.

"I'm sorry."

"Don't be sorry, Charlie. It's not your fault," Grandpa is quick to add.

Charlie shakes his head. "That's what he said, 'I'm sorry.' Nothing else."

"Why, that could mean anything!" Grandma says.

"Maybe there were other texts that didn't go through," Mom says.

Grandpa: "Perhaps that was meant for someone else."

Grandma: "What if he had gifts to bring you and he forgot them all, and that's what he's sorry about?"

"There will always be a million reasons to think the worst," Dad says, surprising everyone by jumping into the conversation. "If you can find even one reason to think the best, you can keep the faith."

For someone who didn't seem on board with having Dario come at all, he is the most helpful in leashing Charlie's worry, which follows him like a mangy, stray dog for the rest of the day.

Charlie goes to work as usual, figuring he's back to needing the income.

Is this what forever looks like for Charlie Moore? Sitting in a sagging chair behind a glass window selling alcohol in Slatington, Pennsylvania?

The Amorina bars have been restocked in the snack stand. Even after everything, they call to him. He exercises restraint. The taste alone would make him lose his hope, and maybe his mind. His father told him to be positive, so he will be.

In his sketchbook, instead of drawing, he writes up a list of all the things Dario could be sorry for instead of standing him up. As his spirits lift with every scribbled bullet point, a car drives up. Charlie is too focused to notice.

The click of dress shoes instead of boots on the cement floor is what pulls Charlie from his brainstorm.

"Charlie," Dario says, appearing in a five-piece suit before him.

Charlie leaps out of his booth and into the chocolate maker's arms. The firmness of his short king confirms he is not a fabrication of Charlie's flowery imagination. Dario Cotogna is in America, in his arms, where he said he'd be. *Where he belongs.*

"Your text—I thought—" Charlie can't form coherent sentences because the familiar smell of Dario's shampoo fills his nostrils.

"I should've never sent that. I had a moment of weakness. I'm so sorry, Charlie," Dario says. He holds Charlie tighter to punctuate his apology.

"What did you mean?" he asks.

Dario pauses. Charlie pushes a few strands of hair back behind Dario's ear so he can see his dashing face better. "I gave in to my anxiety for a moment before leaving. I needed a little push. Emilio came to do that for me," Dario says.

"Emilio?" Charlie asks, unable to conceal his surprise.

The tinted car window zips down behind them. Emilio waves. "Ciao, Charlie. Pretend I am not here!" The window slides right back up.

"I'm sorry if I scared you," Dario says.

"I thought 'I'm sorry' were the last two words you were ever going to say to me," Charlie admits. Good things can come and go so quickly, as he's learned. He didn't want to believe Dario could leave him like that. The situation with Max all over again.

"The whole flight here I was afraid you'd never speak to me," Dario says, hanging his head.

"With this face?" Charlie cups Dario's cheeks in his hands and lifts his gaze again. "Not a chance, Candy Man. I love you."

The words are sweeter than any Amorina bar ever could be. They taste like truth.

Dario beams, and Charlie can't help but squeeze his rosy cheeks. He takes on the appearance of a glubbing fish. An adorably glubbing fish who swam all the way upstream against the raging current of his mental health to be here. Right now. Charlie swans in and kisses him, his brave little chocolatier.

"Ti amo, Charlie. I love you, too," Dario says with his whole chest. They kiss again.

"My shift ends in a half hour," Charlie says, glancing at the clock.

"Are you going to give me a tour then?" Dario asks, gesturing around.

Charlie honks out a laugh. "This is it. It's not going to be much of a tour."

"I gave you a tour of the Amorina Factory," Dario says.

Charlie shrugs. "Fair is fair, I guess."

He points out all the different merchandise—the beer fridge, the seltzer fridge, the shelves of hard liquor. They pass by the self-serve ICEE machines that slosh radioactive-looking drinks around.

"This is the snack shelf where I get my Amorina bars." Charlie dances his fingers over the surface. He loves the oh-so-familiar feel of that shiny wrapping.

Dario lifts the bar off the top and announces he would like to purchase it. Charlie rings it up. The heart in the Amorina logo means more to him now that he has captured the real heart of a Cotogna.

Dario makes a yikes face when he peers into his wallet. "You don't happen to take euros, do you?"

"This one's on me," Charlie says with a wink.

"Shall we share it?" Dario asks, waggling the bar in the air.

"I'd like that," Charlie says.

"Can't I come back there?" Dario asks. "I came all this way and now there's a wall between us."

Charlie points to a sign plastered on the door that says EMPLOYEES ONLY. "Sorry I don't make the rules."

Dario leans in conspiratorially. "If I have anything to say about it, you won't be an employee here much longer, so maybe you can bend the rules this one time."

"Excellent counterpoint." Charlie rolls his chair across the floor and unlocks the door.

A couple weeks have passed, yet their bodies remember what it's like to be in a small space together. A wire runs between them, creating a feedback loop of electricity powering their hearts. The charge is much too great to ignore.

Dario unwraps the Amorina bar. In Charlie's mind, the chocolate bar is Dario, and the wrapping is Dario's clothes. He is overwhelmed by lust and love for this miraculous man who made it all the way to America to propose. There will be a ring, and a wedding, and a whole lot of change, but right now, there needs to be sex. Sex with the man he *loves*.

Dario breaks off a piece of the chocolate bar and holds it out to Charlie. Tipping forward, Charlie takes the entire square in his mouth. His lips graze over Dario's long, outstretched fingers. He leaves the chocolate in his mouth to liquefy, then shares it with Dario through a soft, sensual kiss.

It dribbles a bit down Dario's smooth chin. A single drop lands on his crisp white shirt. Charlie regrets his actions, aware he's ruined a one-of-a-kind garment. But Dario smiles and shakes his head. His eyes beam a message: *I have other shirts, but there is only one you and there is only right now.*

Needfully, Charlie takes Dario by the lapel. Charlie sinks onto the counter in a seated position, and he draws Dario as close as possible with his calves. His ankles interlock behind Dario's waist. There is no denying that they just fit together.

Charlie guides him in by the back of his neck for another kiss.

"My brother can see us," Dario says.

"The windows are tinted," Charlie says. *Kiss. Nip. Lick.*

"That only means we can't see in," Dario says.

Charlie laughs at himself, then leans back and pulls a cord. Wonky blinds plink into place.

"Better?" Charlie asks.

"Much." Dario pitches in for a kiss that gets walled by a loud stomach gurgle.

"Hungry?" Charlie asks.

"Starved," Dario admits.

Charlie bites his lip as he breaks off a piece of chocolate, waves it under Dario's button nose. "Want it?" he asks.

Dario salivates and nods.

Charlie wastes no time fishing his erection out of his shorts. "Beg for it, Candy Man."

Dario slips down onto his knees. His slacks slip up his legs a bit, giving Charlie a view of the garters holding up his semi-sheer dress socks.

Fuck. Charlie never realized calf belts could make his dick throb. He hops down off the counter. With his erection pointing straight out, he balances the bit of chocolate on top of his rock-hard shaft. "Mangia," Charlie instructs.

In the blink of an eye, Dario takes Charlie between his lips and carefully scrapes his upper teeth down his length to retrieve the chocolate. The sensation causes Charlie's knees to buckle. He grips the counter behind him for support.

Dario sits back on his haunches and savors the chocolate. It's simultaneously the cutest and most erotic sight Charlie has ever seen. Half of him wants to take Dario by the scruff of the neck and face fuck him into next week. The other half wants to hold him close and frot with him until they both cum buckets.

Dario licks his fingers clean, then says with a naughty smile, "I'm still hungry."

God, he could do a backflip over how happy he is to have Dario back in his life, back in his space.

"Come here, Candy Man." Charlie beckons him with a finger and a pulse of his cock. "I've got just the thing to satisfy you."

Dario barely gags as Charlie thrusts into his mouth. Charlie clutches the threadbare fabric of his work shirt in the center of his chest. He looks forward to stripping it off one final time and instead of throwing it in the hamper, throwing it straight into the trash bin.

Dario grips Charlie's covered ass, tugging him toward him, faster and harder. The tip of Charlie's dick pummels the back of Dario's throat.

Dario glances up with an innocent and pleased glint in his eyes. It is preposterous how handsome the chocolate maker looks with a mouthful of dick. He ruffles Dario's hair, delighting in the unwashed silkiness of the strands.

Dario stands to pull his well-proportioned, uncut cock free. Charlie lines up their dicks so they are one on top of the other. He slicks them with spit and, using both hands, creates a tunnel for them to thrust into. Back and forth like a double-cut saw.

They kiss, and Charlie can taste both the Amorina chocolate and his own cock on Dario's tongue. If only it were appropriate to package and market that combination of flavors. He'd fucking buy in bulk.

"Don't miss your snack," Charlie says as a general warning.

Dario bends down and works the swollen, sensitive head of Charlie's cock into his mouth again. In under a minute, Charlie shoots four pent-up ropes of protein down Dario's throat. The candy man gulps it all down without wasting a single drop.

Smiling, Dario stands and starts putting his cock away.

"What about you?" Charlie asks through his post-orgasm fog, to which Dario shakes his head.

"I got what I wanted," Dario says. "Andiamo. There's a hotel bed waiting for us. Maybe you've got another round in you."

Charlie wraps a possessive arm around Dario's waist and nips at the tip of his warm, pink ear. "There's no maybe, Candy Man. I've got as many rounds as you need."

Dario twirls inside Charlie's arm so they are chest to chest. "Time to clock out?"

Miraculously, it is.

"Have your driver pull out into the lot so I can close up. I'll be ten minutes, max," Charlie says.

Dario smushes the tips of their noses together. Charlie has never been more certain that those are the eyes he wants to see every night before he shuts off the lights and goes to sleep. Those are the eyes of his dreams.

Loath to have Dario anywhere but at his side, Charlie makes quick work of shutting down the machines, locking the fridges and counting out the register. The little red lights on the motion-sensor security cameras blink each time he passes as if giving him a final salute.

After unpinning his name tag and dropping it on the desk, he grabs a piece of computer paper from the funky printer. It takes him three tries before he grabs a working pen, but once he does, he has no hesitation about writing the date and time, and then: *I quit, effective immediately.—Charlie Moore*

Before exiting, he takes an empty envelope from the box under the desk. He hums Loretta Lynn as he exits the garage and pulls the gate down. Once locked, he slips his keys into the envelope and sails his past through the mail slot.

Twenty-Seven

CHARLIE

When Dario emerges from the bathroom in the hotel room the next morning, Charlie lets out a gasp. He barely recognizes him. "You're wearing...*jeans*."

"Too casual?" Dario asks, checking himself out in the mirror affixed to the wall opposite the bathroom. Charlie gives him his own once-over. He has on a button-up shirt, a seafoam green blazer, jeans and...cowboy boots.

"Not at all, but maybe let's lose the boots? This isn't horse country," he says with an unflattering laugh.

"Will loafers do?" Dario asks, pulling a pair of shiny brown leather shoes from a travel bag inside his suitcase.

"Loafers are perfect. Is the driver outside?" Charlie asks, slipping into his own orange Vans. He texted his family after his shift last night and his mom offered to bring him stuff if he needed, but he refused, not willing to waste a second of his private evening with Dario. Today, he borrows one of Dario's

T-shirts that is too short and a pair of his underwear which is too luxe, but who cares?

As the town car pulls away from the chain hotel several towns over, Dario muses, "America looks different than I remember. In my mind, America is the Empire State Building, the Golden Gate Bridge, and that strange Bean out in Chicago that never fails to make me think of a robot's…" He blushes without finishing his sentence.

Charlie's hands turn clammier the closer they get to the house on Cemetery Street. Last night, it was easy to shuck his clothes and reservations, but today his two worlds collide. The results better be warm and fuzzy instead of fiery and devastating.

"What's in the bag?" Charlie asks to distract himself. Dario brought a zipped-up, designer messenger bag with him.

"You'll see," Dario says, the corners of his lips moving upward.

Five minutes out, Charlie psychs Dario up. "Don't be nervous, okay? I mean, I know that's bad advice, but seriously? They are such kindhearted people who have been through a lot. I swear they are going to be chill. The house has been cleaned within an inch of its life."

Charlie hesitates at the door. Never has this happened before. He is unsure whether to knock or check the knob or use his key. Dario decides for him. A swift knock is followed by an opening of the door. "Buon giorno. Is anybody home?"

Rustling is heard from down the hall. Chairs scrape and papers settle and then all four of the Moores appear in the cramped entryway appearing all kinds of excited.

"Ciao. I am Dario," he extends a hand to Mom first.

"Ellen," she says.

He goes around, saving Dad for last. Charlie holds his

breath. "It is a pleasure to meet you. You have a wonderful home and a wonderful son."

Dario gives him a firm handshake, which goes a long way. A portion of the judgment Dad was clinging to visibly disappears.

"I've brought gifts," Dario announces.

Charlie shrinks away a bit. His father is skittish about gifts and "handouts."

Dario opens his bag and produces five custom Amorina Chocolate bars. The flavor is listed as Amore Moore. Dark chocolate is infused with whiskey and has a layer of caramel inside. "Charlie said that you two used to carry around pocketfuls of hard caramel candies when he was a kid," he says to Charlie's grandparents, then turning to Mom and Dad, "and that you two enjoy whiskey, so I had the artisan chocolate makers in my shop craft these especially for you."

Grandpa is the first to tear into his, but it's Grandma who reads the love note inside since she has her glasses on and can see the small text. Immediately, she tears up.

Charlie steps closer to her wheelchair. He asks, "What does it say?"

Grandma reads aloud, "I hear love in every step when I walk beside you."

"From your card to me," Grandpa says. "How did you—"

"Charlie shared it with me. I hope that's all right," Dario says, bowing with respect.

"This is extremely thoughtful," Mom says.

"Not to mention delicious," Grandpa says, having bitten off a big hunk of the corner. He chews around the words.

"I am glad you think so." Dario beams at them.

"Have you eaten yet?" Dad asks, clearing his throat. He keeps his eyes down on the chocolate bar as if it were a priceless heirloom recovered after centuries.

"We have not," Dario says.

"I'll make French toast," Dad announces before heading toward the kitchen.

Mom follows close behind him to help. Charlie pushes Grandpa's wheelchair toward the kitchen.

"May I?" Dario asks Grandma Opal, moving in behind her chair and gripping the handles.

"I'd be delighted if you would," she replies. "You must have made quite the impression. French toast is Charlie's father's specialty, but he rarely makes it."

"What a treat!" Grandpa peers back and winks. "You done good, boy."

Dario looks to Charlie with an *Is that right?* expression on his face. All Charlie can do is lean in and kiss his cheek.

DARIO

The next day, Dario and Charlie pile into the truck and drive out to the Slate Heritage Trail. Grandpa Al is in his prosthetic, and Grandma Opal is having one of her good days, so she just brought her cane along.

The blacktop trail runs alongside the old Lehigh Valley Railroad, which Dario learns used to be the primary mode of transport for the region's slate. They stay to the left of the wooden fences erected along the tall trees. Squeaking squirrels cut across their path.

Every so often a sign marking a historic place or noting an interesting factoid pops up. Dario stops off to read all of them, not out of obligation, but because he is interested. He strives to understand the Moores, and where Charlie came from, despite the tiredness searing a bit behind his eyes.

On top of the jet lag and the time difference, Dario spent the night crowded beside Charlie on the Moores' couch. It wasn't planned that way. He had meant to go back to the hotel after a glorious BBQ dinner—ribs and burgers and corn on the cob. The American flavors sang for him.

Afterward, Grandma Opal asked if anyone was up for a game. They taught him how to play gin rummy with a stack of old, weathered playing cards. The competitive spirit possessed them all, and they ended up playing well into the night, all of them laughing despite Dario never winning a single round.

By the time they called it quits, it was late, and Dario was half-asleep, and even the fifteen-minute drive to his hotel felt like too much of a chore.

Halfway through the walk, which runs a little over a mile, Dario turns from a placard at a covered bridge and only Mr. Moore is left standing there. The others have gone on ahead.

"Thank you for being kind to Charlie," Mr. Moore says, clearly segueing into a larger topic. "He tells us you looked out for him in Italy, and I appreciate that."

"It was my pleasure," Dario says. They fall into step with one another.

"I'm sorry if I came across like a hard-ass. This all comes as somewhat of a shock to us. Charlie has only ever lived under our roof and has never really dated anyone. For him to win a contest and suddenly go off to another country, I think we— me most of all—were a bit thrown for a loop," he says, scratching at his chin. "If my son had to win a contest to meet the bachelor of a chocolate fortune, I suppose I'm glad you were the bachelor."

"Thank you," Dario says, taking it as a compliment. Up ahead, Charlie glances over his shoulder. His lips are tipped into the tiniest smile. "I understand where you were coming from. I myself did not want to believe my nonno had set this whole scheme up for me, but I discovered it was his way of pushing me out of my comfort zone and back into the world. I can't run a company from my bedroom. Charlie has been immensely supportive by helping me find my peace and confidence again."

"That sounds like our Charlie. Always helping," Mr. Moore says with a proud grin. Dario registers the paternal resemblance in the set of his eyes.

"In Italian, we say 'La famiglia è tutto'—family is everything. I believe that. I lost my father as a teenager, my grandmother as a university student, and my grandfather earlier this year. I think this contest was also a way of reminding me that family means more than blood," Dario says, ruminating on this.

"That's quite nice," Mr. Moore says. He exhales loudly. "I just worry—" He scrapes a hand over his face. "Marriage? You barely know each other. I'm sure Charlie never mentioned about his uncle, but a while back—"

Mr. Moore goes on to tell his side of the story. Of the lawsuit and the settlement and the stolen money. Dario takes it in as if this is new information because it feels like Mr. Moore needs to get this out there to someone outside their immediate circle, and Dario senses them connecting on a deeper level as he speaks. It was something he learned early from his grandfather, that listening is one of the greatest gifts you can give another.

"I'm sorry that happened," Dario says.

"I'm sorry for ever letting that kid anywhere near that bank account. I can usually smell a rancid fish from a mile away. Suddenly, I was nose blind. Do you see what I mean?" Mr. Moore asks.

"You're afraid Charlie will get cheated," Dario says. "That is the farthest thing from my intention."

"And we don't want Charlie moving a million miles away and never visiting us again. If there's even a place for him to come back and visit," he says darkly, glancing out into the trees that are beginning to change.

The yellowing leaves remind him that seasons come and go like people, but Dario intends to stay no matter the weather.

"I would never dream of separating you all from Charlie. We would work that out. All of us, together. I am about to become the head of a worldwide chocolate operation, I know a thing or two about negotiation and compromise," Dario says, trying to sound assured but not boastful.

"I could use a lesson or two," Mr. Moore says reflectively.

"Charlie told me all about the bank and the house. I am fully prepared to assist however I can," Dario says.

Mr. Moore cringes. "Do you really want to take that on?" he asks.

"To me, it is not taking it on. It is sharing the burden. I have the means to help, so I will help. That is what my nonno taught me to do. Business was never about hoarding wealth. It was about making something that brought joy to the world and enriched people's lives," he says.

"While I agree that that's lovely, it's not a world I know or understand. Here, in my world, when you do something for somebody, that somebody expects something in return. What do you get from this other than inheriting Amorina with a legal marriage license?" he asks.

"I hope that I get more family," Dario says from the heart.

Mr. Moore stops in his tracks, really inspects Dario's face. "This isn't all some big marketing charade to sell chocolate? You're not going to make Charlie sign some ridiculous pre-nup and then piss off in six months?"

"I can assure you, sir. There will be no prenups and no pissing off. I love Charlie, and I'd like to make him—and by extension, you all—my family." Dario stands firm behind this statement. Because love, no matter how it comes about, is a gamble. Dario's lost it all before and rebuilt himself. He could do it again if he needed to. Even when his head replays memories of Preston as warnings, his heart reminds him that he's safe with Charlie.

Something breaks—in a good way—inside Mr. Moore. Feelings flood his face until he is crushing Dario in a hug. A dad hug. The kind of hug Dario hasn't had since he was a child. At that, something good breaks inside him, too. A tiny damn of grief gives way to a rushing river of emotion that he finally has a paddle for.

"Everything okay back here?" It's Charlie come to check on them.

Dario peels back and looks at the tearstained Mr. Moore. He nods at him. "Va bene," Dario says. "Lead on."

Twenty-Eight

DARIO

A chocolate maker and a soon-to-be tattoo apprentice walk into a courthouse.

This sounds like the start of a joke, but rather, it is the start of a lifetime.

The late-August heat gives way to strong air-conditioning as they march, hand in hand, toward the Marriage License Office. They have an appointment, both with an official there and with their future.

Mr. and Mrs. Moore along with Grandpa Al and Grandma Opal all come as witnesses wearing their best dress. Emilio, who dashed off to New York for most of the week to meet with some friends and begin the legal process for his divorce, returns in the nick of time to hold up his phone; his mother shines on video chat from a bustling dressing room in some other country, looking the part of the happy diva, exclaiming,

"Please don't make me cry too much. I don't want to have to redo my show makeup before the opening scene."

The plain room and the monotoned officiant do nothing to mire the happiness sparkling within his chest. How could they when he's entrapped by Charlie's already gleaming eyes?

His tattooed American cleaned up nicely. There was no time to rush-order him a Gabriele tux or get Michelle's design custom-made, so Charlie borrowed one of his dad's old black suits that somehow fits him perfectly. He dyed his hair back to blond. Crouched over the bathroom sink, he said, "I don't want to cringe when I look at our wedding photos ten years from now."

A warmth seeped through Dario at that. Charlie imagined revisiting photos from this day ten years from now, and envisioned them still happy and in love. That meant the world to him.

Even he had to settle on whatever he packed for what was meant to be a brief trip to America. Never did he imagine wearing jeans to his wedding, but the casualness seemed all too fitting, for he was done keeping himself always buttoned up and cordoned off. From this day forward, he shows the world the Dario underneath it all.

"Do you, Dario Cotogna, take Charlie Moore as your lawful, wedded husband?"

"Si. Lo voglio. I do," Dario says with a smile.

"Do you, Charlie Moore, take Dario Cotogna as your lawful, wedded husband?"

Charlie grips Dario's hands tighter. "I do."

"And now, with the power vested in me by the Commonwealth of Pennsylvania, I pronounce you partners. You may kiss."

The pronouncement may come out lifeless, but their kiss is anything but. It says everything they would've said to each other in vows they didn't have time for in the fifteen minutes allotted for the ceremony. Who cares? This no-frills, no-flash wedding rings more authentic than any big party ever could have.

Sometimes, the simplest recipe yields the sweetest results.

Epilogue

CHARLIE

Two years later

The house on Cemetery Street no longer stands on Cemetery Street.

Board by board, window by window, it was deconstructed, driven, sailed and shipped to a scenic hilltop in the village of Montecolognola, in the province of Perugia, Italy. The Moore family's new address.

After Dario settled affairs with the bank and permanently moved back into Villa Meraviglia, they tore down the barn house and replaced it with an utterly American-style home with origins in Slatington, Pennsylvania. Of course, it looks a little different now since not every piece could be salvaged, and all the appliances are now in tip-top working order, but it has the same bones, the same heart.

Turns out, it was never the house Charlie was determined

to save when he entered that contest years ago. It was home, and home always will be wherever his family is.

Today, they all gather in a tent staked into the lawn between the two houses—both alike in dignity—to celebrate their second wedding anniversary.

The table is laid with an impressive spread. Paola and her staff ensure no dish is ever empty. Charlie gives her air kisses as she flies past. He still does not understand how such an old woman can move so speedily.

Mom and Dad sit near the head of the table still in their Amorina polos. They would not dream of early retirement—both making quips about idle hands—so they settled on factory floor manager and tourism admin roles respectively.

Grandpa comes out from the house in his new prosthetic, fitted and more high-functioning than any he has had before. "Did you start without me?" he asks.

"We got hungry," says Grandma, who feeds herself a hearty arancini. After the move to Italy and with the right care team, Grandma's symptoms have abated. No more bibs or Charlie cutting up her food. Her restored autonomy has made her happier than ever.

"Can somebody pass the olive oil?" asks Michelle as she takes a piece of fresh bread from the basket Emilio hands her. They reconnected post-divorce and post-graduation, and she might be wearing one of her own wedding dress designs down the aisle in the near future.

Populating the far end of the table are Beau and Selina. Bygones are bygones.

Beau gave up his obsession with challenges and job shifts as soon as he started playing the blues. He became a permanent member of the band he performed with two years ago and comes to stay at Villa Meraviglia any time a European tour passes through.

Selina's online fame brought new recognition to Gabriele Vitale's expert tailoring, so she and Dario crossed paths quite a bit over the past two years. They buried the hatchet, and while it's not exactly a close friendship, their connection remains strong over their love of finely crafted menswear.

"Anyone seen Dario?" Charlie asks, finding his seat at the crowded table.

"Sono proprio qui!" he calls. *I am right here.* Charlie is crushing his Italian lessons. Though having your sexy husband as a teacher can be quite distracting at times, especially when they get to the more romantic words and phrases. "I was helping Mamma with something."

Dario kisses Charlie as they sit.

Holding a microphone, April appears on the pool deck in a stage light Charlie had no idea was set up. Behind her, a pianist sits at a keyboard he's never seen. "Before we eat, I would like to say a huge congratulations to Dario and Charlie on two years of wedded bliss. An extra congratulations to Charlie, who just two days ago did his first flash design as a newly minted tattoo artist."

Charlie smiles as he earns a round of applause. Marcella made good on her promise to take him on as an apprentice. While it was slow-going at first due to their language barrier, they settled into a flow that worked for them.

"Can we see?" Emilio asks.

"I can show you all later," Dario says, leaning in and kissing Charlie on the cheek. Dario is both his muse and his canvas, at least the areas he can easily cover with his business attire.

"And, if I may," April says, calling the group back to her, "I'd like to dedicate a song to you both. It's an Italian American classic." The pianist does a little flourish. "If you know it, feel free to sing along."

The whole group gives out a delighted little gasp of recognition. April sings about the moon looking like pizza, then turns the microphone on the table.

They all sweetly shout back, "That's amore!"

★ ★ ★ ★ ★

Acknowledgments

Special thanks to the many people who made this book as sweet as can be: Samantha Fabien, John Jacobson, Stacy Boyd, Anna Kupstova, Mireille Harper, Robert Stinner, Melanie Magri, Alison Cochrun, Blake Waters, Susie Dumond, Stephanie Kersikoski, Kasee Bailey, Simone Richter, Laynie-Rose Rizer, Hannah Walker, Matt Chisling, Sara Quaranta, along with my parents, extended family, friends, and even my enemies (you know who you are). Lastly, to you, the readers new and old, grazie!

LET'S TALK

Romance

For exclusive extracts, competitions and special offers, find us online:

MILLS & BOON

THE HEART OF ROMANCE

A ROMANCE FOR EVERY READER

MODERN — Prepare to be swept off your feet by sophisticated, sexy and seductive heroes, in some of the world's most glamourous and romantic locations, where power and passion collide.

HISTORICAL — Escape with historical heroes from time gone by. Whether your passion is for wicked Regency Rakes, muscled Vikings or rugged Highlanders, awaken the romance of the past.

MEDICAL — Set your pulse racing with dedicated, delectable doctors in the high-pressure world of medicine, where emotions run high and passion, comfort and love are the best medicine.

Love Always — Celebrate true love with tender stories of heartfelt romance, from the rush of falling in love to the joy a new baby can bring, and a focus on the emotional heart of a relationship.

HEROES — The excitement of a gripping thriller, with intense romance at its heart. Resourceful, true-to-life women and strong, fearless men face danger and desire - a killer combination!

 — From showing up to glowing up, these characters are on the path to leading their best lives and finding romance along the way – with plenty of sizzling spice!

To see which titles are coming soon, please visit

millsandboon.co.uk/nextmonth